STORM'S NIGHTMARE

AMELIA STORM SERIES: BOOK EIGHT

MARY STONE

AMY WILSON

Mary Stone

To my readers, who are the best ever. You mean the world to me. Thank you from the bottom of my grateful heart.

Amy Wilson

To my one and only, my husband and best friend, and the best boys a mother could dream of, who all worked with me to make this all possible.

DESCRIPTION

Some nightmares never end...

When a confidential informant hands FBI Agent Amelia Storm the flash drive containing the information he gave her brother Trevor before he was killed, Amelia realizes she's holding a time bomb waiting to explode. Especially when its contents reveal the extent to which the senator on the FBI's radar has infiltrated Chicago's law enforcement system.

But Amelia's investigation into her brother's murder is put on the back burner when the body of a young girl with her eyes gruesomely removed is found in the trunk of a black Nissan scheduled for processing at a local junkyard. Better yet, the salvage yard is run by the Leónes, the mafia family suspected to be behind Trevor's death.

Is the murderer tied to the Leónes...or a serial killer smart enough to dump his victims in a mafia-affiliated junkyard? The only thing Amelia knows for sure is the clock is ticking before the killer strikes again.

From the wickedly dark minds of Mary Stone and Amy Wilson comes Storm's Nightmare, book eight of the Amelia Storm Series. But beware. Sometimes the eyes aren't the windows of the soul, but the reflection of something more sinister.

1

"Be safe, hon!"

Sammie Howard smiled and waved goodbye to Diane Beischel, the manager behind the counter of the convenience store Sammie worked several nights per week. As much as she hated working later than ten, she was always glad to be able to catch a shift with Diane.

"I will. Have a good night."

Pulling up the collar of her faux Sherpa coat, Sammie shouldered open one of the spotless double doors. The glass sparkled as brightly as the day they'd been installed—thanks to the mindless cleaning she'd done for the last chunk of her shift—and stepped out into the February night.

"Crisp, my ass," Sammie muttered, quoting the weatherman from earlier that day. The temperature wasn't *crisp* so much as it was damn near frigid.

Sammie clamped her teeth together to keep them from chattering. The weather app on her phone promised a warm-up in a couple days, but the pleasant temperatures would be short-lived. Such was the norm for the tail-end of winter in the Midwest.

When most people pictured that part of the United States, they imagined cornfields, tractors, and silos. Sammie lived in Chicago, though. One of the largest cities in the country. She couldn't remember the last time she'd seen a field not holding a sports team or a tall building not made of steel and glass.

As she took the first few steps away from the well-lit gas station, her paranoid brain took the moment to remind her that a city as large as Chicago came with an equally large crime rate. To be sure, she loved her hometown. She loved the amount of culture sprinkled throughout the area, the diverse backgrounds of her fellow Chicagoans, and of course, the food. The Windy City was great, *fantastic* even, but even the best things came with downsides.

Glancing from the fuel pumps to the coffee shop and pizza joint across the street, both of which were closed at ten in the evening, she shoved both hands into her pockets and hurried onto the sidewalk, scanning shadows as she went. She didn't mind the actual work during these late-night shifts when the flow of customers slowed, but she never looked forward to her walk to the L.

Chicago's elevated train system was one of the city's major forms of public transportation. Though the train stop itself was well-lit and boasted plenty of security cameras, the walk to get there was a different story. Sammie wasn't in a bad part of town, so to speak, but she wasn't exactly out in the 'burbs with all the rich people.

Sammie wished like hell she had her own car, but buying a vehicle was more challenging than it seemed on the surface. She'd been fighting an uphill financial battle for what seemed to be most of her twenty-one years, and things had gotten much worse recently. The situation wasn't due to college debt like one of her friends and a couple of her coworkers, but medical debt. Six months ago, Sammie's mom, Amy, had been the victim of a hit-and-run accident when she was walking home from the grocery store.

Sammie shuddered at the memory. She'd been so scared she was going to lose her mom, her only real family, all because some jackass had decided to run a stop sign. Because he was so damn important, he couldn't wait a few more seconds to get to his destination.

What a prick.

And as it turned out, a broke, uninsured prick who only received a fine and a slap on the wrist for essentially ruining Amy Howard's life...and Sammie's to a much lesser extent.

Since the accident, Sammie opted to continue living with her mom in their two-bedroom apartment. She'd earned a full-time position at the gas station, allowing her to help pay for the necessities.

The going was tough, but as her mom healed, things were looking up. Better physical health meant Sammie's mom could work more, which meant Sammie could start saving some money.

At the thought, Sammie's heart lightened. Deep down, she knew they'd be okay. She and her mom had always been on their own, and they'd always persevered without anyone else's help.

"I can do this."

With her chin held high, Sammie quickened her pace down the sidewalk. She'd left her workplace behind and had just passed a closed thrift store on the right, which meant the worst part of the walk was just ahead. She needed to be vigilant.

She hated walking past the damn bar. Even if she didn't make eye contact with any of the drunks out front smoking, they'd still catcall her or hurl wolf whistles in her direction.

Her mom told her to ignore the creeps, but Sammie wished she could conjure up some ninja fighting skills and pummel them all into oblivion.

As she approached the establishment, she eyed the front of the bar with her peripheral vision. Lit only by the neon signs in the windows and a sputtering streetlight, the place sure *looked* like the perfect spot for creepers to congregate.

Fortunately, on a Sunday night, there weren't many patrons present. Only a few cars sat in the adjoining parking lot, and no one was standing outside smoking.

Sammie permitted herself a mental sigh of relief.

No catcalls tonight. Thank god.

Despite the moment of reprieve, the hairs on the back of her neck still prickled like she was in the midst of an electrical storm. Was someone watching her?

A host of nightmare scenarios ran through her head. The details of all the gruesome homicides from the true crime shows her mom loved to watch assailed her at once.

"Hey, kid." The man's greeting slurred together into a single word. Maybe even a single syllable, if that was possible. "Can I ask a favor?" Again, the words blended together. As he moved closer, the scent of booze assaulted her.

Sammie wrinkled her nose and took a step back. "Booker, hi. And I think I know what you're going to ask me, and you ought to already know the answer." She tried her best stern teacher voice, hoping the tone would convey decisiveness without being hostile.

Booker's face fell, his glazed eyes rolling back in his head as he let out an exaggerated sigh. "Seriously? Come on, kid. They cut me off across the street, y'know!" He waved a hand at the bar for emphasis. "Said they won't serve someone drunk like me. A *bar* won't serve a drunk! Isn't that ridiculous?"

You're a little beyond drunk, buddy.

She kept the thought to herself. "I'm not going to buy you booze, Booker. You should go home and get some sleep."

He held out his arms, his face contorting in an expression of disbelief. "No, no, you don't have to buy me nothing. I've got the cash, okay? I'll even give you a few bucks for your trouble."

The offer to pay for the task was new. Until now, their back and forth had simply involved Booker begging her to take his money and buy him a six-pack. He'd never mentioned compensation.

A couple dollars was chump change in the grand scheme of things, but Sammie couldn't deny she was tempted by the offer. Chump change or not, a few bucks was a few bucks. If all she had to do was go back to her workplace and buy the guy a six-pack or a bottle of rum...well, that might be worth the minimal effort.

But giving in to him now means he'll keep on asking in the future. Who knows where it'll stop?

"Well?" Booker held both hands in front of him like a prayer. "C'mon, kid. Please?"

Sammie pressed her lips together and squared her shoulders. "I'm sorry, Booker. I really need to get home. You should get home too."

With a loud groan, Booker's head lolled back like a petulant toddler about to throw a tantrum. "Of course you do. Ain't got no time for the dumbass failure across the street, do ya?"

Sammie flinched at the sudden increase in volume. She held up a hand, backing away another step. "Look, I don't want—"

"Hey, leave the young lady alone!"

Sammie spun to face the newcomer, then relaxed a little

to find a clean-cut man heading her way. He appeared to be about her age and wore a black leather bomber with jeans.

Relieved but still wary, Sammy took another cautious step away. "It's okay. He's just drunk. You were about to head home to sleep it off, weren't you, Booker?"

Booker was old enough to be Sammie's father, but in that moment, she knew their roles were reversed. Muttering something unintelligible, Booker began to amble past the newcomer. As he stepped into the street, the toe of his shoe caught the edge of the curb.

With catlike reflexes, New Guy caught Booker's arm and shoulder to keep him from pitching forward. Miraculously, the drunk was able to get both feet beneath himself.

Booker's bloodshot eyes flitted from the newcomer to Sammie and then back as he regained his balance. Blinking repeatedly, possibly in an effort to focus his double-vision, Booker combed a hand through his hair and muttered a grudging thank you.

New Guy stared at the drunk's back as he crossed the street. Once Booker was out of earshot, he turned to Sammie. "You okay?"

Sammie offered the younger man a nod. "Yeah. I'm fine."

It was a lie.

Now more than ever, Sammie wanted to get home. Back to her mom, to the delicious chicken marsala her mom would reheat, and the new show they'd started last week. She wanted to be away from the chaos created when all she'd done was walk down the street.

She tucked a strand of hair behind her ear. "Well, thank you for intervening…um…"

Flashing a quick smile, New Guy stuck out a hand. He was vaguely familiar, but she couldn't quite place him. "Sorry. I should introduce myself. I'm Gavin, and you're

Sammie, right?" The fabric of his jacket hitched up just high enough for her to make out part of the shape of a circular tattoo on his wrist, and that's when she remembered. She'd interacted with him at the gas station a couple times that week.

Sammie accepted the handshake. "Yep, that's me. Nice to meet you, Gavin. Well, I guess we've met before, but you know what I mean."

He swept an arm at the sidewalk in front of them. "I don't suppose you're headed to the L, are you?"

Despite the unease tingling at the base of her spine, Sammie maintained her smile—a skill she'd honed after years in customer service. "Yeah. I just got off work." She didn't want to give him too much information.

She'd learned from her mom's cop shows that astute stalkers could pick up on a person's routine from a seemingly casual conversation. The technique was much like the stupid so-called surveys littered on social media. Shared chain posts asking about a person's upbringing, such as the first car they owned, first job, and so on. Questions that just so happened to match the security questions for most websites. Subtle but purposeful.

Gavin's knowing chuckle suggested he knew the suspicions shifting around in Sammie's head. "I was headed that way too. Mind if I walk with you?"

Though Sammie figured Booker was most likely harmless, the way he'd emerged from the shadows like a shapeshifting vampire had left her nerves frayed.

What if the drunk came back? Or even followed her home?

She suppressed an involuntary shiver. "Sure. You're probably ready to get out of the cold too, huh?"

He jammed his hands in his pockets as they started to

walk. "A little, yeah. I usually drive, but I was meeting a buddy for a few drinks tonight, so I took the L. Being responsible and all that, you know?"

"That's good. Smart."

See, he didn't want to drink and drive. He's even leaving the bar at a reasonable hour.

Sammie hoped they'd make the trek in silence. She'd used up most of her kindness dealing with customers all evening, and she wasn't sure how much longer she'd be able to make herself seem agreeable.

"How long have you been working at the gas station?" Gavin's query shot her hope out of the sky like a hunter at the peak of duck season.

"Coming up on two years." Her response was almost robotic. She couldn't say for sure how many times per day she answered that exact question. Fifty? Maybe seventy?

"Are you in college? Taking any classes at all?" The genuine curiosity in his tone was all that kept Sammie's irritability at bay. Chances were, he was just making conversation to pass the time as they grew closer to the L.

"Not right now. I took some when I got out of high school but just couldn't find anything that really held my interest."

Gavin chuckled. "I know the feeling. My dad's always pushing me to get my shit together and plan my future. But I don't know." He lifted a shoulder and let it fall. "It's not that easy, is it?"

For the first time, Sammie could relate. Her mom never pushed her, at least not since the accident. Beforehand, however, she'd been on Sammie's case to find a subject to study. To attend college and get a degree in *some*thing.

Hell if Sammie knew what, though.

Ever since her mom had needed financial help, the narrative had changed. Sammie's aimless wandering through the start of her twenties was finally beneficial to the two of them. Not that Sammie wanted to work at the gas station the rest of her life. Most of the time, the customers drove her insane. If she could find something she didn't hate, then maybe she'd take her mother's advice.

She could have given voice to her conundrum. Maybe the contemplation would have sparked an interesting conversation for her and the stranger at her side, something to alleviate the air of awkwardness remaining between them.

Sammie didn't want to give Gavin the wrong impression, so she kept the thoughts to herself. He must have picked up on the cue because he didn't try to rekindle the conversation.

Thank god, a person who gets it. Someone who doesn't have to fill the silence with small talk and force me to think of civil responses.

She feigned pleasantries for a living. She sure as hell didn't want to continue the activity after she'd punched out for the day.

Apartment buildings stacked on top of store fronts—some of which were still in business, and some of which had floundered with recent economic hardships—loomed to either side of the street, and the skeletal branches of leafless trees cast spiderweb shapes in the glow of the dim streetlamps. Despite the light poles placed at regular intervals, this part of her walk to the L always felt so damn *dark*.

"Did you hear that?" Gavin's hushed query cut through Sammie's thoughts like razor wire. He stopped in his tracks, and Sammie followed suit. She turned to him, expecting to be met with a contemplative look.

Blood pounded in her ears as she noted his wide, haunted eyes, his face pinched with worry. She licked her lips and willed her voice to remain steady. "Hear what?"

Slowly, as if he'd draw too much attention if he moved too quick, Gavin turned to face the dark mouth of an alley just ahead of them. "I heard a baby crying. It was faint, though...more like a whine than crying, I guess."

Sammie's knee-jerk reaction was to ask if he was messing with her, but she bit her tongue. "A...a baby? I didn't hear anything." But she'd been absorbed in her own thoughts. If a quiet whimper had come from the alley, she might not have noticed.

Gavin cocked his head. "Did you hear that?"

Sammie stepped closer to the mouth of the alley, putting all her focus into her ears. "No. I don't—"

A hand clamped over her mouth, and before she could think to scream, she was hauled into the darkness, swallowed by the inky black.

※

As SAMMIE's brain strolled back toward the world of the waking, she was convinced she'd fallen asleep on the couch after stuffing her face full of chicken marsala. She lifted her head and groaned. Her skull pounded with each beat of her heart.

Little by little, her senses returned. The first sensation she noticed was the hard wood of a chair digging into her back and then the numbness at the tips of her fingers. Something was wrapped around her wrists, and the bind was tight enough to restrict blood flow to her hands.

This was definitely not the couch. She hadn't fallen asleep at home. She'd never even *made* it home.

Panic swirled in her gut like the event horizon of a black hole.

Gavin.

The alley.

It had all been real.

Dragging in a sharp breath through her nose, she snapped open her eyes. All she saw was darkness. A musty odor permeated her nostrils. Was she underground?

She blinked to clear her vision, hoping her eyes would adjust to the low light. But they didn't. Nothing came into focus, just more darkness.

Her breath caught in her throat, panic burning its way into her gut. Had she gone blind? He'd hit her, she remembered, but had the blow been so hard that it had somehow eliminated her eyesight?

A twinge of anger pushed aside the anxiety. She opened her mouth to yell, but her lips wouldn't budge, either. Tape tugged on the skin of her cheeks, a painful explanation for why she was unable to speak. Her mouth had been taped shut.

"Welcome back, Sammie." The familiar voice was like shards of ice stabbing her eardrums.

With a click, a faint glow lit up in Sammie's periphery. She almost sagged back in the chair with relief. He'd blindfolded her. She still had her sight.

The reprieve lasted only a beat.

Fabric rustled, and the faint scent of cologne mingled with the must as the person she could only assume was Gavin tugged the thin piece of fabric off her head. As she suspected, she was surrounded by the bare cement walls of a basement. The room was small, lit only by a single lightbulb hanging from the ceiling.

Shelves lined one wall, and the contents were normal enough. Bug spray, salt for the sidewalk, weed killer. To her chagrin, there was nothing to give her a better indication of *exactly* where she was.

Turning her gaze back to Gavin, she was face-to-face

with the unabashed hatred burning in his eyes. He was so different from the man who'd saved her from Booker.

The abrupt transformation in his demeanor was enough to give her mental whiplash. Where he'd first been so concerned, rage now contorted his features into a mask of hatred. The fires of anger burned in his dark eyes like the smoldering embers of a blacksmith's furnace.

The fingers of fear sank into Sammie's heart, sending tendrils of dread spiraling through her veins where they touched. Time slowed to a crawl as the implication of the events became clear.

She didn't have the first clue what had changed in Gavin's head, didn't know what had transformed this man from Dr. Jekyll to Mr. Hyde.

Was there a mysterious serum in his pocket that had started the transformation?

No. She knew the idea for what it was—bullshit. The truth was, Gavin had always been Mr. Hyde. He'd only hidden the monstrous persona.

And Sammie had bought into the charade. Hook, line, and sinker.

Gavin tore the tape from her mouth, stinging her skin.

"What do you want from me?" She tried to pose the question, but all she managed was a muffled groan.

Yellow light from the bulb overhead glinted off the polished steel of a hunting knife as Gavin brought it from behind his back and waved the blade in front of Sammie's face. The blood froze in her veins, failing to bring life-giving oxygen to her brain. Her entire focus snapped to the six-inch blade.

Her forearms ached as she strained against the duct tape binding her wrists. She tried to move her legs, hoping perhaps she could tip over the chair to break a piece free, but they didn't budge. Not only had Gavin bound her wrists, but he'd restrained her ankles as well.

Gavin had done his best to make sure she'd never leave this hell hole. And the knife? She didn't even want to think of what he planned to use *that* for.

Perspiration dripped into her eyes, adding a new layer of pain. Blinking rapidly, she strained against the tape, but the effort was both Herculean and pointless.

She knew it. Just as she knew she couldn't give up.

Chest heaving, breathing more difficult with each passing second, Sammie glanced around the room again. Searching for what, she didn't know. Something. *Any*thing.

A low chuckle drew her gaze back to the crazy man before her. There was no mirth in his laugh, only mocking derisiveness. Contempt.

He dropped down to a crouch, bringing them eye-level. "You people just think everything in this world is yours for the taking, don't you? You see a guy show up out of nowhere, and you just assume he's there to help you, right? You can't tell me that's not what you did. I was there."

Sammie didn't have the first clue what he was ranting about. She had no idea who *you people* were. Was he referring to gas station employees? Broke daughters of single moms? College dropouts?

There's no point trying to make sense of this lunatic. You need to get out of here, stat.

She couldn't linger on the hopelessness of the situation. She had to try.

Straining against the duct tape, she tried to rotate her wrists. If she could get any leeway, then she might be able to tear the tape a little. One slight rip was all she needed, wasn't it?

Her hopes sank when her wrists didn't budge. Gavin had made the binds too tight for her to move. If he intended to keep her captive, maybe she could achieve some success over time, but for right now…

There was no way out.

The slightest smirk played across his face, almost as if he could sense her hopelessness. "You're not getting out of here alive."

Even as terror pulsed through her, Sammie threw her weight to one side and then the other, hoping to tip over the chair. If the wood broke, maybe she wouldn't need to rip herself free from the tape.

For the second time, Gavin seemed to read her thoughts. In a single fluid motion, he snapped up the knife, holding the tip of the blade level with her bottom eyelid, freezing her every movement. "Try it. Try breaking the chair. Try moving at all."

Terror she didn't know was possible nearly caused her heart to explode against her ribs. She wanted to scream. To cry. To beg. To lament the unfairness of the entire situation. She barely knew this man, but somehow, he held a grudge against her that was so deep-seated, he wanted her dead.

Why?

What had she done to him?

Nothing. I've done nothing to him. He's a psychopath.

He eased the blade closer, and Sammie pulled her head away as far as she could manage in the stiff-backed chair.

The smirk returned to Gavin's lips. He inched the knife closer. "These are mine now."

As the cold steel cut into the tender skin beneath Sammie's eye, she tried to open her mouth to scream. But as the blade sank deeper, as pain lanced through Sammie's skull, her lips wouldn't part.

Help.

The silent plea would have done no good, even if it had been shouted from the rafters. No one would be able to save her from this madman, she knew, as she began to pray for the pain to be over.

As Sammie's world grew dark, Gavin's laughter took on an even more maniacal tone.

"Mine…mine…mine…mine…"

The blade touched Sammie one more time, and it really didn't even hurt before all her other senses disappeared.

2

A s FBI Special Agent Amelia Storm pulled her car to a stop in the shadow of a decrepit warehouse, she was struck with a strangely calming sense of familiarity. Six weeks earlier, she'd parked in almost this exact same spot, unsure of what to expect from the person who'd requested the meeting in the first place.

Josh Young.

Senator Stan Young's son and the former confidential informant of Amelia's brother.

She still couldn't believe it.

Her brother—Detective Trevor Storm, who'd been killed in a gunfight on the streets of Chicago three years ago—had been working with Josh.

Or had he?

She still wasn't entirely sure if Josh truly had information he wanted to share or if he had wanted to meet so he could ensnare her in some sort of trap and take her back to his father like some prized turkey.

It had been January at the time, a little late for Thanksgiving, but who knew with these people. The Young family's depravity had no limits. Their dubious morality undoubtedly extended to holiday traditions.

She would have been a fool to trust anyone with the last name of Young, and Amelia Storm wasn't a fool. She met Josh armed both with her service weapon and with Zane Palmer, her partner and lover, as backup. Luckily, she hadn't needed either.

Would she need them tonight?

She wasn't sure.

The first meeting had been cryptic, and she'd left with only a slip of paper.

"This is the login information for an email address with a disposable domain." He'd handed her the handwritten note. *"You know how disposable email addresses work, right?"*

"Yeah, I do."

Amelia wasn't a cyber crimes specialist, but she was indeed familiar with disposable email addresses or DEAs. A person could set up an account with one of the temporary— or disposable—email domains and then use the address for a limited period before deleting it. The ability to throw away the email address after a single message, or a string of messages, made them nearly impossible to track.

"Okay. I'll send you a message when I figure out when we can meet next. And next time, Agent Storm." He released his grip on the paper but didn't break eye contact. *"Come alone. Actually alone. You might trust your fellow agents, but I don't."*

Six long weeks had passed since that night, and Amelia had met with Josh on only one other occasion. Josh had provided Amelia with a few tidbits she was able to verify. Things only someone with insider information would know. Amelia was hopeful Josh could be trusted. Gnawing at the back of her mind, however, was the fact her brother had trusted this man, and Chicago PD Detective Trevor Storm may have paid for that trust with his life.

Though Amelia's meeting with Josh had been productive in terms of establishing trust, they hadn't yet gotten to the proverbial meat and potatoes—the murder of Trevor and the extent to which Stan Young's malevolent tentacles had invaded Chicago's law enforcement system.

In addition to verifying the intel Josh had provided before today's meeting, Amelia had researched the senator's son until she felt she knew him as well as she knew her own family members.

Josh Young, thirty-two years of age, was born to Senator Stan Young and his late wife, Grace Young, née Sutton. Grace had been killed in a car accident when Josh was only a few months old, leaving Stan a single father in his early twenties. Josh graduated from Chicago Booth School of Business with a master's in business administration at age twenty-three, then was handed control of the Young's agricultural empire when Stan Young first won his senate seat.

For the past eight years, Josh had technically been at the helm of Happy Harvest Farms. Josh's title at the multibillion-dollar agricultural giant was largely for appearances and to make the senator appear aboveboard to the Senate ethics committee. The practice wasn't uncommon among the Washington elite, specifically those who owned successful businesses. On paper, they stepped away from the business when they became an elected official. In reality, they were just as invested in the business as they had been beforehand.

Over the summer, Amelia and Zane had taken down one of the Young's many agricultural sites. A Kankakee County farm working under the Happy Harvest umbrella had a rogue management team trying to pocket some extra cash while running a forced labor trafficking ring on the site.

Although the FBI had shut the operation down, the blame had fallen solely on the management of the Kankakee County location. The agricultural behemoth's C-suite officers, including Josh Young, apparently had no clue about the illegal activities, though Wall Street briefly punished the stock.

Poring over Josh's history, as well as the limited information she'd found regarding Trevor's final case, Amelia had found no involvement between Josh and the criminal underworld. Knowing what had occurred at the Happy Harvest Farms location in Kankakee County, Amelia had closely scrutinized the details of that case to make sure Josh had not been involved, even if only to turn a blind eye to make an extra buck. She'd found no link to Josh. His father's hands were not so clean.

Two rival Italian mafia families—the D'Amatos and Leónes—called Chicago home, along with the ever-present Russian mob and a couple cartels who hated one another. Each criminal organization commanded a piece of Chicago's illegal pie, with the Leónes and D'Amatos especially well-entrenched. So far, all signs indicated to Amelia that Stan Young was in bed with the Leónes.

Hopefully, she'd learn much more soon.

Amelia stepped out of her car and into the strip of sunshine that made it over the warehouse. The light would soon be overtaken by shadow as the sun continued its journey across the sky. Reflexively, Amelia tugged on the collar of her knee-length trench coat. The temperature was much more pleasant today than it had been, but without the warm glow of the sun, she still froze her ass off.

The cold winter wind whipped her long dark-brown, blonde-tipped hair into her face and, to her chagrin, her mouth. She spat out the strands and shoved the hair back over her shoulder, hoping Josh didn't notice the goofy look on her face as she did so.

Amelia still didn't know what Josh had revealed to Trevor that had gotten her brother killed, but she was determined to find out. Her fingers brushed the barrel of the tiny Beretta she'd stowed in the coat's pocket in case she was, in fact, being set up. It would be easier to reach than the service weapon she also carried under her layers of clothing.

Approaching the run-down bus stop and its rusted metal bench, Amelia lifted a hand in greeting. "Nice to see you again. And that's not sarcasm, trust me. How's your day going?"

The corner of Josh's mouth turned up with a faint smile. He raised two fingers from the paper coffee cup cradled in his hands. "It's fine. Glad you could make it on such short notice."

"It's not a problem. It sounded like this was important, so I didn't want to make either of us wait." Amelia wished she'd taken the time to pick up her own coffee. If nothing else, she could have tossed the hot brew at anyone sneaking up on her.

Stop with the paranoia. Get the information you need and get out of here.

Taking a sip, Josh lowered himself to sit on the edge of the old bench. Considering the amount of dirt and debris littering the actual seat, she couldn't blame him for his caution.

As Amelia followed suit, careful to avoid a pile of dried leaves swept up beside the arm of the bench, Josh's gaze shifted to her.

"You're a good person, Agent Storm."

Amelia blinked, surprised. Josh's voice was quiet, but the words appeared to be genuine, like a compliment given to an old friend. "Thanks. I, um…"

He snorted and waved a dismissive hand. "You don't have to lie and tell me I am too. I know who my father is. I know what our 'family business' gets away with every year."

A pang of sympathy struck Amelia's heart like a chime.

"Yeah, but you're trying to change it. That's worth something, right? It's dangerous, and you know it's dangerous, but you're doing it anyway."

His jaw tightened, his gaze becoming distant. "I'll be honest, Agent Storm. It scares the hell out of me."

Amelia didn't blame him. If anyone learned that Josh had been her brother's CI and was now talking to a Fed, a man like Senator Young would make him disappear, related or not.

"You think your own father would kill you?" It was one of the questions Amelia had asked him during the first meeting.

"There's no doubt in my mind. See, when you're stuck being surrounded by billionaires for most of your life, you pick up on a few of their universal truths. You'd think having ten or eleven figures in an offshore bank account would be enough to make someone happy for the rest of their life."

She'd nodded. *"I suppose."*

"That's the thing, though. The thing about guys like my dad. There's no such thing as enough. *They always want more, and they never stop."*

Goose bumps raised on her arms at the memory, and she still felt worry for the young man. Josh was right. Men like his father never stopped, and they didn't care who they had to destroy to get what they wanted.

Amelia's family wasn't perfect, but when it came to being the child of a genuinely evil human being, she couldn't relate.

Her father had succumbed to an alcohol addiction for seventeen years, having only cleaned up a few years ago. But Jim Storm wasn't a bad man, not even a bad father. He'd just been…hurt. The loss of Amelia's mom, of his beloved wife, had broken him, and he'd taken nearly two decades to pull himself together.

Trevor had been a corrupt detective for the Chicago Police Department, but even his work with the D'Amato family wasn't *bad*. The D'Amatos were criminals, sure, but they dealt primarily in cyber-crime and counterfeit goods. Amelia would know. Back in high school, she'd dated the son of one of the crime family's capos. Alex Passarelli was now a capo himself, but he wasn't a bad person, either.

Stan Young was a different story. Amelia couldn't imagine what it must feel like to be the child of such a detestable human being.

For now, she'd stick to what she and Josh *did* have in common. Their shared paranoia. "There was an investigation a few months back where another agent tried to frame me for killing someone. When they realized that wasn't working, they decided to try to kill me. It was a...tense couple of weeks."

"No doubt." Josh twisted the paper sleeve around his cup. "I think...I think it's time I tell you what I told Trevor. The information I think he must have done something with, something to put him on my father's radar."

Amelia held her breath even as her pulse picked up speed. This was the moment she'd been waiting for. Needing to see his face and read his expression, Amelia straightened and turned to fully face Josh. "Okay. I'm listening."

Silence greeted her. For several long, drawn-out moments, the only sound between them was the distant bustle of the city. Just as she was sure she'd have to prod Josh to talk or wind him up like an old-school wooden toy soldier, he met her gaze. "You know I worked with your brother. He never wrote my name down anywhere or kept records, none that were maintained officially by the CPD anyway."

Amelia was aware. After first receiving Josh's note under the windshield wiper of her car, she'd scoured high and low to find even a shred of evidence to indicate the identity of

Trevor's CI. But both Josh and Trevor had covered their tracks.

Josh slipped a hand inside his coat, and Amelia reflexively stiffened, her body preparing for a fight.

However, Josh produced not a weapon but a nondescript flash drive. "There's no legally admissible evidence here, nothing that would hold up in court, but it might be enough for you to flesh out and actually get somewhere. I don't think your brother and the city had the proper resources, but the FBI might."

As he handed the device to Amelia, she had more questions than answers. She figured she'd start with the simplest. "What's on it?"

Josh sipped his coffee. "Dates, names, locations. Photos of old documents. Some notes I added about what I was able to dig up. Your brother and I would trade this flash drive back and forth. Honestly, it's just dumb luck that I had it when he was killed. If it had been on his person, I'd have been assassinated right along with him."

Amelia suddenly got the feeling she was holding a miniature bomb. Gritting her teeth, she cupped her hand around the flash drive. This was why Trevor had been killed. Why, though?

As if he could sense her query, Josh held up a hand. "Sorry. I'm getting ahead of myself. I need to give you some context. You know Stan has been married to Cynthia Young for twenty-six years, going on twenty-seven this spring. And you know Cynthia isn't my biological mother. My mother was killed in a *car accident* when I was about six months old."

Amelia didn't miss his emphasis on two key words. "You don't think it was an accident?"

"No, I don't." His expression was akin to that of a person who'd just bitten into a lemon. "I've been digging for a long time, Agent. And I've found some discrepancies between reality and what Stan's told me over the years. My mom, my *actual* mom, was planning to file for divorce when she was killed."

Anticipation flooded Amelia's bloodstream, and she gripped the flash drive a little tighter, almost as if she was afraid it would fly away if she let it. "I never saw anything about that in my research. How do you know this?"

"She left me her journal. It was locked in a security deposit box until I turned eighteen. Once her lawyer carried out the final portion of her will—giving me the key to access the journal—I'd moved it and other items I needed to keep out of Stan's sight into a storage unit I rented under a pseudonym. My mom knew Stan was having some type of relationship, and she'd hired a private investigator to get proof of it. Stan made her sign a prenup, but the prenup would have been void if she could prove Stan was cheating. She'd have gotten half of his stake in Happy Harvest Farms, half of his fortune, half of everything."

Having lost her own mother at age ten, Amelia could relate to what Josh had been through. "That's terrible. I'm... I'm genuinely sorry to hear that. There has to be something we can do with this, right?"

"Not by itself. The investigation of the car crash turned up no signs of foul play. The cops who worked the case didn't even have a reason to look at Stan's marital status. The only reason *I* looked into it was because of that journal. There are scanned copies of the pages of everything I've shared with you on that flash drive. I don't know if the records are even accessible anymore. After your brother was killed, Stan probably had someone go in and scrub anything incriminating."

Her hopes of progress sank. "So, that's how Trevor is connected? He was getting too close to figuring something out, and Stan had him killed for it?"

Josh appeared to mull over her words. "Yes and no. That's not where the story ends. My mom had figured out *who* Stan was sleeping with. Her private investigator even got a few pictures to prove it. Not surprisingly, the PI wound up dead a few weeks after my mom. Stan made sure to get rid of all the loose ends. We've talked about Stan's connections to the Leóne family, but the woman he was screwing was from the other side of the fence."

Amelia bit her tongue to keep her eyes from popping open wide. "A D'Amato woman?"

The sour expression returned to Josh's face. "Sofia Passarelli, formerly Sofia Lettiero."

For a beat, Amelia's heart froze into a block of ice. She knew who Sofia Passarelli was. Sofia was the mother of Alex Passarelli. The same Alex who Amelia had dated for nearly four years in high school and whose father threatened her into fleeing Chicago.

Clearing her throat, Amelia shoved the sudden shock to the back of her mind. She could process the disbelief later. Right now, she needed to figure out how all these revelations connected. "I take it you think Stan's sexual relationship with Sofia, and my brother finding out about it, has something to do with him being killed? Trevor was investigating Gianna Passarelli's disappearance when he was murdered. Is *that* connected too?"

Steeliness descended over Josh's features. "It has to be. Obviously, the fling between Stan and Sofia didn't end well. Stan isn't the type of person to live and let live, or to let transgressions against him go without some sort of reprisal."

"I've looked over the Gianna Passarelli case seven ways from Sunday, though. There's nothing in there to even remotely indicate Stan had a connection to the Passarellis."

Josh gave his head a single shake. "There wouldn't be. Stan would make damn sure of it."

He had a point. Regardless of the lack of information in the kidnapping case, *Alex* had never hinted about Stan's relationship with his family. Wouldn't Alex have uncovered *something* by now? Alex had loved his little sister, and Amelia knew firsthand how much her loss still pained him. He'd have left no stone unturned, no avenue unexplored in searching for those responsible for her disappearance.

Or did he already know? Had he been sitting on this information without sharing it with her? Amelia pushed the thought aside. After all, hadn't Alex been the one to bring Amelia the damning photos of Agent Joseph Larson cozying up to Brian Kolthoff?

Amelia had done her best to keep her and Alex's relationship to a minimum since her return to Chicago almost eleven months ago.

Now, however, she fully intended to meet with him. Maybe she'd break into his house and wait for him to show up like he'd done after Amelia had ignored his calls and texts.

"There's more." Josh's voice cut through the cacophony of Amelia's thoughts. "Something I'd come to notice shortly before I started talking to your brother. Something about my younger sister."

Amelia bit back a dry observation about Josh's nine-year-old sister being involved in the murder of a homicide detective. "Your sister is adopted, right?"

"Right. Cynthia can't conceive. They tried IVF and all sorts of other methods, but none worked. So, about nine years ago, they adopted Mae. You know what those nine years line up with? Give or take about another nine months?"

A combination of disgust and anger crawled along Amelia's skin like living vines. "Gianna Passarelli."

Alex's little sister.

His grave expression matched the shift in Amelia's mood. "Yeah. Exactly. If you compare pictures of the two of them,

Mae looks just like Gianna. Mae is home-schooled, and Stan seems too afraid to even let her go outside. For a while, I just thought it was sexism because he was never protective like that with me. But now? I think he's protecting her from more than just the media."

Which made perfect sense, given the implication of Josh's observation.

If Josh was right, then Gianna was Mae's mother...

...and Stan Young was her father.

3

Anticipation buzzed through Zane Palmer's system as he pilfered Amelia's cupboards for spices and a handful of canned goods. Keeping his hands busy had started as a strategy to ignore the trepidation grating away at his nerves, but ever since receiving a quick call from Amelia to advise him she was on her way home from meeting with Josh Young, Zane's mood had lightened considerably.

In the dead of a Midwestern winter, the only real activity he could find to busy himself with was cooking. Not in his lonely kitchen, of course. At least at Amelia's apartment, he had her cat to keep him company.

Though he and Amelia had technically been dating for less than two months, they'd been good friends ever since their first case together in the Chicago FBI office. So, when Amelia had entrusted him with a spare key to her apartment, he'd been more than happy to return the favor.

Most of the time, they convened at Amelia's place. Her cat, a long-haired calico she'd adopted from a young woman who was about to go into witness protection, would have been disappointed if they'd chosen to spend their free days and nights at Zane's apartment.

Pulling a can opener from the drawer full of utensils, Zane glanced down to where the calico sprawled on the rug in front of the sink. Hup's green eyes were fixed expectantly on him.

"These are beans, Hup. Not cat food." He waved at the can for emphasis, though he doubted the feline understood or cared. "Do you want a bean?"

Her tail swished, and one ear twitched.

"You don't want a lovely legume, but okay. Far be it from me to decline you the opportunity to try new things." In the midst of his growing anticipation to hear what Amelia had learned, he was more than happy to distract himself by giving the cat a bean she wouldn't eat.

Part of him was looking forward to a piping hot bowl of chili after a solid week when the temperature had barely climbed into the double-digits. He wasn't exceptional in the home cooking department, but he knew how to make a damn fine pot of chili.

A little more than six weeks ago, Zane had reached out to his good friend and most reliable CIA contact Nate Tennick, a tenured intelligence analyst. Though Zane had left the CIA and joined the FBI more than three years ago, no one ever *truly* cut ties with the Central Intelligence Agency, for better or for worse.

So far, Zane's lingering relationship with the CIA had been for the better. When Amelia had shown him a couple photos of Brian Kolthoff, also known as The Shark, buddying up with fellow FBI agent Joseph Larson, Zane had offered to corroborate the pictures.

The process had taken some time, during which he and Amelia faced the possibility that Joseph Larson would be promoted to Supervisory Special Agent of the Organized

Crime Division. Fortunately, the process of selecting a new SSA was a lengthy one, and Spencer Corsaw was currently still at the helm of the department. Zane could only imagine how irritated Larson must be with the process.

Good. He hoped the rest of Larson's life was nothing but irritation and discomfort. After the sick bastard had tried to blackmail Amelia into sleeping with him, Zane hoped the guy's life didn't last much longer. If he got hit by a bus tomorrow, the world would be a better place for it.

He snorted at the thought.

Wouldn't that be perfect? Larson doesn't get taken out by one of his shady accomplices or shot in the head to tie up a loose end...he just gets hit by a bus like any normal but unfortunate person.

As he used a fork to scoop a stray bean out of the can, the familiar metallic *click-clack* of the front door drew his attention.

"I'm home!" Zane's heart lifted at the ease with which they'd settled into their relationship. Only a few months previous, they'd shared their first kiss. Now, he was spending almost all his free time with Amelia and Hup. The object of his affection appeared in the foyer, barely visible from his angle in the open-air kitchen.

"Welcome home. I hope the drive was okay. I'm dying to hear what Josh knew." As Hup meowed and rubbed against his legs, Zane suddenly remembered the treat he'd promised the cat. He set the bean on the tiled floor, and by the time he rose to his full height, Amelia had emerged from the short hall.

Her dark hair was windblown, and her cheeks were flushed from the cold. They'd each taken a half-day from work since they didn't have an active case, and Amelia had abandoned her dress shirt and slacks. In place of the formal attire, she wore a pair of skinny jeans and a hoodie. The green hue of the sweatshirt nearly matched her eyes, and the dark shade stood out in stark contrast to her fair skin. Whether she wore a hoodie and jeans or a designer gown, she was a stunning woman.

With a sigh, Amelia moved to the granite breakfast bar and ran a finger down the silky petal of one of the roses he'd given her yesterday for Valentine's Day. He'd stressed over the color to choose and had ended up ordering two of every color the flower shop had to offer. The bouquet was enormous, and costly, but Amelia had seemed delighted with the gift as well as the fancy dinner they'd enjoyed.

"The drive was fine. The meeting was…interesting. It was good. Productive. But, well." She leaned forward to rest her nose on a pink bloom, inhaling deeply. "It's a lot of information."

Helpful information, he hoped. "Really? That's…good, right?"

A half-smile crept to her face as she nodded. As she went over the details she'd been provided by Josh Young, including the flash drive he'd given her, Zane robotically put together the rest of the chili. He was glad he'd made the recipe countless times before. Otherwise, he most definitely would have forgotten an ingredient.

"So," he set the lid on the pot and turned to face Amelia, "Stan Young possibly kidnapped Gianna, a thirteen-year-old girl. A girl who just so happens to be the daughter of a woman with whom he had a romantic relationship. A relationship he potentially killed his first wife over."

Amelia spun a piece of dark hair around her index finger, a common mannerism when she was thinking. "Yeah, that about sums it up. I feel bad for Josh, honestly. He's a good guy, but if even a sliver of this gets back to Stan, Stan will kill him."

Just like he did with Amelia's brother.

Stan wouldn't have pulled the trigger himself, of course.

He'd have hired someone to do the job. Someone he trusted and someone he kept close.

Zane kept the thoughts to himself. He was sure Amelia had already come to the same conclusion. Fortunately, amidst all the questions created by Josh Young's revelation, Zane was glad he could present an answer to one of their problems.

He placed both hands on the counter and flashed Amelia a reassuring smile. "Well, I've got news too, but it doesn't come with a bunch of question marks. I heard back from my contact today."

Her eyes widened, and she dropped the piece of hair. "Really? What did he find?"

The cautious optimism from earlier gradually began to return as Zane made his way to her side of the bar. He powered on his personal laptop and navigated directly to Nate's message. "I talked to my contact earlier, and he explained what we're looking at and why it was recorded in the first place." He opened the first video in a long series of recordings.

In the frozen first frame of the video, the mid-morning sun shone on the host of vessels moored to the docks of a marina. Palm trees were visible on the edge of the screen where they dotted the shore.

"A marina." Amelia leaned in closer until her shoulder was warm against his upper arm. "Where is it? Somewhere tropical, it looks like."

"Florida. About an hour north of Miami. You saw the time stamp?"

Glancing back to the screen, Amelia nodded. "Five years ago."

"Yep." Zane was glad when she didn't ask for any additional information about the recording. Though Zane was comfortable showing her the footage of Kolthoff's yacht, he was less comfortable discussing the CIA operation that had made use of the video.

Half a decade earlier, the Agency had suspected a group of terrorist sympathizers was smuggling weapons via a luxury yacht that traveled between the U.S. and Middle East. Zane hadn't personally worked the operation, but he'd been on standby in case the investigation required more manpower.

Eventually, the CIA had caught up with the arms dealers, just like they always did. The operation wasn't classified as strictly now as it had been five years earlier, but many of the details were still unavailable to those outside the Agency.

Zane shifted his focus back to the still shot of the tropical harbor. Back to Brian Kolthoff, and away from terrorist arms dealers.

"This isn't just any ole marina. It's a private one. Hence the luxurious looking boats." Zane zoomed in on a large yacht moored in its own private section of the docks. "All this footage was taken with the highest-quality equipment available at the time. The recording software allows you to zoom in and out without having to pause the feed. You can't move the camera, obviously, but you can get a nice, close-up look at whatever you're interested in."

Amelia's eyes were glued to the screen. "And this yacht… is it…?"

She left the question unfinished, but Zane knew what she was asking. "It's not the *Equilibrium*, but…" He zoomed a bit closer and increased the playback speed. "It's owned by the same creep. This is the *Server Not Found*, another one of Kolthoff's collection of yachts."

In the silence that followed, he and Amelia watched a well-dressed man emerge onto the second-story deck. His movements were choppy until Zane pressed a button to return the video to its normal speed.

With a glass in one hand, the man strolled to the railing, glanced down toward the bow of the vessel, and then sipped at his drink.

Though he wore a pair of shining aviator sunglasses, there was no mistaking his identity. Zane and Amelia had both stared at his picture enough to identify him with ease.

"There's Kolthoff." Amelia turned to him, lifting a sculpted eyebrow. "I take it there's more?"

"There is. I haven't had a chance to look through all the footage yet, but I looked through enough to find what we were after." Zane's excitement mounted as he closed out of the first video.

The files were massive, and each time period had multiple points of view. Fortunately, Zane had been able to give Nate an idea of what they were trying to find. Nate had done a once-over to ensure the footage was relevant, leaving the rest of the legwork to Zane. It was a tedious task, but Zane didn't mind. The payoff—catching Joseph Larson buddying up with The Shark four years *before* the Leila Jackson case—would be well worth the tedium.

The Special Agent in Charge of the Chicago Field Office had essentially recruited Zane to help her sniff out corruption amidst her personnel. SAC Jasmine Keaton was aware of some of Zane's intelligence background, though she didn't know any specifics of the work he'd done. Of course. The CIA didn't exactly let its former agents list their completed projects on a resumé.

As Zane pulled up the sixth video in line, he promptly navigated to the timestamp he'd memorized earlier in the afternoon. The recordings were divided into twenty-four-hour chunks, beginning at midnight and ending at 11:59:59. Hour nine, minute forty-three, was when their guest star arrived on scene.

Amelia swore under her breath as a man who could only

be Special Agent Joseph Larson trailed out onto the deck after Brian Kolthoff. Both men held mugs, and both appeared every bit as put together as they would be if they were headed to their respective jobs.

Brian swept an arm in front of himself to indicate the entire deck, and Joseph responded with an approving grin. For the hundredth time that day, Zane wished like hell the CIA's advanced surveillance tech had included audio.

The pair lingered near the railing, each man sipping from his mug and occasionally nodding as the other spoke. Clearly, these two men knew one another well.

Zane paused the recording, and Amelia turned to face him, her expression filled with determination, and for the first time since they'd been dealing with Joseph Larson, hope. "This is perfect. This is exactly what we needed to corroborate that photo Alex gave me. This *proves*, beyond a shadow of a doubt, that Larson and Kolthoff were friends before the Leila Jackson case. It proves that Larson *knew* about Kolthoff and still didn't reveal his relationship during our investigation. That's huge."

Zane wholeheartedly agreed. "Barring any unforeseen events, I can take this to SAC Keaton within the next couple days. I just need to clean up the footage a little bit." He couldn't bring the entire recording of half of a covert CIA operation to their special agent in charge.

A hint of disappointment shadowed Amelia's face, and with the expression came a stab of guilt in Zane's chest. Amelia was the one who'd been truly victimized by Joseph Larson, and Zane knew she wanted to be the person responsible for his downfall. He didn't blame her—her vendetta with Larson was personal. But at the end of the day, Amelia was a practical person. She knew how to put aside her personal interests for the betterment of the greater good. As long as the job got done and got done *right*, Amelia wasn't the type to demand credit.

Still, a pinprick of guilt persisted in Zane's heart. "SAC Keaton recruited me to the Chicago Field Office to find corruption. I mean, I had all the duties of a field agent, but with the added expectation that I keep my eyes and ears open to find the leaks that were coming out of this office."

Amelia shifted her weight from one foot to the other. "Yeah, I know. It's definitely the best way to handle it. Plus, then maybe you'll get a raise or something." She shot him a sarcastic wink and nudged his arm.

Zane rolled his eyes, feigning exasperation. "If I get a raise, then maybe I can afford to keep buying treats for your cat."

Crossing her arms, Amelia turned toward the living room where Hup was perched on the arm of the sectional couch. "Yeah, she is getting chunky. Weird how that coincides with you being over here more often."

Zane held up both hands in a gesture of innocence. "She's persistent, okay?"

Amelia threw back her head and laughed, which was a truly beautiful sound. "You have no idea."

His spirits a bit lighter, Zane joined in her mirth. Hup was a regular source of comedic relief for them. Whether the cat was stealing Amelia's hair ties, licking Zane's feet after he got out of the shower, or stalking the occasional bug that wandered inside, she never ceased to amuse.

As silence settled over the room, Zane assumed he and Amelia were both processing the information they'd each received over the course of the day. The intel was good, but there was still a long road ahead of them.

When Amelia spun on one heel to face him, Zane abruptly jerked his attention away from the half-asleep calico. "What?"

She snapped her fingers victoriously. "You know how Cassandra Halcott and I have been looking into Michelle Timmer's disappearance, right?" Amelia and the Assistant U.S. Attorney had become closer over the past six weeks. After Amelia had escaped what would have undoubtedly been her death at the hands of none other than Joseph Larson, the two unlikely friends had become convinced a terrible fate had befallen Michelle Timmer. Timmer was a brilliant young woman with an undergraduate degree from Yale and a master's in forensic science from the same fine institution.

"Right." Zane had also kept his ear to the ground around the building maintenance staff he'd befriended since his transfer to the Chicago Field Office.

She gestured to the laptop screen. "Maybe something like this can help us figure out what happened to her. We've been looking at Jane Does who've turned up across the country, but so far, none of them have been a match to Michelle. We can't find her dead, and we can't find her alive. But maybe we can find her...somewhere in between? During the Leila Jackson case, we thought Kolthoff might have kept girls on board his yachts. Couldn't hurt to look."

Zane kept his expression carefully neutral. Asking for favors from his old CIA contacts was a risky endeavor. He still had a few favors he could cash in from Nate and a couple others, but what would he do when his so-called chits ran out? Then, if he wanted help from the Agency, he'd owe *them*. Stepping back into the world of covert operations wasn't a move he wanted to make. He'd endured his share of trauma, and he'd never had any intent to go back to the job.

I don't have many favors left, but I'll have to make the ones I do have count.

Finally, he offered Amelia a slow nod. "I might be able to find out something."

She touched his shoulder and smiled, a hint of sympathy in her green eyes. "Don't do any more than you're comfortable with, okay? We'll get to the bottom of this. With me, you, and Cassandra all looking for Michelle, we'll figure out what happened to her. And if Joseph's responsible, then we'll make sure he hangs for it. Literally or figuratively, either one is fine with me at this point."

Laughter bubbled in Zane's chest at the comment. "I can't say I disagree."

They'd both sleep better after Joseph Larson's sins were dragged out into the light. But in doing so, what other monsters would they unearth?

Larson was well-protected by his billionaire friends and figuring out where their influence began and ended was half the battle.

Information was power, and Zane prayed his connections would give him the upper hand.

4

When Amelia had gone to bed after stuffing her face full of chili, she'd expected to wake up to Zane's alarm at six o'clock sharp. Between her tenure in the military and the day shift she usually worked at the FBI, Amelia was accustomed to rising in the wee hours of the morning. It wasn't her favorite activity on the planet, but she was a creature of habit.

Midway through a pleasant dream of raking leaves with her sister-in-law, niece, and nephew, a pervasive but familiar melody pierced through the crisp afternoon air. Gripping her rake with both hands, Amelia glanced over at Joanna, Hailey, and Nolan, wondering if one of them held the source of the sound.

In a single heartbeat, their images faded from view, replaced with only blackness. Amelia's eyes shot open as she jerked to sit upright. At her side, Zane grumbled something unintelligible and pulled the comforter over his face.

Resting a hand over her pounding heart, Amelia turned to the digital clock.

Four-thirty? What the hell?

She snatched her phone off the nightstand before it could buzz again. Noting that the caller was Supervisory Special Agent Spencer Corsaw, she cleared her throat in an effort to make herself come across more like a human being. "Storm here and ready for duty."

The SSA chuckled. "Morning. You sound about as happy to be awake as I am. Unfortunately," he sighed, though Amelia suspected the gesture was also a yawn, "we're not getting any sleep in the near future. We've got a case, and the scene is still fresh. A body was found in a junkyard, and it looks like it might be mob-related."

"Mob-related?" The announcement gave her a shot of much-needed energy. "How do we know that?"

Beside her, Zane lifted onto his elbows without making a sound. Amelia tapped the speaker icon so he could hear every word.

"The junkyard where she was found has been under surveillance by the Bureau for a while. It's suspected that it's involved with a chop shop run by the Leóne family. We need you and Agent Palmer down here ASAP. You're two of our experts on the Leónes."

With the mention of the Leónes, Amelia was wide awake. "All right. Send me the info, and I'll be there as soon as I grab Agent Palmer."

"Roger that. See you soon."

She pulled the phone away from her ear and disconnected the call. To her relief, Zane was already on his feet, not even bothering to ask any questions. They each hurried to get ready, and Amelia thanked her good sense for renting an apartment with two bathrooms.

Amelia sized up her partner and boyfriend five minutes later. Zane was dressed as impeccably as an actor pretending to *be* an FBI agent, a feat that somehow came as naturally to him as walking and talking came to other people. They filled their thermoses with freshly brewed coffee and headed out into the frigid morning.

By the time they arrived at Paulie's Scrap and Salvage, the sky was still dark. Red and blue lights flashed atop the squad cars lining the street in front of the junkyard. A pair of crime scene vans were parked near the entrance to the yard, which was a tall, wrought iron fence topped with razor wire and backed by chain-link to prevent a person from slipping between the bars.

The barrier struck Amelia as a bit excessive. What would someone steal from a junkyard?

If it's run by the mob, then that's all the explanation we need for the extra defenses. The Leónes don't want to just keep out the riffraff. They want to keep us *out.*

They stopped the car at the barricade that blocked off-street traffic, showed their badges to the pair of officers stationed in front of the collection of orange cones, and parked behind one of the police cars. Amelia swallowed as much of the still hot coffee as she dared before shoving open her door and stepping out into the cold.

Another pair of officers guarded the crime scene tape that now marked the entrance to Paulie's Scrap and Salvage. To their side, a young, clean-shaven man with a Chicago P.D. badge draped around his neck—a detective, Amelia gleaned —was in the midst of a conversation with a middle-aged fellow wearing a bulky parka and flannel pajama pants.

Amelia tilted her chin at the pair and shot Zane a knowing look. According to the follow-up information she'd received from Spencer Corsaw, the CPD had been first on the scene and were currently sticking around to lend their assistance where it was needed. She assumed the young detective was talking to the owner of the junkyard.

In response to her wordless comment, Zane pulled out his badge.

Amelia followed suit, clearing her throat to draw attention to them. "Morning, officers. Detective."

The detective's expression relaxed as he turned to them. "Morning. I'm Detective Murray."

Amelia introduced herself and Zane. "Do you mind if we have a word with you quickly?" Turning to pajama pants man, Amelia gestured for him to stay put. Zane stationed himself next to the annoyed individual, just in case Amelia's message hadn't been clear.

Walking out of earshot of the junkyard's owner, Amelia asked the detective to bring her up to speed.

"Not much to tell you at this point. We'd just begun questioning Russel Armstrong." He nodded toward pajama man.

"Then maybe we can finish doing that together?"

Not even appearing to be the least bit pissed about her and Zane joining his case, the detective gave her a little salute and began walking back the way they'd come.

Amelia let her gaze drift over the guy wearing pajamas. "You're Russel Armstrong? Are you the owner of this business?"

He stood a little straighter and lifted his chin. "My uncle, my dad's brother, was Paulie Armstrong and the previous owner. Uncle Paulie left me the yard when he died. Didn't have no kids of his own, and I'd been working here since I was a kid. So, here we are."

Amelia doubted the junkyard owner was usually so forthcoming with his family information, but he *had* been in the middle of an interview with a CPD homicide detective, and he *was* talking to an FBI agent. That tended to loosen lips. "Do you know anything about the body that was found on your property this morning?"

Armstrong gave a vehement shake of his head. "Don't know nothing about 'em, Agent. I manage a business that crushes cars and sells 'em as scrap metal. Don't know a damn thing about no dead kid."

Zane waved a hand at the massive gate behind Armstrong and the detective. "As the owner of this fine establishment, how about you save us some time and a few legal headaches and give us permission to search the whole yard?" Zane pinned the man with an expectant stare, the type he'd used effectively on numerous suspects during his tenure with the Bureau.

After a brief moment when the only sound was the squawk of police radios and distant chatter of crime scene techs, Armstrong broke away from the intense look. "I could, but I won't. You can get a warrant if you want to look outside that area you all taped off in there."

Amelia ignored the spark of annoyance in her gut and flashed the man a smile. "We'll do that, then. Nice talking to you, Mr. Armstrong."

"Uh-huh." Armstrong's suspicious expression told Amelia there was more to his knowledge of the junkyard than he was willing to provide without some form of legal persuasion. Not that she'd doubted Spencer when he'd told them the place had been under surveillance for its ties to a Leóne chop shop. But for the owner of the place to squirm under pressure from a pair of federal agents was more than a little interesting.

After locking eyes with Detective Murray and shaking her head to let him know the owner had not revealed anything beneficial to her, Amelia and Zane headed for the open gate. Amelia pushed Russel Armstrong out of her mind. He'd be there after they'd had a chance to look at the crime scene. For the time being, she wanted to get a good look at the place while everything was still fresh.

Dirt and debris crunched beneath Amelia and Zane's feet

as they made their way toward the halo of light created by the CSU's portable work lamps.

The area leading to the car compressor was relatively clean, or at least as clean as Amelia could have expected from a junkyard. A row of crushed vehicles along the perimeter blocked the line of sight to the street and created a wide path. The width of the makeshift aisle permitted plenty of leeway for the forklifts, tow trucks, and other machines to navigate to the work area.

As Amelia and Zane neared the hustle and bustle around the car compactor, Amelia noted the rows of flattened vehicles looming in the background, creating a labyrinth in the darkness. Were those cars simply empty vehicles awaiting their day for the final step of processing, or were they a clever mafia graveyard?

The curiosity nagged at the edges of her psyche as she spotted Spencer Corsaw, along with who she assumed, based on the silver badge clipped to his belt, was a Chicago homicide detective—the partner of the younger guy who'd been speaking to Russel Armstrong.

Spencer waved them over. "Good morning, Agents. This is Detective Cordell Hamilton with the CPD homicide unit. Detective, this is Special Agent Amelia Storm and Special Agent Zane Palmer."

Detective Hamilton's dark wash jeans, hooded sweatshirt, and leather jacket were nowhere near as formal as Zane's designer suit, but he wore the attire with poise and dignity. The faint lines on his face put him in his late thirties or early forties, but Amelia didn't spot a hint of gray in his close-cropped black hair.

"Nice to meet you." The detective extended a hand to them both. "I'm sure you two are wondering about the person who called this in, yeah?"

Right down to brass tacks. Amelia liked Detective

Hamilton already. "We were, yes. Are they here? Can we talk to them?"

Hamilton shook his head. "No, I'm afraid not. We're sending the recording of the 911 call over to the FBI so your analysts can take a closer look at it."

Zane crossed his arms, appearing contemplative. "Much appreciated. What more can you tell us about it?"

A hint of amusement came to light in Detective Hamilton's eyes. "You're not going to believe this. The call was made from a payphone."

Shaking his head, Zane chuckled. "I'm surprised any of those things even exist anymore."

"Only one around here." The detective lifted a finger. "At a gas station about three blocks south of here. We're going to pull CCTV footage from the place, but none of the cameras are pointed at the payphone well enough to give us a clear picture of who made that call."

Amelia wasn't surprised. Security at places like gas stations was focused on the store and the pumps, not the payphone outside. "What else can you tell us about it? What did the caller say?"

Hamilton rubbed his hands together, reminding Amelia briefly of the sub-zero temperature. "The caller sounded like a teenager, more than likely a male. He didn't leave a name and didn't go into much detail about why he was at the junkyard in the middle of the night. If you ask me, there's only one reason anyone would be here in the wee hours of the morning, though."

"They broke in." Zane gestured to the main building and then the rows of derelict cars on the other side of it. "Most of the cars parked out there probably still have parts left in them, or metal, at least. The 911 caller was probably hoping to scavenge something of value and wound up over here."

For the second time, Amelia wasn't surprised. She and

Zane had theorized as much on the drive to Paulie's Scrap and Salvage. At first, they hadn't been quite sure how a group of thieves could have managed to bypass security at a facility operated by the Leónes. However, Paulie's was under investigation for being *affiliated* with the family, not being directly involved.

Many businesses throughout the city were affiliated with the Leónes, meaning they were friendly to the family and would occasionally do favors when asked. The level of actual involvement with the criminal underworld varied. Where Paulie's rated on the scale, they'd have to find out.

"As of right now, we've got no reason to think the 911 caller is affiliated with this place." Spencer scratched his temple. "We'll keep looking and try to figure out who they are, but like Agent Palmer hinted, someone calling in a dead body in the middle of the night probably isn't connected to the junkyard or with the Leónes."

To Amelia, especially with what she knew of the Leónes and their commitment to loyalty, the reasoning was accurate. "Let's focus on what we do know." Amelia glanced over to the handful of crime scene techs hovering around the vehicles stacked on a shelf near the car crusher. "This property is huge, and the owner already declined when we asked him for permission to search anything beyond the crime scene."

Spencer frowned. "We'll have to get a warrant if we want to go through anything else here. I'm sure the agents who've been surveilling this place are chomping at the bit to sift through all the cars in the lot. But, like you said, Agent Storm, we'll focus on what we've got. And right now, we've got a dead young woman whose body was stuffed in the trunk of a car next to a compressor."

The SSA was right. The Fourth Amendment of the Constitution protected private property that was out of the immediate vicinity of a crime scene, even when that crime was murder.

Since the victim's body was found in one of the vehicles next to the car compressor, the Bureau was allowed to search a reasonable distance around the area. Until they received a warrant—*if* they received a warrant—they would have to be careful not to overextend their reach. A savvy defense lawyer could have an entire case thrown out if law enforcement was found to have violated any of the accused's rights.

Spencer pointed to the crime scene. "Storm and Palmer, I want you to follow up with the forensic pathologist and the CSU. See where we're at on that front. Detective Hamilton and I will have Russel Armstrong call in all his staff so we can start interviewing them."

Zane snorted. "Good luck with that. He's not exactly the cooperative type."

A smirk made its way to Spencer's face, the type of look a person got when they were the only one privy to an inside joke. "He's not, but we'll see how long that lasts. He can hold out on a warrant all he wants. That's his right. But it's *our* right to make sure we scour this crime scene with everything we've got. Who knows how long that might take? Sure would be a shame if the flow of business here at Paulie's Scrap and Salvage came to a halt because they couldn't compress any cars."

Detective Hamilton grinned at the SSA's comment, and the four shared an amused expression. In Amelia's dealing with the Leóne family, the best tactic was always to hit them where it hurt. And in almost all cases, that meant their wallet.

With the understanding they'd reconvene soon to compare notes, Detective Hamilton and Spencer set off to chat with Russel Armstrong. Amelia stuffed her hands in her pockets as she and Zane strode toward a familiar man standing beside a gurney.

Dr. Adam Francis had wheeled the corpse away from the derelict vehicles and their metal shelving, and he appeared to be wrapping up his part of the crime scene examination. The black body bag on top of the gurney had been zipped closed, concealing the face of the poor soul inside.

The bright work lights glinted off Adam Francis's clean-shaven head as he glanced up from his clipboard. Though his expression remained mostly stoic, his dark eyes warmed when he spotted Amelia and Zane. "Agents, good morning. I'm glad to see you've been assigned to this case."

Flattery wasn't something Amelia usually attributed much value to, but she could tell Dr. Francis's comment was genuine. He wasn't kissing ass—not that Amelia was even sure a man as professional and intelligent as Adam Francis *could* or would do such a thing. The pathologist meant what he said.

Amelia offered him a slight smile. "Good morning to you as well, Doc. I appreciate you saying that. What do we have so far?"

"Let's start off where we found Jane Doe." Dr. Francis clicked his pen, hung the clipboard on the side of the gurney, and produced a box of vinyl gloves. Once he'd handed identical ones to Amelia and Zane, he beckoned them to follow him over to the vehicle that was the subject of so much scrutiny.

A three-tier metal shelf, capable of holding nine vehicles in total, stood off to the side of the car compressor. As the crime scene tech snapped another photo of the black sedan on the bottom shelf, she turned to acknowledge the newcomers. Her blonde ponytail and bright blue eyes were familiar, though Amelia hadn't crossed paths with her in several months. Bailey Howison was a lead crime scene tech with the FBI's own lab.

Bailey lifted two fingers from the Nikon in greeting.

"Howdy. Don't mind me. I'm just taking some more photos now that we've removed the body. Documenting as much of the vehicle as I can before we really start tearing it apart."

Amelia studied the other two cars, both of which occupied the shelves above the black sedan. "I assume we're able to look through both of those too?"

Bailey followed Amelia's gaze. "We are. These cars, the shelving, and then the compactor, plus the open area around it. It's going to be a little tedious to sift through everything here, but we're hoping there'll be something that'll allow us to secure a warrant for more of the property."

As Amelia recalled the stacks of flattened vehicles, she mentally shuddered as a flash of crushed bodies went through her mind.

Please, God, don't let this place be a human graveyard too.

Dr. Francis took the lead, gesturing to the opened trunk as Bailey knelt for more photos. "The trunk was open when we arrived, presumably by whoever made the 911 call."

"We think," Bailey paused, and the camera's shutter clicked, "the person who made the call was checking the trunk for anything of value. And that's when they saw the body. It must've freaked them out enough that they just bolted."

Nodding, Dr. Francis pulled a small flashlight from the pocket of his thick coat. The length of the shelf, presumably built to accommodate much larger vehicles as well as the small cars, left plenty of room for the pathologist to maneuver behind the sedan. "Which is why we were able to pull out the body before truly processing the vehicle. It'll give me a head start on the post-mortem while the CSU keeps working here."

Amelia couldn't help but admire the efficiency of the entire team. Dr. Francis and the medical examiner's office were separate from the Bureau's crime scene techs, but they all worked together like a well-oiled machine. "That's good. What do we know about our Jane Doe so far? I take it she didn't have any ID on her person?"

Dr. Francis clicked on the flashlight. "Correct, there was no ID. Though her clothes were tossed into the trunk alongside her, she was naked, and she had no purse or wallet." He shone the beam on the interior of the trunk. "This is where she was found, jammed in here like a ragdoll. We have plenty of photos you'll be able to review. There was no evidence of defensive wounds or any indication she tried to get out of the trunk. That, combined with the limited amount of blood inside, suggests she was killed elsewhere and deposited here later."

Leaning in as close as she dared, Amelia scanned the gray lining of the trunk. Aside from a single, dark brown splotch of blood roughly the size of a dinner plate, the material was as clean as could be expected. "There's just the one blood stain, meaning the body didn't move around at all, right?"

Zane hunched down, scrutinizing the trunk more closely. "Unless she was wedged in by other items that were later removed. It's pretty clean for a dump site."

As Zane straightened, Dr. Francis turned off his flashlight. "The victim's position leads me to believe she was dumped here shortly after being killed before rigor mortis set in. It would seem she was unceremoniously thrown in the trunk, and then her limbs began to stiffen, locking them in place."

Amelia pondered the other elements of Dr. Francis's summation. "With no evidence that she tried to escape once in the trunk, can you say definitively that she was dead when she was placed here?"

Dr. Francis tapped the flashlight against the heel of his hand. "It appears at some point the victim was bound. There are marks on her wrists and what appears to be adhesive residue as well. While the killer could have dumped her in the trunk, still alive and bound, that means he removed her bindings before he left. Anything is possible, but that seems unlikely."

Moving close enough to inspect the roof of the trunk, Amelia searched for any visual evidence of marks that might show the woman had attempted to escape with her hands. "Any wounds on her fingers or palms?"

Dr. Francis shook his head. "I'll do a more thorough search in the lab, but I didn't see any sign of her attempting to use her fingers to pry open the trunk."

"Any idea of how long she was here?"

Frowning at Amelia, Dr. Francis lifted a shoulder. "Since it's doubtful she was in the position we found her in before the killer threw her in the trunk, then we can use the stage of rigor mortis to approximate when she was tossed into this vehicle. The average timeframe for rigor mortis is two to four hours, but that can be impacted by temperature. In colder temperatures, like we've experienced today and yesterday, the onset of rigor mortis is slowed. Rigor is part of the decomposition process, and just about every form of decomposition is slowed by the cold."

Amelia glanced to the gurney as she ran through a few rough calculations in her head. "How long do you think she's been out here?"

"Out *here*, specifically? I can't say for sure. As for her time of death, well, that's not much easier to calculate at this point. Rigor had begun to wear off when we pulled her from the trunk, so as of right now, I'd put the TOD somewhere in the two- to four-day range."

Zane backed away from the car, flexing his fingers, likely in an effort to restore some of their warmth. "We can probably get a better feel for the time she was dumped here as we examine this car. We'll check the records of when it was brought over here to be crushed." He pointed to a forklift on the other side of the compactor. "The yard uses forklifts to transfer the vehicles from place to place, and that's not a smooth ride. If she was in the trunk when they transported the car across the lot, then there'll likely be some signs of it."

The taste on Amelia's tongue soured. She had personal experience with being jostled about in a trunk. During fellow FBI agent Glenn Kantowski's attempt to frame her for Ben Storey's murder, the agent's lackey had knocked Amelia unconscious, bound her, and stuffed her in a trunk before Amelia eventually awoke in a moving vehicle.

"Correct, Agent Palmer." Dr. Francis's voice cut the memory short. The pathologist pocketed the flashlight and stepped away from the car. "Come on, we can take a look at the body before I load her up and take her to the M.E.'s office."

Suddenly glad to be away from the sedan and all memories of her time as a prisoner in the trunk of a different car, Amelia fell in beside Dr. Francis, Zane right on their heels.

Without preamble, Dr. Francis tugged down the zipper of the black bag to just above her naked breasts. A young female with her limbs still stiff from rigor lay on her side. Bending down, Amelia was struck by the impossibly pale face and the concave shape of her closed eyelids. Streaks of dried, flaking blood coated the one cheek Amelia could observe.

Though she kept her expression neutral, a rush of anger and sadness warmed her skin. "What happened to her? Why is her cheek covered in blood?"

Dr. Francis's face turned grim. "I'll get a better idea of how it happened once she's on my table, but right now, I can tell you her eyes are gone."

"Gone?" Zane echoed. "How?"

The pathologist lifted a shoulder in a slight shrug. "The

'how' still isn't clear to me, Agent. Judging by the blood on her cheeks, this is something that happened while she was upright, probably before she died." He pointed to the one visible cheek. "See? The blood runs *down* her face, not to the side. Meaning she was sitting or standing when this happened."

Amelia's stomach did a maneuver that would have made a fighter pilot proud. "She was *alive?*"

"I'm not sure. But that kind of blood loss only happens if a wound is inflicted antemortem, Agents." Dr. Francis pulled the zipper down farther to reveal an angry, dark red slash in the young woman's chest. "This is what I presume is the cause of death. A stab wound to the approximate location of her heart, made by a fair-sized blade. Again, although it is difficult to tell from this angle, you can see the blood stain is moving *down*. So, she'd have been upright when she was stabbed in the chest."

Amelia pointed to the mark on the young girl's neck. "Was she strangled too? That's a bit of overkill, isn't it?"

The medical examiner rubbed his hands together, presumably to warm them in the freezing temperatures. "That abrasion on her neck is approximately the width of a person's arm. I've seen injuries like this a fair amount in my career. It's typically indicative of a choke-hold."

Beside her, Zane growled under his breath. "Choke-hold on a woman this small. Damn coward."

Ignoring the agent's mutterings, Dr. Francis held his hands out to his sides before continuing with his observations. "I'm going to have to analyze this in the lab, but the angle of penetration to the wound to her chest seems to indicate the killer used their left hand. There are many variables, but once I can examine the depth of the wound, the angle at which the knife sliced through the tissue and organs, and the injuries to her eye sockets, I should be able to give you a definite answer on that. For now, consider it an educated guess."

Calling the excising of a human being's eyes an *injury* struck Amelia as a grave understatement. For the sake of the unnamed young woman in the body bag, Amelia *hoped* the wounds had been sustained postmortem. If the killer was indeed left-handed, that would be quite helpful. Amelia didn't know the statistics on left-handed murderers, but she would be sure to run the information through ViCAP once Dr. Francis could declare positively which hand was used. They didn't have much to go on, but Amelia welcomed any information that could narrow the suspect pool.

She swallowed against the sudden dryness in her mouth.

All these cars, and all this space.

What other macabre discoveries would they make in this little slice of hell? Was Paulie's Scrap and Salvage more than just an affiliate of the Leónes?

Were they responsible for the disposal of bodies for the affluent crime family?

Determination washed over Amelia. She would do everything within her power to secure a search warrant for the rest of the junkyard. Her vendetta with the Leóne family was personal, and this poor young woman had just added another reason for Amelia to take that damn family down.

5

A s I pulled down the overhead door to my storage unit, sealing off the outside world, I groped along the wall for the light switch. I blinked a few times at the abrupt change in illumination, but my eyes adjusted quickly after being out in the morning sun. I'd told myself I wouldn't come here today, that I'd go about my normal routine like any other twenty-two-year-old man.

Fresh out of the shower, I'd been committed to a day of normalcy when I'd heard the news.

"Early this morning, authorities discovered the body of an unidentified young woman on the site of Paulie's Scrap and Salvage, a vehicle scrapyard southwest of the Chicago metropolitan area. Sources confirm the young woman's body was found in the trunk of a car scheduled for its final processing later today."

The cops had found her. Not another victim of the mafia's never-ending war, no. Not some grizzled enforcer or a suspected drug kingpin, but a young woman.

Sammie Howard.

They didn't know her name yet, but I did.

As my heart thundered in my chest, I turned my attention

toward the black metal gun safe in the corner of the room. I needed to calm down, but I wasn't sure how to deal with this level of uncertainty. So, I'd come here. To the one slice of privacy I had left.

I didn't actually store weapons in the fire-resistant cabinet, though I'd recently thrown together a go-bag to keep in this location. I had a total of three different go-bags, one at home, a second in a separate storage unit I used for old furniture and household items, and now a third bag that was here.

Ever since I was a teenager, my father had stressed the importance of being prepared for the unexpected, for the worst-case scenario. It was just a part of our way of life, he'd told me.

Clenching and unclenching my hands, I took a deep breath to calm my rapidly fraying nerves. I was still trying to wrap my head around the fact that the cops had found Sammie's body.

That hadn't been part of my well-crafted plan.

Why had she still been at Paulie's in the first place? Wasn't that damn Nissan supposed to be crushed, the scrap metal shipped off to a client in Japan? That's what had happened with almost all the others.

I gritted my teeth and entered the six-digit code for the lock on the gun safe. I wasn't a novice of disposing of corpses at the junkyard.

None of the other bodies had ever been found—I'd made damn sure of it. I *knew* the crushing schedule at Paulie's like I knew the schedule for my favorite television show. Paulie's scrapyard was consistent and reliable, which was the whole reason we worked with them in the first place.

I hadn't screwed up. I'd gone through the same routine I'd used fourteen times already, not counting the very first one, Jeffrey Atkinson.

The memory returned some semblance of calm to my frazzled mind. Rolling my shoulders, I tried to displace the tension I'd let into my muscles.

Glancing over my shoulder, I half-expected to discover someone had followed me into the storage unit. Of course, that was ridiculous. My rational mind knew such a feat was impossible, but my rational mind wasn't exactly calling the shots right now.

Satisfied I was alone, I pulled open the door to the safe.

Jeff Atkinson's eyes greeted me from the top shelf. The once light brown of his irises, ringed with green along the edges, had been concealed by a white film in the five years since I'd submersed them in formalin—a mixture of formaldehyde and water I'd learned about in a high school biology class.

I blew out a long, relieved breath. The eyes were still in the mixture, no longer out in the world where they could hurt me so badly.

Anger sparked at the edges of my mind like an electrical storm as I gazed upon the orbs. I hated those eyes. They'd always been there, ever since I was a kid. Watching me. Judging me. Torturing me.

Just like the bitch I'd taken care of already, and that kid at the burger place...

No, I couldn't think about him right now. It was too much. Those eyes were everywhere.

Dragging in a sharp breath, I snatched the jar from the shelf, glaring down at the only remaining piece of Jeff Atkinson. Picturing his green-tinged stare brought back a wave of memories, of points in time throughout my life when I'd been tormented by eyes just like his.

No more, though. I was in control now. The discolored film over his irises was proof of that.

I was here to remember. I needed to remind myself the

cops had searched for Jeff's killer too, and they'd come up empty.

I was safe. Safe. Safe. Safe.

Like Sammie, Jeff's body had been found, though he'd floated in Lake Michigan for several days before being pulled from the water. Even if I'd left any trace evidence, which I knew I hadn't, the lake would have washed it all away.

Back then, at the tender age of seventeen, I hadn't nailed down a reliable process like I had now. After I'd finished with Jeff, I'd wrapped his body in a tarp, loaded him into the trunk of my car, and driven to a private marina used by my father and some of his cohorts. I doubted Jeff's corpse was the first to have been dumped off that pier.

Sammie hadn't spent four days in Lake Michigan, but I was *certain* I hadn't left behind any physical evidence. There was nothing that could link back to me. I'd killed her in the basement of a vacant house that had been on the market for more than half a year.

Killing her had been a spur-of-the-moment decision, maybe even a mistake.

No, definitely not a mistake. She'd needed to die. She had those damn eyes. The same eyes as Jeff, the same eyes as him. *Andre. The one who'd tortured me.*

Bullying didn't quite encapsulate Andre's level of cruelty when I was a kid. Growing up around a mafia lifestyle was hard enough for a little boy with one eye that turned in toward his nose, but Andre had taken it upon himself to make the experience much worse. He and his posse of like-minded drones, the type of lackeys who'd ask "how high" if Andre commanded them to jump, had been relentless.

They'd tripped me, given me wedgies, dunked my head in a toilet right after one of them had taken a shit. Once, they'd even waterboarded me. At the time, I hadn't known what they were doing, but the realization dawned on me when I became older.

And, of course, they'd filmed the entire thing. Every time, one of them would pull out their phone to record themselves tormenting the little cross-eyed kid who was too young to defend himself properly.

Rage clenched around my heart like a phantom fist. I tightened my grip on the jar, forcing myself to peer down into those diabolical orbs.

Andre was dead, though not by my own hand. I'd not *witnessed* the life leave his miserable, pig-nosed face. Because of that, whenever I saw those damn eyes, I knew part of him was still alive. I'd keep killing him over and over again until the cacophony in my head finally quieted.

That was precisely why I kept the eyes, why I preserved them. They were the proof, the cold, hard evidence that Andre's reign of terror was gone. *I* was the one in control now.

Which brought me back to the reason for my visit to the storage unit this morning. I wasn't here exclusively for Jeff, and I sure as hell wasn't here for Andre. His eyes weren't even a part of my collection.

Sammie. This visit was about Sammie.

I returned Jeff's jar to the shelf, scanning the other fifteen sets of eyes until I found Sammie's. They were organized in chronological order, though I didn't label any of them. I knew who they were. After all, some famous quote talked about the eyes being the window to the soul for a reason.

Turning the cool glass over in my hands, I finally let out the breath I'd been holding.

I'd been on a temporary assignment for the family in a part of town I didn't usually frequent, helping out some of the other guys after they'd received a shipment of stolen luxury vehicles. I hadn't minded the change of scenery, but then I'd walked into that damn gas station one day on my lunch break.

All I'd wanted was an energy drink and a bag of chips, but *she* was there. She'd been behind the counter, ringing up my items, staring at me, judging me with those hazel eyes that set my brain on fire.

My work assignment didn't end soon enough.

Less than a month after my last kill, I'd tried to resist the urges. I'd made a valiant effort.

In the end, the urge had been too strong. The desire—no, the *need* to eliminate those eyes, to rid myself of her mocking stare, had driven me to make an impulsive decision.

I should have planned better, but here I was. After knocking her unconscious in an alley, I'd driven to a vacant house that had been on the market for more than six months. My father and the rest of the family kept their fingers on the pulse of real estate in the parts of Chicago under their control, and it just so happened that an affiliate of ours was trying to sell their house. He was asking far too much for the place, and I'd taken to using it for my own purposes. I counted on the family keeping the cops away, or at least forcing them to jump through a hundred legal hoops.

I'd taken the precaution of bringing Sammie to the house, right? Hell, I'd even laid a tarp out beneath her to catch the blood. After breaking apart the chair to which I'd bound her, I'd used the wood to start a fire to burn the sheet of blood-stained vinyl as well as her clothes.

Nothing. There was nothing on her body that would lead the cops to me.

Rolling the jar between my hands, I finally allowed myself to relax. It would be okay. The cops wouldn't find me, and neither would the family.

My phone buzzed in the pocket of my coat, grounding me further in reality. Today was a normal day, complete with normal responsibilities, including the work I did at the chop shop.

I squeezed the jar before returning the eyes to their place on the shelf. With another deep breath, I closed the gun safe, locked it, and retrieved my phone.

Unsurprisingly, the text was from my father.

I need to meet up with you as soon as possible. I've got news about work.

My father had never been a man of many words. He'd always exuded the quiet, tough-guy vibe, and the demeanor showed through in his text messages. Despite the vague request, I was confident I knew why he wanted to meet with me.

Sammie's body. Paulie's junkyard. The family would be forced to temporarily shut down its operations at the chop shop, which would cost them money.

A lot of money.

And if they found out I was the reason for the corpse the cops had found at Paulie's?

When a shiver rolled down my spine this time, it was for an entirely different reason. I had first-hand experience with how the family treated those who interrupted its flow of business. They went about their disposal a bit differently, choosing to dispose of bodies by cremation.

It's what I should have done as well, but I shuddered at the thought. I wanted my bodies to be in one piece, not released on the smoke to follow me through eternity. Besides, my dumping ground had served me well...until now.

I spared one last glance to the gun safe before pulling open the door and shutting off the light. As I started down the well-lit hall to exit the building, my stomach grumbled.

My thoughts immediately shot to the cashier at the fast-food restaurant. The guy I'd first spotted two days ago, less than twelve hours after I'd killed Sammie.

So soon after a kill, I should have been able to look that little shit in the eye with a smile on my face. Instead, I'd almost turned around and left for fear I'd reach out and grab his throat in front of God and everyone. I'd told myself such a visceral reaction was simply the result of stress. Work had been hectic lately, and my father had been getting on my case to contribute more to the family.

Now, however, I wasn't so sure. The urges were getting stronger, and the time between them shorter.

Perhaps, if I dealt with this one, then the universe would finally allow me a break.

6

After three hours of interviewing the workers at Paulie's Scrap and Salvage, Amelia wasn't sure if she'd rather take a nap or flip over a table. Taking a long drink from the can of soda she'd purchased from an overpriced vending machine, she shifted her weight from one foot to the other. For most of the morning, she'd been sitting on her ass, repeatedly asking the same questions.

She and Zane had commandeered the breakroom to question the employees of the junkyard one by one. Finally, after a morning filled with tedium and non-answers to more questions than she cared to count, they were nearing the end of the list.

Russel Armstrong had called in all the employees who'd been scheduled to work over the past three days—the timeframe matching Dr. Francis's approximate time of death thus far. They couldn't be sure if Jane Doe had been in the trunk of the black Nissan for that entire time, but they'd decided to proceed as if she had.

To the surprise of no one, the junkyard had no security cameras around the area used to crush cars.

Armstrong's exact words had been, "Why the hell would we waste money putting cameras in there? Ain't no one stealing a busted-ass car that's been compressed into a damn pancake."

Amelia could admit the reasoning made sense. The junk-yard *did* have cameras placed throughout the lot where the partially intact vehicles were kept, but Armstrong had refused to give up the footage without a warrant. Besides, the video was deleted on a rolling twenty-four-hour basis, meaning anything captured around the time of Jane Doe's murder was long gone.

To Amelia's side, Zane leaned back in a creaky plastic chair and stretched both arms above his head. "We've got the shift manager up next, Dennis Barrett. Guy's been scheduled for the past five nights, from one p.m. 'til when they close at nine."

Amelia forced away the fog that had settled in her head during their short break, her attention turning to Zane. "Then he'd have almost definitely worked on the night Jane Doe's body was dumped. Not that he'd have been here when it happened, but still."

Zane drummed his fingers atop the table. "Well, I guess we'll see what he has to say."

They waited in silence for only a moment before a knock at the door heralded the arrival of their newest guest. A uniformed officer ushered Dennis over the threshold, reminding Amelia of a child being escorted into the principal's office. The CPD had been quite helpful in keeping all the employees isolated from each other so they couldn't corroborate alibis or concoct lies based on the questions being asked. As the door closed behind the shift manager, she almost laughed aloud.

Dennis Barrett's pale blue eyes darted around the room

like he was an antelope, and Amelia and Zane were a pair of cheetahs.

Amelia waved at the chair across from Zane. "Have a seat, Mr. Barrett. We've got a few questions to ask you, same as we've been asking everyone else who's been working over the past few days."

The man's dark eyebrows drew together as he pulled out the chair. Still a good two feet away from the table, he dropped down to sit. "Okay. What kind of questions? Do I need to call my lawyer?"

Interesting that the shift manager of a junkyard has a lawyer on-call.

Outside of the agents at the FBI, Amelia wasn't aware of anyone who had a lawyer saved in their contact list.

Maybe Alex...?

She pushed aside her curiosity. Though there was no official confirmation yet, they *were* dealing with a junkyard that had ties to the Leóne family. "That's entirely up to you, Mr. Barrett. If you've got the spare change to call up an expensive defense lawyer just so he can sit and hold your hand while we ask you some routine questions, then far be it from me to stop you."

Barrett narrowed his eyes and snorted. "Yeah, we'll see how routine these questions actually are. What do you want to know?"

Zane tapped the printed work schedule he'd pulled off one of the breakroom walls. "You've worked every night for the past five days, is that right? Including Saturday through Monday?" He slid a picture of the dead girl's face across the table. "Did you see Jane Doe on any of those days?"

The exasperation dissipated from Barrett's face as he glanced at the image. It was almost as if the query had made him more comfortable—like he was perfectly fine answering questions about Jane Doe but not about the junkyard itself. "I worked those days, but I've never seen that girl before. Why? Is that when you all think that girl was killed or something?"

"That's correct." Amelia set down her soda, lamenting for a beat that it wasn't strong coffee. "Did you see anything out of the ordinary over the last three or four days? Was anything around the yard out of place, like maybe it'd been tampered with overnight?"

Rather than the sarcastic responses Amelia had received a handful of times so far that morning, Barrett appeared thoughtful as he scratched his cheek. "No. I didn't notice anything weird. Just the usual."

Zane beat Amelia to the follow-up question. "And what would the *usual* be? What kinds of security measures do you guys use here?"

Barrett lifted a shoulder and let it fall. "Same as any junkyard, probably. We don't waste our resources on the scrap over by the crusher, though. I figure the razor wire on top of that big ass fence would be enough to keep kids from breaking in, but they find ways around it."

Amelia was glad Barrett was at least slightly more forthcoming than some of his employees had been. Then again, if they truly were affiliated with the Leóne family, Barrett might have more authority, and therefore more leeway when it came to speaking about the business. "Are break-ins a regular thing around here?"

The man crossed his arms and shrugged again. "I don't know about regular, but yeah, they're something we've got to deal with. That's why we've got cameras by the vehicles with anything of value still left in them."

From a business perspective, the rationale made sense to Amelia. Junkyards like Paulie's typically kept a lot full of vehicles in various states of disrepair, which they'd permit paying customers to sift through to find parts. Selling the parts from those types of vehicles was the primary source of income for many junkyards. When resources were finite, it was best to spend them on protecting the more valuable assets.

A lack of security cameras also made perfect sense for a junkyard where the mafia scrapped stolen vehicles. Though Amelia and Zane's primary focus was the dead body found in the Nissan, she doubted a murder victim showing up in a location affiliated with the Leónes was a coincidence. Odds were, the dead girl was somehow connected to the Leónes, possibly even to the suspected chop shop that used Paulie's as a dumping ground.

If they could only prove any of it.

Amelia turned the idea over in her head a few times before she spoke. To get to the bottom of one criminal act, they had to get to the bottom of the other. "Mr. Barrett, you don't think it's weird that the FBI is interviewing you right now, and not the city police?"

Barrett's jaw tightened, though only for a split second. The gesture was enough to tell Amelia the man was squirming beneath his calm persona. "Agents, I manage a junkyard. I'm not a lawyer. I figure if you two are here doing these interviews, then there's probably a reason for it. It's not my job to figure out what that reason is."

The man's articulate responses so far had already told Amelia he was smarter than he let on. How much smarter remained to be seen. "I'm not sure I believe all that. You seemed pretty defensive when you first came in." She made a show of weighing her hands. "If we get a warrant to search beyond the car compactor, do you suppose we'll find the VINs of a few stolen vehicles?"

Zane's eyebrows lifted as if he'd just been enlightened. "That's a great question. Suppose we discover that Paulie's Scrap and Salvage is harboring a lot full of stolen, scrapped vehicles?"

To his credit, Barrett's face remained calm. "I wouldn't know anything about that, Agents. I was under the impression you two were here looking for the person who killed that poor girl."

Amelia shot the man a reassuring smile that was only partially sarcastic. "We are, Mr. Barrett. But I'd find it hard to believe that those two things *aren't* connected, if you follow my meaning. But..." she held her hands out to her sides, "earlier, you said you didn't know who the girl in the trunk is? Are you sure you haven't seen her around, maybe?"

Something resembling relief passed over Barrett's face. Odd to be relieved to talk about a murder instead of stolen cars. But that silent relief spoke volumes to Amelia. "No, I hadn't seen her before. I've got no idea who she is."

Zane shuffled around a couple papers. "According to the vehicle crushing schedule your boss was kind enough to provide, the Nissan with the girl's body in its trunk was scheduled to be flattened yesterday. Why wasn't it?"

Barrett rubbed his temples and sighed. "The truth? We were short-staffed. You talked to most of my guys already, and you probably noticed that not a lot of them were at work yesterday." He gestured to the window at the other end of the room, the blinds of which had been drawn. "Usually, we don't like to leave any vehicles stacked by the crusher, but we weren't able to get through them all."

Amelia kept her expression carefully blank. Internally, however, she was more than a little perplexed.

If the mob had dumped the girl's body in the trunk of a car for disposal, wouldn't they have prioritized the vehicle over all others? Why did they leave Jane Doe intact for an entire extra day?

Clearly, Barrett knew more about the yard's connection to the Leóne family's chop shop than he was willing to admit.

His cluelessness regarding the victim, on the other hand, appeared genuine.

Zane's voice pulled her from the contemplation. "How close are you to your staff, Mr. Barrett? Do you know if any of the guys on your team were having marital issues?"

Barrett blinked a few times, his eyebrows knitting together. "We get along here at the yard, but I wouldn't say I'm buddies with any of them. To answer your question, even though it's weird as hell, no. Not that I know of. One of them went through a divorce a few months back, but that wasn't anything out of the ordinary. Why? What does that matter? You think one of my guys killed that girl because of some *marital* issue?" He let out a derogatory snort. "Yeah, right."

The smile that spread over Zane's face was as cold as ice. "Statistically speaking, most female homicide victims are killed by a male acquaintance. Oftentimes, that acquaintance is a boyfriend or a husband. So, if you don't mind, we're going to need the names of every employee who have access to this place."

Barrett crossed his arms. "Does that request come with a warrant?"

Placing both palms on the table, Amelia leaned forward to pin the man with a withering stare. "Mr. Barrett, if you make me get a warrant for this, it will become my personal goal to make your life as big a pain in the ass as you're making this investigation. I will drain your entire bank account with how often I make you call your lawyer, and I will throw every obstruction charge at you that I can find. The Assistant U.S. Attorney is a personal friend of mine, just so you're aware."

Though scarcely noticeable beneath his beard, Barrett's face blanched. Amelia had gotten across her point. "Fine. I'll get it for you. Anything more than that, and you're going to need a warrant, though."

Amelia offered him a sugary sweet smile in response.

Russel Armstrong, Dennis Barrett, and the entire staff at Paulie's Scrap and Salvage were hiding something. Something big. Though the shift manager's willingness to discuss Jane Doe was curious when compared with his obstinance at giving details of the junkyard's likely side business, Amelia found it hard to believe the two were unrelated. If she wanted to avoid tunnel vision, she had to keep an open mind.

She'd read about killers using derelict vehicles for body disposal, and the method had even been present in movies and television shows.

Were they dealing with a crime of passion, where the killer had dumped Jane Doe's body at the junkyard to get rid of evidence? Or maybe a man whose advances Jane Doe had turned down? An ex-boyfriend, an abusive spouse...the list went on.

Or were they facing a calculated serial killer who'd chosen Paulie's Scrap and Salvage specifically because he knew a mob-related junkyard would stir up a heap of unrelated baggage for the FBI to sift through before they could truly investigate the murder?

Could it be it was a mob dumping ground? It appeared to be the ideal place to dispose of corpses.

Or was it something else entirely?

Amelia's gut told her they were only scratching the surface, and her experience from the past few cases—investigations that had ended in brutal serial killers claiming more lives before Amelia could catch up to them—prodded her to waste no time.

7

Special Agent Joseph Larson shrugged out of his wool coat and handed the garment to the neon-haired woman at the nightclub's coat check desk. Her ruby-red lips curled into a flirty smile as she handed him a ticket for his coat. He returned the expression, but only for the sake of being polite.

She wasn't ugly, but she also wasn't quite his type. Joseph preferred women who held higher statuses in life. Women he could break. Something about the coat check girl's demeanor told him she'd already been through the wringer. There was no challenge in breaking a woman who was already broken, though it could be a fun way to pass the time.

Well, maybe not. Cassandra Halcott had proven that much.

As Joseph navigated his way past the bar and toward the entrance of the club's exclusive VIP section, he fought to keep the sour expression off his face. Blue and purple icicle lights twinkled overhead, lending the entire place a futuristic feel. A crowd of dancers in the center of the large, open room gyrated to the beat of a current techno song while others sat at glowing tables and post-modern lounge areas with their drinks.

At age thirty-six, Joseph's clubbing days were mostly behind him. But this place, Exhale, wasn't just any ole nightclub. Only a specific sect of the population was permitted through the solid metal doors upstairs.

Exhale wasn't affiliated with any specific criminal organization, though Joseph figured the majority of its regulars were either friends with the Leóne family or the Russians. As luck would have it, the man Joseph asked to meet him here for drinks was friendly with both organizations.

Straightening his suit jacket, Joseph approached a familiar man stationed at an unremarkable metal door. As soon as his gaze fell on Joseph, the bouncer straightened to his full height and reached for the door handle. "Evening, Red. Nice to see you again."

The reverent tone of the man's voice brought a slight smile to Joseph's face. "Nice to see you too, friend."

Exhale didn't use real names, not even for its staff. Some had acquired nicknames or codenames, like Joseph's own moniker, Red. There was a sense of comfort in the anonymity, though many of the staff did, in fact, recognize Joseph on sight.

Not that any of them would ever rat him out. They were paid well for their work, and those who performed reliably were given the added benefit of protection by the Russians and Leónes. Being friendly with either of those two groups was a fast-track to being financially comfortable in the city. All they required in return was loyalty, which most were happy to give.

Around here, Joseph commanded *real* authority. Not like his time at the FBI office, where he was forced to answer to the Supervisory Special Agent, and then the Special Agent in Charge, and then…the list went on.

With a grin, the bouncer pulled open the heavy door and ushered Joseph through. A set of concrete stairs greeted him, the faint purple glow of more icicle lights visible at the top. Joseph hurried up the steps. He'd been cautious about meeting with Brian Kolthoff tonight, just as he had been for the past several months.

The Leila Jackson case had royally fucked up Joseph's usual mode of operation. Before Leila, Joseph hadn't worried about being spotted with Brian. At that point, Kolthoff had been a law-abiding citizen. He had been classified as a successful D.C. lobbyist and a former venture capitalist, but never a criminal.

Leila had changed everything. Why in the hell Brian had been so damn dead-set on buying the sixteen-year-old when there was so much scrutiny on her, Joseph couldn't understand. Of the three of them—Joseph, Stan, and Brian—Brian had always been the most cautious. Stan had made his share of blunders, and whether or not Joseph liked to admit it, so had he…

He gritted his teeth as he emerged on the landing. A short hall brought him into a spacious room that sported a wall of tinted glass to look out onto the club's floor. The bar along the back wall of the VIP section was only about half the size of the main bar, but the stock of liquor was high-end. In accordance with Brian's request, no one staffed the luxurious suite when he was here.

Joseph had learned over the years that Kolthoff was a hands-on sort of man. Though Kolthoff's net-worth had continued to climb, even in the months after he'd slipped out of charges for nearly buying Leila Jackson, the guy always mixed his own drinks and cooked his own meals.

Maybe he's paranoid. Thinks someone's going to poison him.

The idea was ridiculous at first, but there was some merit to it. Plenty of powerful men had been poisoned by their enemies throughout history.

Clearing his throat to announce his presence, Joseph strolled over to the bar.

Brian glanced up from the glowing screen of his phone and straightened in his large, overstuffed chair. "There you are. I was starting to wonder if you were going to bail on me."

Joseph waved a dismissive hand. Even with their rapport, Joseph knew better than to ghost someone like Brian. "No, I just had some work shit that ran late. A body was found at a junkyard the Leónes like to use to get rid of stolen vehicles they scrap for parts."

One of Brian's eyebrows quirked up. "I'd heard about that. Have the Feds made any headway on identifying the Doe?"

As Joseph poured whiskey into a stout crystal glass, he shook his head. "No, not yet. There was no ID on her person, and her prints aren't in the system. The M.E. sent her DNA off for analysis, but if her prints aren't in the system, I doubt her DNA is, either. Could be a relative or something in the database, though. We'll see." Though he didn't have much of a stake in what had happened at Paulie's Scrap and Salvage, he preferred to keep his ears and eyes peeled regarding any Leóne-related cases his department caught.

Setting his phone on the frosted glass coffee table in front of him, Brian picked up his own drink and swirled the contents a couple times. "They don't use that yard as a dumping ground, do they?"

"I've got no idea. As far as I know, no. When they need to make a body disappear, they've got connections to an actual morgue, including the incinerator." Joseph added the finishing touches to his whiskey sour. Leaning against the bar, he took a sip. He wasn't the best bartender in the world, but he was pleased with his handiwork.

"That makes the most sense, but a junkyard isn't bad, especially when they're compressing the material and selling it as scrap." Brian pushed to his feet, stretching as he rose. "But I gather that's not why we're here tonight, is it? Seems we've got more pressing things to deal with."

Joseph tried to ignore the patronizing tinge to Brian's statement. Their inner circle hadn't been firing on all cylinders lately, but Joseph knew damn well it wasn't exclusively his fault.

"No." Joseph took a deep drink of the whiskey sour, savoring the way the liquor burned its way down his throat. "I'm here because I'm being…" he waved a finger in the air as he searched for the proper term, "*proactive,* I think is the best way to put it."

Brian drained his own glass and made his way to the other side of the bar. "Proactive about what, exactly?"

Flattening his palms against the cool glass surface of the bar, Joseph heaved a sigh. "About Michelle. I think it's time we get rid of her."

"You know that's not possible." Brian met Joseph's stare, his gaze steely, like a parent interrogating their kid after he'd come home past curfew. "Personally, I don't care either way, but Stan said she was off-limits."

Anger threatened to crack through Joseph's cool composure. He clenched one hand and inhaled deeply. "Since when does he call all the shots? It's not for him to say. I can find him someone else. Someone who's *not* an ex-girlfriend of mine." He forced his irritation down along with another sip of his drink. "One of my contacts in the CPD told me someone on the outside's been looking into Michelle's missing persons case."

"I'm not happy this mess is bubbling to the surface." Brian's blasé demeanor fell away, revealing a hint of exasperation. "What the hell's going on?"

Joseph mulled over his next words for a long moment before he spoke. His contact hadn't been able to tell him *who* had requested the records from the CPD, but Joseph had narrowed the list down to two potential candidates. "I believe the person investigating Michelle's disappearance is either Amelia Storm or Cassandra Halcott."

Maybe both.

Midway to reaching for a bottle of vodka, Brian froze. "Excuse me? Did you say that an FBI agent and an assistant U.S. attorney might be looking into the disappearance of your ex-girlfriend? Why? What the hell is going on?"

Joseph dragged a hand over his face, suddenly exhausted. "Because they're bitches, Brian, that's why. Cassandra broke up with me a month and a half ago, but she can't seem to let this shit go. I know she's been collaborating with Amelia Storm, and if you ask me, there's only one thing the two of them would have to talk about."

"And that's you." Brian's tone was flat and unimpressed. "You've got to be shitting me. What is it with you and Stan and your fascination with women who don't want you?"

"You're not one to talk, all right?" Joseph barely managed to rein in his anger before he spat out a remark he'd surely regret. He felt like he was running a race in reverse. "You remember Leila Jackson, right? And how you *had* to go through with that sale, even though the FBI was all over it?"

Brian's head rolled on his shoulders. "It was a mistake."

"So is this!" Joseph almost shouted his rebuttal. If he was talking to anyone other than his friend, he'd have been tempted to punch them in the jaw. "We help each other out when we make mistakes, don't we? That's what we did when Stan decided to hire someone to kidnap Gianna Passarelli out of the fucking blue. We tied up all the loose ends there, didn't we? Then, we did the same for Leila Jackson. Now, all I'm asking is that we do that for Michelle Timmer. You see where I'm coming from?"

Silence descended over them like a thick blanket of fog. The only sound was the rhythmic thud of the bass downstairs.

Finally, when Joseph was convinced Brian intended to ignore his question altogether, his old friend raked a hand through his brown hair. "You're right. We'll clean it up. We've got to be especially careful with getting rid of Michelle, though. We can't let anything be found. You're going to need to do your due diligence here, all right? Make sure there are no witnesses who can put the two of you together too close to her disappearance. Tie up loose ends."

Joseph held up his hands like he was surrendering in a war. "Consider it done."

"And…" Brian paused, locking his scrutinizing stare onto Joseph's, "you're going to forget about Cassandra Halcott and Amelia Storm, yeah? If they keep sticking their noses in our business, we'll deal with them. But the best way to deal with them right now is to cover our tracks." His eyes narrowed. "No more high-profile women, Joseph. No law enforcement either. Not even a fucking meter maid."

Slowly, Joseph nodded. He'd already suspected Brian would advise him to sever ties with Amelia and Cassandra. That Brian thought he could give Joseph orders grated on his nerves, but he bit his tongue before a rebuttal could manifest.

Logically, he knew Brian was right. The same stern warning had been given to Stan when he'd gone off on his Gianna Passarelli tangent.

Just as well. He'd gotten sick of the teacher he'd screwed

on the side toward the end of his and Cassandra's relationship, but he'd find another plaything. One who wasn't an FBI agent or an assistant U.S. attorney. One he could use up and throw away, just like Michelle.

He wasn't finished with Cassandra, though, just like he wasn't finished with Amelia. Despite Brian's order, Joseph decided he'd merely put the two women on the backburner.

Joseph wasn't a man who ever gave up.

He'd get back to them.

One way or another, he'd make them pay.

❄

BRIAN KOLTHOFF WATCHED the patrons of the club mill about on the ground floor with little interest as he swirled his half-empty drink. Joseph had departed a half-hour ago, leaving Brian to his own devices in the VIP suite of the secret nightclub.

When he was younger, back before he'd made his first billion, the idea of having such a luxurious space all to himself was exhilarating. Reserving the room wasn't cheap, at least not to most people. Now, at nearly fifty-six, with more money piled up in offshore accounts than he'd ever be able to spend in ten lifetimes, the VIP suite at Exhale was just another weekday.

Speaking of just another day...

Glancing down at his vodka tonic, he finally allowed himself to heave the sigh he'd been holding ever since Joseph left.

What in the hell was he going to do with that man? Joseph was only half right when he'd said the Michelle Timmer issue was no different than Stan Young's obsession with Sofia and Gianna Passarelli.

Not that the sentiment was of much comfort to Brian. And for Joseph to bring Leila Jackson into the conversation?

Brian's chest tightened as a spell of anger rolled over his body. Closing his eyes, he took in a deep, steadying breath. This was neither the time nor the place for him to give himself over to the simmering rage.

Leila had been a mistake, plain and simple. Unlike Stan and Joseph, Brian's screwup didn't stem from an uncontrollable urge or an obsession. Brian had simply miscalculated. He'd overestimated Emilio Leóne's capacity for discretion, and he'd been caught in the crossfire. Instead of Emilio's underlings delivering Leila to him, he'd come face-to-face with none other than Joseph's recent infatuation.

Amelia Storm had brandished her service weapon, cuffed him, and read him his Miranda rights, but he'd never lost his cool.

How would Joseph react in that same situation? Would he keep his mouth shut, obey the FBI agent's orders, and politely ask for a lawyer? What about Stan, for that matter?

He snorted. Doubtful in either case. Stan liked to present himself as a cool, collected individual, but it was all a charade.

Unfortunately, as Brian had begun to realize, the answer to his question held more and more weight.

These two women, Cassandra Halcott and Amelia Storm, were going to be Joseph's downfall. Brian didn't want to believe it. He wanted to think his old friend would have the common sense to back away from the lawyer and the agent, but...

Brian threw back the rest of his drink, the bitterness of the vodka tonic no match for the sour taste that had filled his mouth.

If Joseph went down, then Brian and Stan would be up shit creek without a paddle. Even their amassed billions wouldn't be enough to bail them out of that storm. Or, if they did manage to escape prison time, their reputations would be irreparably tarnished. Stan would lose his senate seat to the next Ben Storey, and the politicians with whom Brian rubbed elbows would be too afraid to be spotted in public with him.

What if Amelia Storm and Cassandra Halcott were to disappear, never to be seen again?

He tightened his hand around the cool glass. Killing both of them would be one hell of an undertaking, and chances were good their murders would raise more suspicion than they would quell.

Unless the deaths looked like accidents.

No, modern-day forensics would find *some*thing. Brian was certain the Bureau would pull out all the stops to find who'd killed two of their own.

For the time being, leaving Amelia and Cassandra alive was the best option. Instead of killing them, the men had agreed Brian would help Joseph mislead the two women, ensuring they found neither hide nor hair of Michelle Timmer.

Just like the last time someone got too close.

Trevor Storm had been on the cusp of breaking open Stan's closet full of skeletons, but Joseph had seen to him. Perhaps that was why he was so infatuated with Amelia. After killing her brother, Joseph must have been propelled by some sick sense of fascination, some desire to screw the younger sister of the man he'd murdered in cold blood.

Killing Trevor had been an obvious decision. None of them were sure where Storm had gotten his information, and despite their efforts to unearth the source, they'd come no closer. Considering the time that had passed since Trevor's death, the general assumption was that the detective's murder had sent a message.

A message Amelia Storm and Cassandra Halcott had apparently chosen to ignore.

Brian would keep his law enforcement contacts close in the coming weeks. Offing the two women wasn't the best option right now, but Brian hoped that would soon change.

8

For the second day in a row, Amelia was out the door before the sun had crested the horizon. Fortunately, she and Zane were more prepared for the early start this time.

Slumping down into the warmed passenger seat of Zane's Acura, Amelia fastened her seat belt and pulled a tablet from her handbag. Ever since returning to Chicago, she'd come to loathe driving in the city's traffic. Fayetteville, North Carolina, the city where she'd been stationed during most of her military career, was relatively populous, but its rush-hour was nothing compared to Chicago.

Since Amelia hadn't learned to drive until after leaving to join the armed forces at age eighteen, she'd never truly become used to bad traffic. Switching from Norfolk, Virginia to Boston had been a jarring experience. For the first two weeks of her time in the Boston FBI Field Office, she'd been late every day except one.

Gradually, with much frustration and a great many swear words, she'd adjusted to the change. She didn't *enjoy* navigating Chicago or Boston traffic, but she'd come to a point where she could make the drive without turning into the Incredible Hulk.

Zane, on the other hand, had been born and raised in Jersey City. Nightmare traffic was practically second nature to him. In fact, Amelia was fairly sure she experienced more road rage in the passenger seat than he did at the wheel.

Any time the opportunity presented itself to toss him the keys, Amelia took it. She'd much rather conduct research during the trip than get cut off by some asshat who thought the blinker on his fancy car was an optional extra.

As Zane shifted the Acura into gear, Amelia brushed off the memories and tapped out the PIN to unlock the tablet. She used so many different electronic devices for work, she was surprised she could keep all the PINs and passwords straight. Luckily, she had a head for numbers as well as a unique system of jotting them down in case she ever forgot.

"Any new messages from the M.E.'s office?" Zane's voice pulled her away from where she'd been staring blankly at the tablet.

Amelia blinked a few times, still clearing the cobwebs of sleep from her brain. "No, just the ones from last night setting up our visit this morning. Dr. Francis put in a rush on the tox screens for our Jane Doe."

After their mostly pointless conversations with the employees of Paulie's Scrap and Salvage, Amelia and Zane had spent the remainder of their day searching through missing persons reports.

Dr. Francis had provided them with an official time of death estimate of two-and-a-half to three days, or sixty to seventy-two hours. The TOD had narrowed down Amelia and Zane's search to young women who'd last been seen sometime on Saturday.

When they included Jane Doe's hair color, height, weight, and approximate age, the list had shrunk to only three—Lily

Schultz, Sammie Howard, and Shana Patton. Through the blood and grime that had coated Jane Doe's cheeks in the crime scene photos, Amelia and Zane hadn't been confident enough to say for sure whether or not they had a match. Hell, if Amelia didn't know any better, she'd have thought the three young women were sisters.

By comparing Jane Doe to the three young women once Dr. Francis had finished the postmortem exam and cleaned off her face, Amelia was sure they'd be able to tell if Lily, Sammie, or Shana was the poor girl who'd been found at Paulie's Scrap and Salvage.

Or maybe Jane Doe wasn't any one of them. Maybe she was some out-of-state visitor who'd been in the wrong place at the wrong time. If that was the case, only god knew how much time would pass before they could identify her.

Amelia opened Lily's case file, scrolling through to ensure no new information had been added overnight. When she spotted nothing different, she turned to Sammie's. Again, no change. Sammie Howard and Lily Schultz were both still missing.

As Amelia pulled up Shana Patton's file, her eye was immediately drawn to a line near the top. "Oh." When she shifted her attention away from the tablet, she was met by Zane's curious stare.

"Oh what?" He glanced back to the traffic light as it changed from red to green.

"Shana Patton's missing persons case was closed last night. She was found." A chuckle slipped from Amelia's lips as she scanned the case summary. "Shana was camping down near Springfield, and she didn't have cell service. She'd told her boyfriend, but apparently, he forgot."

Zane snorted. "Camping in February? You'd think he'd have remembered something so unusual."

Locking the screen of the tablet, Amelia couldn't disagree. "It's warmer down south, but still."

After the moment of shared amusement, the rest of the trip to the medical examiner's office passed largely in silence. Neither Amelia nor Zane were much for conversation so soon after waking, and she was grateful for the shared understanding. If Zane had tried to strike up a more in-depth discussion about camping when Amelia had only been awake for forty-five minutes, she might have lost her mind.

Whether due to the coffee she'd drunk on the car ride or the wall of cold air that greeted her when she stepped out of the Acura, Amelia was wide awake when she and Zane made their way through the front doors of the medical examiner's office. The concrete exterior of the building gave the place the feel of a fortress or a prison, but fortunately, the aesthetic didn't continue once they were inside.

The young man behind the receptionist's desk buzzed them in, advising that Dr. Francis was waiting for them downstairs. Amelia and Zane had visited often enough that they had no need for directions.

As she approached the set of double doors leading to the body storage area, Amelia rapped her knuckles against the stainless steel. "Dr. Francis?" She shouldered open the door, and the pathologist donned in scrubs looked up from his own tablet.

His face warmed as he spotted Amelia and Zane. "Good morning, Agents. I appreciate you two coming in here so early. I've got quite the workload today, and I wanted to make sure I got all my notes and takeaways to you ASAP."

Amelia returned his smile. She also had a long day ahead of her, provided they could identify Jane Doe. If they couldn't, then, well. She'd be sitting on her hands until they could. "We'll try to get out of your hair." Her face warmed. "Er...I mean..."

Dr. Francis ran a hand over his bald head and chuckled. "It's all right, Agent. It's a common figure of speech. I'm bald by choice, anyway. Hair's just too much of a hassle at my age."

Zane's cheeks were tinted red, and Amelia could tell he was holding back laughter. He ran his own hand through his hair as if checking that the strands were all where they were supposed to be. "There're plenty of days I can relate."

At the remark, Amelia briefly pictured what Zane would look like if he shaved off his neatly styled, sandy brown hair. She was sure he'd still be handsome, but he'd look...weird. Some people could pull off the buzz cut or bald look, including plenty of women, but Zane? That would take some getting used to.

She gave herself a mental shake, clearing the imagery from her mind. "What've you got for us?"

Expression turning from bemused to focused, Dr. Francis set the tablet aside and began the process of pulling on his personal protective equipment while Amelia and Zane did the same, though to a much lesser extent.

The entire room was stainless-steel and white tile, as sterile as sterile could be. Two entire walls were taken up by square metal doors, many of which were labeled with the names of the deceased. Still, others remained unoccupied, waiting silently for their next visitor.

With a hiss, Dr. Francis pulled open a drawer on the middle left of the wall near the room's entrance. "I looked over the missing persons reports you sent me last night, Agent Storm, and I think I've identified Jane Doe."

Relief and anticipation threaded their way through Amelia's veins. "You did? Who is she?"

Shaking his head slightly, Dr. Francis pulled down the white sheet to reveal a pale, lifeless face. "I'd like to hear your thoughts before I give you mine. Just to make sure we're all in agreement." He pointed to the counter where he'd acquired his PPE. "There are eight-by-ten photos of the three young women in that folder over there. There are also copies of my notes for you to take with you back to the field office."

Zane strode over and scooped up the documents. "One of the three cases was closed overnight. Shana Patton was camping and didn't have any cell service."

Dr. Francis's eyebrows furrowed. "Camping in February? To each their own, I guess."

Zane chortled. "That's what we said. It narrows the possibilities down to Lily Schultz and Sammie Howard." He pulled two photos from the folder, keeping one while he handed the other to Amelia. Each eight-by-ten was a printout of the girls' DMV picture.

As Amelia stared down into Sammie Howard's hazel eyes, she noted the young woman was about as happy to be at the DMV as Amelia usually was. Her skin tone was a touch paler than average, though that wouldn't help them much right now. The young woman in front of them was almost as white as the sheet used to cover her.

Amelia glanced back and forth between Sammie's picture and the girl lying on the steel table. The hairstyle of the girl in the photo was slightly different, but the dark blonde shade was still the same. And the missing eyes...

I need something that doesn't change. Something like a birthmark or a tattoo.

She leaned in closer to Jane Doe, holding the photo beside her impossibly pale face. Jane Doe had no birthmark, no tattoos, but...

"There." Amelia pointed to a small mole on Sammie Howard's upper lip. One which was mirrored on Jane Doe. "She has the same beauty mark as Sammie, and they both have another mole on their right cheek. What about Lily?"

Zane lifted Lily's DMV photo for Amelia to examine.

"No. Lily has a scar on her left eyebrow, but I don't see one on Jane Doe's face."

Amelia turned to Dr. Francis. "Jane Doe is Sammie Howard."

The pathologist dipped his chin. "That was my conclusion as well."

Passing the photo of Lily Schultz to Amelia, Zane dug his phone from the interior pocket of his coat. "All right. Sammie Howard's mother reported her missing. Let me give her a call so we can get her down here for a positive ID."

Dr. Francis gave Zane an appreciative nod. "Thank you, Agent Palmer. We'll wait to go over the victim's injuries until you get back."

So early in the morning, Amelia briefly worried Zane might not be able to get ahold of Sammie Howard's mother, Amy.

That woman is missing her only child. There's no way she won't have her phone right beside her, even if she's sleeping.

Zane returned after a few minutes, his expression even more solemn, if that was possible. "She's on her way here. Should be about a half-hour."

Being in the same room with the body of a young woman whose life was stolen from her far too young was like a gut-punch no matter how many crime scenes Amelia worked. But coming face-to-face with a grieving mother made the entire scenario even more heartbreaking. Even if Amelia worked the rest of her life in the FBI, she'd never get used to breaking the news to a victim's family.

Perhaps she was different from her peers in that way. After having lost her own mother to cancer when Amelia was ten and then losing her father to alcoholism for seventeen years, she was uniquely familiar with loss and mourning. Two years ago, when she'd received the news that her brother had been killed in the line of duty as a CPD homicide detective, her heart had shattered all over again. The feeling was familiar but in the absolute worst kind of way.

Rolling her shoulders, Amelia returned her focus to the ghostly white girl and the forensic pathologist. "What can you tell us about how she died?"

The little cloud of melancholy—the moment of silent reflection upon learning a grief-stricken mother was headed their way—that had held the three of them in place drifted away, and they were back to business.

Pushing down the white sheet, Dr. Francis pointed a gloved finger at a garish wound on the young woman's chest. The bright red of fresh blood was long gone, leaving in its place a deep, bruised coloration. "Her official cause of death is a laceration to the right ventricle of the heart. We took some measurements, which I've included in my notes."

Amelia leaned closer. "Straight through the ribs."

The M.E. nodded. "You'll recall when we were at the junkyard, I noted that the wound was caused by a stab from someone holding the knife in their left hand. While a person could use their non-dominant hand to stab someone, they wouldn't be able to excise the eyeballs without using their dominant hand. Far too much skill is necessary for that very precise task. Based on the trajectory of how the knife penetrated the subcutaneous tissue and the angle with which the optic nerve was severed, your murderer favors his left hand. Also, as you can see based on the size of the stab wound on her chest, the murder weapon is a relatively large knife, which appears to be at least partially serrated on one side."

Zane frowned, his gray eyes shifting from the body to the pathologist. "A tactical knife?"

"Correct." Dr. Francis replaced the sheet. "No signs of sexual assault, and no other injuries below the stab wound to the chest."

Amelia breathed a silent sigh of relief upon learning that

Sammie hadn't been sexually assaulted. Amelia and Zane's most recent case had involved a serial killer who'd raped and then killed three different men and also murdered their families. Sammie Howard's death was a tragedy, but at least she hadn't had to experience *that* before she was killed.

Dr. Francis gestured to Sammie's throat. "The abrasion we noted in the field was indeed caused by a person's arm. The measurements align with the vic being placed in a choke-hold."

Slowly, Sammie Howard's final moments came into focus. "She was probably choked unconscious, then, right?"

Zane crossed his arms, his gaze fixed on Sammie's body, expression unreadable. "Knocked unconscious and abducted, more than likely."

"More than likely." Dr. Francis gestured to Sammie's concave eyelids. "Now, for the part I'm sure you've been wondering about."

"Her eyes." Amelia had heard of cases where killers cut a piece of the victim's hair or even pulled a tooth to keep as a trophy, but there was something far more intimate about excising a person's eyes.

"Right." The pathologist pursed his lips, appearing contemplative before he spoke. "Both eyes were removed with a tool, a sharp knife most likely, possibly even a scalpel. The cuts were clean, and damage to the surrounding tissues was…minimal. The perpetrator was familiar with what they were doing."

A couple months ago, Amelia and Zane had investigated a serial killer who'd carved Bible verses into his victims' flesh, but cutting out a person's eyes was a whole new level of messed-up. "You said when we were first looking at her body that the blood on her cheeks meant she was upright when her eyes were cut out and that she might have been alive."

"I did, and she was. Her eyes were cut out before she was

stabbed in the heart, and the direction of blood flow indicates she was either standing or seated upright when those wounds were inflicted. Now, the pattern of liver mortis also indicates she was on her side at some point, but that would have occurred after she was killed." He paused to lift up one of Sammie's arms. "The trace analysis of the adhesive found on her skin along with the width of the residue indicates her hands were bound with duct tape or a similar product."

The picture painted of Sammie's last moments was horrifying and flames of anger licked at the edges of Amelia's heart, but she pushed the sentiment aside. "Why would the killer cut out her eyes? Were they trying to send a message?"

The question was largely rhetorical. She doubted Zane or Dr. Francis knew any more about the killer's motivation than she did.

Zane scratched his temple. "I don't know. As far as I know, it's not a calling card for any active contract killers in the city. We can double-check when we get back to the office, though. It's possible we're looking for an enforcer or a hitman who's new in the area."

If that was the case, Amelia wanted to put an end to their career. She filed the possibility away for later. "Was there any other evidence found on her body?"

"Unfortunately not. I scraped beneath her fingernails, but they were quite clean. I sent the little bit of dust over to the FBI lab. I also checked between her teeth but didn't find anything promising there, either." Dr. Francis pulled the sheet over Sammie's face, pushed the drawer closed, and snapped off his gloves. "As far as the lividity of her body is concerned, it appears to back up the theory that rigor mortis set in after she was deposited into the trunk of that car."

Zane lifted an eyebrow. "And since the blood on her cheeks indicated she was upright when her eyes were cut out, she'd have been moved not long after she was killed."

"Exactly." The pathologist stuffed his hands in the pockets of his scrubs.

Amelia's curiosity was piqued. "So, the killer more than likely knew he was going to have to dump her body before he killed her. That would be true of a contract killer, but it could also fit someone just trying to cover up their crime."

Zane frowned but nodded his understanding. "In a sense, it tells us nothing."

Amelia held back a sigh. "Basically. Her eyes could've been cut out because a mob hitman was trying to send a message that she'd seen something she shouldn't have. Or the killer could've cut out her eyes because he has a sick fascination with human anatomy or some sort of hang-up about people looking at him funny."

Dr. Francis scratched his neatly kempt goatee. "I've had bodies come across my table with their tongues excised, some of which were the victims of contract killers. It's not an uncommon message for organized crime to send to those who testify against them. I can imagine that symbolism extending to sight as well. In any case, it's a safe assumption the removal of the eyes and the reason for it are relevant."

Though the removal of Sammie Howard's eyes had led Amelia to think they might be dealing with another serial killer, the lack of evidence so far still left her with doubts. "We'll have to do a deep-dive into Sammie's background and the background of her family. See if there are any connections to the Leónes or any other criminal organization. If nothing else, then to rule out that angle. And while we do that, we can see if there are any family enemies or connections like that."

For the next fifteen minutes, Dr. Francis gave them a rundown of the rest of his examination. The rushed tox screens had all come back negative, indicating Sammie had been sober as a judge when she died. No sedatives had been found in her blood, which made sense when Amelia considered the bruise she'd sustained from a probable chokehold.

Once Dr. Francis had finished his synopsis, Amelia and Zane made their way back to the front room of the office to wait for Amy Howard.

Even if Amelia hadn't had the opportunity to quickly research the Howard family before Amy arrived, she'd have known who the woman was as soon as she stepped through the door. Dark circles shadowed the skin beneath her blue eyes, and her red-tinged eyelids were evidence she'd been crying.

She'd maneuvered her dark hair into a messy bun, and her fashionable peacoat contrasted sharply with her gray and black striped slippers. A taller woman accompanied her, and though the stress was evident on her face, she was in better shape than Amy.

Heart squeezing for Sammie's mother, Amelia introduced herself and Zane before leading both women to a small meeting room. Contrary to fictional depictions, most victim identifications didn't involve an in-person viewing. Photos taken of the deceased were usually enough to make a positive ID.

The instant Amelia flipped over the first picture of Sammie, her mother's eyes filled with tears. There was no need to provide the woman with a second photo. She knew.

Swiping her cheeks with a tissue, Amy sniffled. "That's her. That's my Sammie."

Amelia slid the photo back across the table and replaced it in the folder. "We're so sorry for your loss, Ms. Howard."

Amy blew her nose with hands that shook so bad Amelia was surprised she could hold the tissue. "Thank you. Just call me Amy, please."

To Amelia's side, Zane threaded his fingers together. "We have some questions we'd like to ask you, but if it's too difficult right now, we can set up a later time instead." His voice was kind but still quiet and somber.

"No." Amy dabbed her nose and shook her head. "Ask your questions now, Agents. I'd rather get this over with."

The other woman, Brandy Maynard, squeezed her friend's shoulder. "It's all right, Amy, don't push yourself."

"I know. I know. I'd just like to get this done with so I can go home and have a minute to myself."

Amelia flipped open a notepad. "We'll get through the questions as quickly as we can." She turned to Zane, and he nodded.

As they ran through the first few routine questions, they received routine answers. Amy had last seen her daughter before she left for work on Saturday, and she'd last heard from her when she sent a text message advising she was on her way home. Though Amy wasn't familiar with the exact route her daughter took, she confirmed Sammie took the L since neither of them had a car.

Sammie hadn't been dating anyone and hadn't had a relationship in more than a year. She'd not had a spat with any of her friends and was generally well-liked by Amy's acquaintances.

Amelia was still sympathetic to Amy's grief, but she'd become more determined as the interview went on. "What about Sammie's coworkers? Were you familiar with any of them? Did she have any issues at work, maybe a problem with management or something like that?"

"No, I didn't really know any of them." Amy started to shake her head but froze midway through. "Wait, there was that one guy. Sammie said that a customer had been pestering her repeatedly to buy him booze after he was cut off at the bar near there. He made her uncomfortable, but management wouldn't do anything about him because he never harassed her on their property. All they did was recommend she walk to the L with someone else."

Amelia tightened her grip on the pen to keep her sudden rush of anticipation from sweeping her brain away. The lackluster response from Sammie's boss sent a jolt of anger through her, but it was still a lead. Less than twenty-four hours into the investigation, discovering a lead was imperative if they were to catch Sammie's killer.

She and Zane wrapped up the questions shortly afterward, each of them handing cards to Amy and Brandy and reiterating that they should call no matter the time of day if they remembered anything.

Amelia practically sprinted to the car, and she wasn't surprised Zane kept pace with her.

They had a lead, and time was of the essence.

9

As Zane followed Amelia into the manager's office of the gas station, the scent of roasting hot dogs made his stomach groan. He reminded himself that, in his experience, food on the rollers at gas stations always smelled ten times better than it actually was. Unfortunately, the rationalization did little to ease the pangs of hunger. He and Amelia had been in such a hurry to get to the M.E.'s office that morning, he'd skipped breakfast altogether.

He hoped the hangry mood would hold off until after they'd finished interviewing Sammie's manager and coworkers.

Once the door was closed behind them, Zane turned to the manager—Diane Beischel, according to her shiny name tag—as she took a seat behind a messy desk. Pushing a pile of papers aside, she gave them a nervous smile. "Sorry about that. We just don't want to disrupt the customers out in the store, you know?"

He returned her smile, though he doubted his expression held much warmth. "That's all right. We'd rather talk to you and your employees in a quieter space, anyway."

The manager straightened. "Right. What can I help you with? We get a lot of cops through here, but not many FBI agents."

Zane glanced to the single chair facing the desk and then to Amelia, raising his eyebrows expectantly. She replied to his unanswered offer with a slight shake of her head. If there was only one chair, then they might as well both stand.

Amelia pulled a notepad from her coat pocket. "We're here about one of your employees, Sammie Howard. By now, I'm sure you've noticed she's been missing."

Expression falling faster than the temperature at sunset, Diane started to wring her hands atop the desk. "Yeah. She was scheduled today, actually. We...we haven't been able to get ahold of her, and her mother told us she hadn't seen or heard from her either. That's when I got really worried."

A pang of sympathy pushed aside Zane's hunger-driven irritability. "Sammie Howard's body was discovered early yesterday morning. She was murdered."

Diane blanched, her hands freezing in place. "Oh my god. I'm...I don't know what to say. Sammie was great. We're not supposed to play favorites or anything, and I don't, but I always liked working with Sammie. She was so nice, and not just to customers. She was a nice person all around."

Amelia's face was filled with empathy as she clicked her pen. "We're very sorry for your loss, Ms. Beischel. We do have some questions we'd like to ask you, as well as anyone who might have worked with Sammie on her shift Saturday night. Who was the manager on duty that night?"

Clenching her hands, presumably to keep from fidgeting, Diane licked her lips. "I...I was. Sammie and I both hate swing shifts, but we always wind up stuck on one per week. Usually Saturdays."

As Amelia scrawled out her notes, Zane took his cue. "Amy Howard told us Sammie had confided in her about a man who'd been bothering her at work. A drunk who kept asking her to buy him booze after he'd been cut off, from what I understand."

"Oh, *him*." Diane's knuckles turned white. "I think by now, he's asked all of us to buy him booze after he's cut off. I'm just a shift manager, so I don't really have any...*authority*, I guess you could say. To kick people out of the store, or ban them, or what have you, that has to be approved by the general manager, Jackson Grippe. He's kind of passive and super nonconfrontational. His dad owns the store, and he put Jackson in charge. So the GM wouldn't let us ban Booker. Er, sorry, that's the guy's name. Booker Gilbert."

A name to go with a possible suspect? This is too good to be true. What's the catch here? Are we on that old Ashton Kutcher show where he jumps out of the woodwork to tell someone they just got Punk'd?

He peered up at the camera mounted in the corner, but he doubted it was used for a practical joke television show. "What else can you tell us about Booker? How long has he been hanging around here? You said he's asked all of you to buy him booze by now. So, is Sammie not the only person he harasses?"

Diane shrugged her slim shoulders. "I wouldn't call it harassment, at least not as far as what I experienced. It's annoying, but it's the same kind of annoying as the panhandlers asking for money, you know?" She pressed her lips together and shook her head as if she was coming out of a haze. "That's just my experience, though. Um, as far as how long he's been around? I couldn't say exactly, but it's been at least a few months. I noticed one weird thing...he was wearing a wedding ring when I saw him the first time, but that was the only time I saw it on him."

Zane glanced to Amelia, and he was confident they were thinking the same thing. A drunk who'd been through a divorce had the potential to be a loose cannon. Even if Booker was a perfectly nice human being on an average day, if the man felt like he'd hit rock bottom, there was no telling what could set him off.

But how did Booker and his divorce tie back to the Leóne family? Or Sammie, for that matter? Zane doubted someone unaffiliated with the Leónes would just happen to break into a junkyard that operated in conjunction with a Leóne chop shop.

Pushing aside the litany of questions that remained, Zane turned his attention back to the manager. He was eager to leave the gas station to find Booker Gilbert, but he and Amelia still had to be thorough. "Do you know if Sammie was dating anyone? If not dating, then maybe seeing anyone casually? We've spoken to her mother, but we're aware that people Sammie's age aren't always as forthcoming with their parents as they are with friends."

A weak smile passed over Diane's face. "Sure, I understand that. But no, Sammie wasn't involved with anyone I knew about. We'd talk about relationships occasionally, especially after my boyfriend and I broke up a couple months ago. Sammie's last relationship was almost a year ago, I think, and she said she wasn't in any hurry to get back into one."

Amelia tapped the pen against her notepad. "Do you know if Sammie maintained any contact with this ex? Did he ever show up around the store, or call her, text her over social media, that kind of thing?"

Diane shook her head. "No. He'd moved across the country for college, which I think was a big part of why they broke up."

Well, that rules out the person who's statistically most likely to commit the murder. The thought didn't give Zane much reprieve. Victims killed by bitter spouses and ex-spouses were tragic, but those sorts of crimes were far likelier to be solved than a homicide committed by a stranger.

It still might not be a stranger. There's still Booker Gilbert, and Sammie might've been seeing someone she'd kept secret from her mother and her coworkers.

Unlikely, but still possible.

Zane filed the thought away for later. "Back to Booker Gilbert for a moment. Has he been here since Saturday night?"

Diane absentmindedly straightened a handful of papers atop the desk. "I don't think so, no. I've worked every day since Saturday, but I've been here during the day. You might want to ask some of the clerks who work the swing shift."

As Amelia and Zane ran through the remainder of their questions, no other clues immediately came to light. After speaking with Diane, they interviewed all the employees on shift in hopes of learning more about Sammie's personal life.

To Zane's disappointment, Sammie's coworkers all confirmed what her manager had told them. Sammie was kind and polite, even when she wasn't dealing with customers, she had no enemies as far as they knew, and she wasn't romantically involved with anyone.

With regards to Booker, the employees were all of the same mindset. Booker was obnoxious when he was drunk, but he'd never given off the impression of being dangerous. As far as Zane could tell, the main reason other workers had reported Booker to the general manager was because he wasted their time while they were on shift. If he wasn't asking them to buy him a six-pack, then he was talking their ears off about random subjects.

None of the information absolved Booker. However, the employees' accounts of their interactions with the man reminded Zane that this case might not be the slam-dunk he was hoping for.

The first forty-eight hours of a homicide investigation were critical to the successful outcome of the case. Many thought that meant they had to solve the case in the limited timeframe, but what they truly required was a solid lead. So far, Zane and Amelia had acquired plenty of information, but Booker was their first true lead.

Now, the question at the forefront of Zane's mind was a simple one.

Was Booker a key witness, or was he the perpetrator?

10

Amelia pulled open the door of the modest apartment building, holding it as Zane trotted down the sidewalk. They'd wrapped up the interview of the remaining gas station employees within a couple hours. Amelia and Zane had left plenty of business cards behind, encouraging the employees to reach out if they remembered any details, no matter how small.

From there, they'd put in a request for assistance from the local police precinct. The officers who patrolled the neighborhood were more familiar with businesses and goings-on around the area, and they'd be more easily able to locate security cameras that might have captured some of Sammie's last moments. There was still plenty of ground to cover in the investigation, and Amelia was grateful for the CPD's aid.

Having covered all their bases around the gas station, for the time being, Amelia and Zane had headed straight to Booker Gilbert's current address—less than a five-minute drive from the convenience store. Easily within walking distance.

As she waited for Zane, Amelia scrutinized the

surrounding buildings. A couple large, Victorian-style houses stood across the street, but for the most part, the block was occupied by three-story apartment buildings circa the seventies and eighties.

Based on what they'd learned so far, Booker had moved three months ago, which was consistent with the timeline of his divorce. As Amelia and Zane had pulled into the neighborhood only moments earlier, she'd been struck with how...*normal* the whole area appeared. They weren't in a ritzy part of town, but the area was well maintained, nothing to point out that a "wino" lived in the area.

Shooting Amelia a grin, Zane followed her inside. "You're such a gentleman."

She chuckled, grateful for the moment of humor amidst what had otherwise been a tense, fast-paced day. As they climbed to the second floor, Amelia mentally ran through the brief research they'd conducted before heading into the building.

Most notably, Amelia had found no indication of a link between Booker Gilbert and the Leóne family. Aside from a single speeding ticket received twenty years ago, Booker's record was clean. He had two kids, both of whom were out of state attending college.

Booker wasn't a wealthy man, but he also wasn't in debt. His financial status reduced the possibility of him borrowing money from the mob to pay his bills or of him doing a favor for the Leónes for a bit of cash. Amelia had been surprised to find that, two weeks ago, Booker had been laid off from his management job at a call center for a popular electronics manufacturer. She'd wondered if the loss of his steady income had sent Booker spiraling, but Zane had reminded her that most layoffs came with some sort of severance, especially for middle-management. After a chat with the HR director Zane's theory had proven to be true.

Financially speaking, Booker Gilbert was sound, despite the fact he'd recently lost his job. All records pertaining to his divorce indicated the dissolution of marriage had been a long time coming and hadn't been a sudden, earth-shattering bombshell. However, the records kept by the court and the reality of the situation could still be vastly different.

Rapping her knuckles against the door of Booker's apartment, Amelia was almost certain they'd find the man gone—having fled due to his involvement in Sammie's murder or out on another bender.

Seconds ticked away in silence. With a quick look at Zane, Amelia knocked again. "Booker Gilbert, open up. This is the Federal Bureau of Investigation."

Right away, she caught a faint utterance from the other side of the wooden door. A handful of curse words, if she'd heard correctly. "Hold on!"

Anticipation tingled her scalp as both she and Zane automatically stepped to the side, their training kicking in without any thought. Their suspect hadn't bought himself a one-way ticket to Panama, hadn't even elected to lay low at a hotel on the outskirts of town. He was *home*, and Amelia was prepared to get some answers.

Before she could turn to Zane to comment on the situation, the door creaked open, revealing a middle-aged man with a head full of salt-and-pepper hair and a beard to match. Though the beard had been well-maintained in his driver's license photo, his facial hair was now every bit as bedraggled as the rest of him. Plaid pajama pants, slippers, and a hooded sweatshirt seemed fitting of someone with no place to go and no plans to be seen.

Squinting through bloodshot eyes, he examined the agents. "Did you say you're with the FBI? Are you fucking with me? I mean, you *look* like Feds, but what the hell are you doing *here*?"

The lackadaisical response was far from what Amelia had anticipated and served to pique her curiosity more. "We're with the FBI, Mr. Gilbert." Amelia produced her badge, followed by Zane.

Booker's eyes went from slits to the size of dinner plates. "Holy shit." He blinked a few times, and the awe dissipated. "Wait a second, did Brenda...did my ex-wife send you? What the hell is she trying to pull? She already got the damn house! What else could she possibly want?"

For a beat, Amelia was just as puzzled as Booker appeared, though she kept her face calm and neutral.

She and Zane were at this man's apartment to ask him questions about a murder he might have committed, and he was worried his ex-wife was pulling a stunt? If Booker had killed Sammie only a few nights ago, wouldn't the murder be the first concern on his mind?

Maybe he was so drunk he forgot he did it. He could've blacked out and killed Sammie in a rage.

No, that didn't make any sense. Sammie's eyes had been carefully removed. That wasn't something easily achieved, especially if the perp was out of it. And it didn't match with what Dr. Francis had learned so far in his analyses. The entire process of Sammie's murder had taken far too much time to be attributed to a single, drunken blackout.

Maybe Booker Gilbert was a well-trained liar used to covering his tracks.

"Sir, we're not here because of your ex-wife." Zane's voice was as calm as his expression, but Amelia sensed a note of her own curiosity in his demeanor. "Do you mind if we come inside to talk to you?"

Booker rubbed his eyes, reminding Amelia of a small child trying to will away the outside world. "You're *sure* Brenda didn't send you here? You're not following up on some shit she's trying to pull? Not that I even know what the hell she *could* pull to get the damn Feds involved, but..." he shook his head and pulled in a deep breath, "yeah, come in, Agents. Whatever you're here for, I'd rather deal with it somewhere my neighbors can't overhear."

Wordlessly, Amelia and Zane made their way after him, closing the door behind themselves. The faint aroma of pine wafted past them as they followed Booker into a small dining area next to the kitchen. Aside from a handful of family photos hanging in the dining and living rooms, most of the walls were bare. A few empty beer bottles lined the counter beside the sink, but otherwise, Amelia was surprised at the man's tidiness.

What was more surprising was Booker's hospitality. His behavior so far was much more consistent with a normal witness, not a suspect. Suspects—the guilty ones, at least— were often cagey, even rude.

The smart ones aren't rude, though.

Booker might not come across like a criminal master- mind, but the true geniuses never did.

Waving to the dining table, Booker shambled into the kitchen. "I'm going to make myself some coffee. All I've got is Folgers, nothing fancy. But if you want a cup, let me know."

Amelia was alert and observant, keeping an eye out for any abnormality, but she couldn't recall the last time a suspect had offered her coffee. "That's all right. You seem like you probably need it more than we do."

Booker half-laughed, half-snorted. "You're right about that one. Okay, if you don't want any coffee, and you're not here because of Brenda, then what do you need from me?" His attempt at humor fell short, and he came across as more nervous than anything.

As she took her offered seat, Amelia observed the tremor in Booker's hands as he prepared the pot. Was he nervous simply because he was talking to the FBI, or did he have something to hide? Or perhaps the shaking was another hangover side-effect. "Mr. Gilbert, you're familiar with the Fast Trip convenience store located a few miles south of here?"

The man nodded as he poured water into the carafe. "Uh-huh. I, uh...I've been at the bar down the street from there quite a bit lately. It's convenient, having the Fast Trip right there. But I guess that's why it's a convenience store, huh?"

There was a hint of a different emotion besides his nervousness, and it took Amelia a moment to place the sentiment.

Embarrassment.

Booker was almost sheepish when he mentioned the gas station and the bar—as if he'd done something he'd rather forget.

Not on the level of what you'd expect from a murderer, though.

Zane turned away from where he'd been focused on the photos on the wall and pulled out the chair at Amelia's side but didn't sit. "Were you at all familiar with one of the clerks at the Fast Trip, Sammie Howard?"

A flush crept up Booker's neck, and his eyes darted around the small galley kitchen. "Um, well, yeah. She...she's a nice kid. You know, when I show up there hammered drunk and start talking about space and planets and shit, she actually talks to me about it instead of telling me to piss off. The kid's a saint."

Amelia didn't miss his use of the present tense when referring to Sammie and made a mental note of it. Confusing past and present tense in conjunction with a victim was often the beginning of a suspect's downfall. "Mr. Gilbert, several of the employees at Fast Trip complained about you harassing them. Asking them to buy you booze after you'd been cut off."

He heaved a sigh that would've made a leaf blower proud.

Covering his eyes with one hand, he slumped back against the wall. "Those aren't my proudest moments, all right? But, honestly, how stupid is it that a bar won't serve a drunk guy a drink?" He dropped his hand to his side. "Okay, sorry, that's not what you want to hear. Yeah, I've been around there a little too much since my divorce. Been spending too damn much money and time at that bar."

Zane tilted his chin at the beer bottles. "I take it you've decided to stay home to do your drinking recently?"

Though Amelia hadn't thought it possible, Booker's cheeks turned an even darker shade of red. "Yeah, actually. Less likely to make an ass of myself if I'm at home. Is...is that really why you two are here? Because I've been acting like a fool asking some younger kids to buy me booze when I'm cut off? I mean, I guess that might be illegal? Something about circumventing having to show my ID?"

As far as Amelia could tell, his cluelessness was genuine. The man legitimately thought she and Zane were here because he'd been pestering a handful of gas station employees. "We're here because of Sammie Howard. She's dead."

In the blink of an eye, all the color drained from Booker's cheeks, leaving the dark circles beneath his eyes even more pronounced. "D-dead? How? Like...from cancer or something? Or was she..." He trailed off, his shocked stare fixed on Amelia and Zane.

Zane sat down and clasped his hands together atop the table. "She was murdered."

They'd decided to keep the details about Sammie's missing eyes out of the press. Only a handful of people—Dr. Francis, his assistant, Amelia, Zane, and Spencer—knew about the garish wounds, and they'd keep it that way for as long as possible.

Booker raked a hand through his hair. "Jesus, that poor kid." Suddenly, his stance went rigid, his gaze jerking back to

Amelia and Zane. "Wait a second. You're here because you think *I* had something to do with that? Just because…because I asked her to buy me a six-pack? No, I didn't touch her. That wasn't me. Search my place if you want, run whatever tests you want. You want DNA? It's yours. I didn't hurt that poor girl."

"Did you see her on Saturday night after her shift?" Amelia kept her voice calm and level, holding her curiosity at bay. "According to her pass for the L, she never boarded the train at her stop. Which means she disappeared somewhere between Fast Trip and the L."

Booker opened and closed his mouth a couple times, his gaze vacant. "Yeah, I saw her. I think she was headed toward the L… I'm sorry. I was pretty hammered, and I'd just been booted out of Danny's. I wasn't ready to call it a night, and I'd learned from experience they wouldn't sell me any liquor at Fast Trip in that condition. So, I offered her a few bucks to go pick me up a six-pack." He held up both hands. "But that's all I did. I wasn't blacked out or anything. I'd remember if I hurt someone."

Producing his phone, Zane leveled Booker with an expectant glance. "Do we have your permission to record this?"

Amelia expected Booker to protest, but the man continued to surprise her. "Go ahead. Record whatever you want. I didn't hurt her, okay?"

As Zane set his phone in the center of the table, he motioned to one of the chairs across from them while providing the pertinent date and time information for the recording. "Have a seat. Booker Gilbert, can you tell us where you were on Saturday night?"

Half-rambling, Booker did his best to recount his Saturday—from the time he woke up to what he ate for lunch to heading to Danny's Pub and some of the people he interacted with there. His recollection grew less detailed the deeper into the evening he got, ending with tales of the rounds of darts he won and lost at the bar. "I was sitting on the bench across the street from Danny's Pub. I won't lie, I was waiting for someone to walk by so I could ask 'em to get me a sixer. That's when...when Sammie showed up. I don't know how long I'd been sitting there. It's possible I dozed off waiting. When I noticed her and approached her, I think I scared her a little, like she didn't know I was there."

"What did you say to her?" Amelia kept her tone non-accusatory. She wasn't convinced Booker was their guy, but she had to keep an open mind until they could officially rule him out.

"I think I asked her if she could do me a favor, then mentioned how the bar wouldn't serve me anymore. I *do* remember offering her a few bucks to buy me a sixer." Expression focused, he rubbed his temple like he was a brilliant scientist on the cusp of a new discovery, not a regular Joe trying to recall what he'd done during a bender a few days earlier. "It seemed like she was thinking about it, and this dude showed up."

If Amelia had an antenna, it would have shot up the instant Booker mentioned another man.

Over the past few days, Booker had plenty of time to fabricate the entire story. So far, however, Amelia had spotted no signs that Booker was trying to deceive them. With any luck, the local police around the area would be able to find a security camera to corroborate Booker's account of the events.

She tempered the sudden rush of anticipation. "What did this dude look like? Did you know him?"

Booker licked his lips, still concentrating. "I didn't get a long look at him, and I wasn't exactly totally with it. But he didn't look familiar. It seemed like he came from Danny's, but I don't recall seeing him in there. I don't know where the hell he came from or what he'd been doing."

He was waiting.

Amelia kept the thought to herself. Provided the strange man was actually real, he'd have been lurking in the shadows waiting for his chosen victim to happen by the vicinity. He wouldn't have shown up in the bar because he didn't want to risk being identified later on.

"Did he say anything to you or to Sammie?" Zane's curious tone told Amelia he shared her cautious optimism.

"Yeah, he said something about leaving her alone. It seemed a little excessive, the way he paraded out of the shadows and told me to get lost, but then I'm not sure if I looked menacing to an outsider." Booker's eyebrows furrowed, and he finally returned his gaze to Amelia and Zane. "It's not like I was catcalling her or begging her for cash. For Christ's sake, she reminds me of my daughter. But I wasn't about to try to reason with that guy. Seemed like he was the type trying to make himself come across all gallant so he could score points with Sammie. Like a peacock, you know? How the males fan out all their pretty feathers to attract a mate. I knew that guy would've clocked me if he had the chance. It would've been like he was showing off his feathers."

"A peacock?" Zane echoed.

Booker didn't acknowledge him. The man's stare had become distant, even crestfallen. "Do you think that was the guy? He walked with her. I think they were going to the L." He dropped his face into his hands. "Oh my god, could I have stopped him? I should've done something, shouldn't I?"

Despite the lingering uncertainty, Amelia was struck by a pang of sympathy for this man. "You couldn't have known his intentions. And if he's the person who killed Sammie, then he would've more than likely been armed."

Zane dipped his chin. "My partner is right. There's no way you could've known, and there's always the possibility this isn't the person who killed Sammie. He could be another witness, but we need to find him to figure out his role. Could you tell us what this man was wearing, whether or not he had an accent, things like that? No detail is too small."

Booker straightened in his chair, nodding vehemently. "It was a little dark, and I'd been drinking, but I did see his face, and I'm very good at recognizing faces. He was a white guy, young, about the same age as Sammie. Dark hair, dark eyes. Nice looking leather bomber jacket. When he walked away, I remember thinking there was an emblem or something on the back of the jacket, but I didn't get a good look at it."

Beside her, Zane shifted in his seat, and Amelia wondered if he was thinking the same thing that she was. For a man who'd been tossed from a bar for being drunk, Booker Gilbert was showing a great deal of recall. Was it true or fake in the hopes of tossing them away from his own foul stench?

Booker closed his eyes, and Amelia watched the thin skin of his eyelids move back and forth, as if their owner was watching a video rewind. She and Zane remained quiet while their suspect spent nearly a minute reviewing his mental "film."

His eyes popped open, and he sat up straighter. "He was wearing jeans and some kind of boots, like the kind construction people wear, you know? He was maybe a few inches taller than me. I'm five-ten, so maybe he was six-foot, something like that."

Amelia forced herself not to frown at the description. *Dark hair and dark eyes* sounded an awful lot like so many of the mafiosos she'd encountered over the years. "Did he have any distinguishing features? A cleft chin, dimples, tattoos, scars?"

"No scars or anything that I saw. Oh, wait." He snapped

his fingers. "There was a tattoo. Me, being the drunk dumbass I was that night, sort of tripped over the curb. He grabbed me to keep me from face-planting onto the concrete, and that's when I saw the tattoo on his wrist."

Keeping any hint of excitement from showing on her face, Amelia gave the man an encouraging nod. Even if the young guy in the bomber jacket—if there truly had been such a man—hadn't killed Sammie Howard, he could very well be a key witness. "Do you remember what the tattoo was?"

"Yeah, actually." Booker tapped his temple, almost like he was attempting to get all the dots in his mind to align correctly. "It was pretty unusual and reminded me of my daughter. She's always been big on philosophy, and she's minoring in it in school. I'm pretty sure, from what I saw of the tattoo, that it was the ouroboros." He drew a circle on the tabletop with his finger. "My daughter tells me it's a philosophical symbol that represents eternal life through reincarnation. The new feeding on the old, or something like that. Anyway, that was his tattoo."

Zane tapped an index finger along his wrist, a tic Amelia often noticed when he was thinking. "It's usually depicted as a snake biting its own tail."

"That's what it was, yeah. The part of the image where the snake is biting its tail was near the heel of his hand. Like I said, if it weren't for my daughter, I probably wouldn't know what it was called."

Amelia wasn't entirely sure where the discovery would lead them, but she was grateful to have found a lead so soon. "Mr. Gilbert, do you mind coming back to the FBI office with us? We'd like to take you up on your offer to provide DNA, if that's still on the table. And perhaps you'd be able to work with a sketch artist?"

"Yeah, sure. Whatever I can do to help. I'm not sure how

many details of that guy's face I'm going to be able to recall, but I'll do what I can."

Booker's cooperation—innocent or contrived though it may be—was a breath of fresh air. In the Organized Crime Division of the FBI, Amelia was used to dealing with obstinate individuals like Russel Armstrong and Dennis Barrett from the junkyard.

But was Booker cooperative because he was innocent and had nothing to hide, or was this all a grand attempt to mislead them?

There was only one way to find out.

She had to keep digging.

11

The wooden bench creaked as I slid into the RV's breakfast nook. I'd never been a huge fan of camping, not that it was a regular activity for a city boy like me. My father had taken me on a few trips when I was younger, but we were rarely gone for longer than a couple days. I didn't mind the transition from concrete buildings to nature. In fact, I enjoyed the change, but I always missed the amenities of home.

Turning to peek through the blinds covering the tinted window at my side, I noted the lack of other recreational vehicles throughout the camp site.

"Guess that's what I should expect in the middle of February in Illinois. Only the hardcore camping nuts are out in this shit."

Well, the hardcore camping nuts and the man I'd been sent here to kill.

Rage burned low in my gut as I recalled the conversation with my father that landed me in this frigid wasteland last night. All I'd done was walk through the front door of his lavish residence to be met with the frigid gaze of dear ole dad.

Other than that single look, my father had hardly acknowledged me. With a barely discernable tilt of his head, he'd beckoned me to follow him through the foyer and into the kitchen. Wordlessly, I obeyed. One didn't refuse a man like my father.

Even at almost fifty, he was still a force to be reckoned with. A man's man, a tough guy who never cried, never showed weakness. He was exactly who I'd aspired to be for the first eighteen years of my life.

It had been a hard lesson to learn that I'd never be like him.

That lesson had come at the gym, when I'd finally reconciled with myself that, no matter how much I trained, how fit I got, or how adept I became at boxing, mixed martial arts, or ju-jitsu, I'd never stack up to this man. I'd never make him proud.

Perhaps that's what the guys who'd tormented me as a child had been trying to convey. The best I could do was stomp out the figurative demons one by one and seize their most potent weapons—those damn eyes. The eyes I'd always secretly wished I'd had, at least before the surgery that had transformed me from the cross-eyed little shit into a respectable young man.

After the procedure, the bullies had lost their edge. Their main source of ridicule for me had been removed. They'd moved on to someone else, but their taunts never left me. Never went away.

Never.

Worse, my father's house always drudged up the past, simultaneously welcoming me like an old acquaintance and kicking me in the gut.

Parts of the home had been updated over the years, but

the high-end base was the same. The top-of-the-line fixtures weren't there because of my father. He'd never cared much for the home-based luxuries. Not like my mother had.

A sharp pain manifested in my chest as I recalled the woman who'd brought me into this world. She was gone. Six months ago, cancer had claimed her life, and her loss had left a void in mine. I gritted my teeth and forced the memories into the back of my mind. She hadn't known about what I truly was, and she'd never find out. Part of me was grateful for that.

My father was a different story…

"I know about the girl." My father's intense stare bored into me like a laser from a science fiction movie.

His simple statement jerked me back to reality. "What? What do you mean? What girl?"

But I'd already known.

"Don't play stupid with me. I don't have time for that shit. You know what girl I'm talking about. Sammie Howard, the body the Feds dug out of Paulie's junkyard."

If my father had walked up and punched me square in the jaw, I was sure my reaction would have been about the same. How had he known I was responsible? I'd been so careful. I'd kept my actions secret ever since the first time he'd caught me when he'd taught me how to ditch a corpse so it would never be found.

There was no point in denying that I'd killed Sammie. Not to my father. "How did you find out?"

He crossed both arms over his broad chest, his gaze unfaltering. "Something about you isn't quite right, son. I've known since you were a kid, and that was confirmed ages ago when I had to show you how to dispose of that first body I found." My father's nose wrinkled in distaste at the memory of tracking down the smell of the boy I'd shoved under our back deck. "But, in this life, in this family, there's no real way to tell what's right or normal, is there?"

You're a freak! You're a freak! You're a freak!

I wanted to slap my hands over my ears to shut out the taunts of my childhood bullies but opted to thrust them in my pockets instead. "I suppose."

Father narrowed his eyes. "You've got some proclivities I can't quite wrap my head around. Some sort of need to kill, am I right?"

I'd never pictured my father as a brilliant man, but apparently, he was far more astute than I'd realized.

"I-I d-don't kn-know." *I ground my teeth together, forcing the stutter to a halt, giving myself a moment to pull my shit together.* "I guess. But how is this any different than what you do for the family? I've seen you kill someone, remember?"

My father scratched a spot on his bearded face and sighed. "It's different because I'm doing my job. I've never offed anyone without a damn good reason. Never anyone who wasn't connected to this life, all right? That's the difference. What I do is a means to an end, what you did to Sammie Howard, that's...different."

In a way, his reasoning made sense, though logic did little to quell the storm of anger and defensiveness brewing in my head. "As far as the cops are concerned, it's not different. In the eyes of the law, a murder is a murder, period."

"You might be right there, but that's exactly what's got me concerned, son. Any time I deal with someone for work, I know damn well there's nothing that'll lead back to me." *He spread his arms wide.* "Or any of us. We make sure of it. What about this girl? Did you...did you rape her?"

Disgust rose in my throat like bile. "No. God, no, what the hell do you think I am?" *Even if that was the sort of reprieve I sought—which it damn sure wasn't—I'd never touch someone with those eyes.*

He held up a hand. "Just covering my bases. What about evidence? Did she scratch you? Could there be DNA under her fingernails?"

The rage grew hotter, flowing through my veins like lava. "No. I know what I'm doing."

A flat stare told me my father was unconvinced, and I didn't dare glance at the TV that was paused on a news story about the body. The red and blue lights reflecting off the smashed automobiles seemed to be laughing at me.

"Where did you find her? Were there witnesses? Security cameras?"

I closed my eyes, forcing myself to remember each and every detail. "One security camera outside a thrift store, but I didn't look at it. I kept my head down. There was one guy who saw us, some bum, I think. He was wasted, though. There's no way he'd ever be a reliable witness. I doubt he even remembers me."

"All right." My father paused for a beat, scratching his chin. I could almost picture the gears turning in his head. "Here's the deal. The boss is breathing down my neck about the girl at Paulie's. He's breathing down all our necks, and rightfully so. The Feds have the place taped off as a crime scene, but right now, they haven't gotten a warrant to search any more of the yard. But we have to plan for the worst."

I mentally steeled myself. If the family discovered I was the reason for the magnifying glass hanging over Paulie's, I was as good as dead.

"You need to stop this shit, Gavin. And you need to stop it now. *Look, I don't know what drives you, but I know it's...different. You feel like you need to kill, right?"*

All I could do was lift a shoulder. I didn't know how to articulate my motivations, and even if I could, I doubted a man like my father—a man who'd always fit in, who'd never been bullied or tormented for his appearance—would understand.

My father forged ahead without my reply. "If that's the case, then this is something we can work with. The family has taken some hits recently, and some of our people have been either killed or locked up. I can get you a contract, and you can be working on it as soon as tomorrow night."

The world tilted as if I'd been knocked off balance. My father was looking out for me? He was trying to help *me, rather than just ripping me a new one?*

Was this a trick? A trap to get me to admit what I'd done? No, that didn't make sense. I'd already admitted to killing Sammie Howard.

I leaned against the marble counter to keep myself upright. "Yeah, all right. Okay. I can do that."

"Good." *He gave me a nod of approval but paused to meet my gaze.* "And Gavin, this is it, you got it? No more of this shit. No more killing some random person. If you've got an urge to fulfill, then this is how you do it. You do this contract, and you put that skill set to use for the family. Two birds, one stone. Trust me, there are always people we need gone."

I blinked a few times as the memory of last night's conversation faded. A slat of sunlight pierced through the gap in the blinds, the glow shimmering along the wooden table of the RV.

My father's reprimand still pissed me off, but the anger had lessened in the hours since our conversation. I wasn't a child anymore. I was a full-grown man, adept in hand-to-hand combat and the use of a firearm and deadly force.

When I thought back to the discussion, I realized my father hadn't treated me like a child, not entirely. Perhaps there was merit to his suggestion that I satiate my urges by killing for the family.

Shifting in my seat, I flipped open the folder my father had given me before I'd left for this frozen campsite.

"Brock Dominguez." I made a tsk-tsk sound with my tongue. "You owe the family a hell of a lot of money, don't you? We've only been trying to collect for a year now, and you just keep disappearing instead of paying what you owe."

As I stared down at a paparazzi-style photo of a lanky man in a tacky suit exiting a cab, I wondered what had driven him to his current position in life. Was he motivated by urges he couldn't control, or was he just some nobody who wanted desperately to be somebody?

I chuckled to myself. Of course he was. Why else would he have borrowed so much money from the family? According to the documents given to me by my father, Dominguez had tried and failed in a number of different business ventures. From Ponzi schemes to crypto currency scams to a failed cult, the guy had dipped his toes in just about everything.

Closing the folder, I turned back to the window. My RV was mostly obscured by a thicket of trees, but the position allowed me to look out onto the campsite nearest to mine. In the summer, leaves would have blocked my vantage point. I was freezing my ass off, but at least I could spy on Brock.

From the exterior, Dominguez's RV appeared even nicer than mine. Unlike Brock, I was smart enough to travel in an inconspicuous vehicle.

"There you are."

Dominguez emerged to stand beneath an awning, his attention fixed on the rocky shore of the lake sprawling out in front of the RV. While much of the lake's surface had turned to ice over the winter, the body of water was large enough to prevent it all from freezing.

At first glance, the lakeside campground was the perfect place to carry out a hit and dispose of a body.

However, my father had taught me better. Though the month of February wasn't prime time for camping, there were enough people around the area to make the endeavor riskier than I'd like. The lake was decent-sized, but it was no Lake Michigan.

Brock's current home was an RV, meaning it—and any items inside, such as his corpse—could easily be transported. I'd off Brock, stash his body in a closet, and get one of the guys from the chop shop out here to drive Brock's RV to one of our warehouses so it could be stripped. No one would have the first clue what had become of Brock Dominguez. Frankly, I doubted anyone would care.

I let the blinds slide closed and turned back to the table. Now, all I had to do was keep myself occupied until the sun went down.

With a television mounted to the wall across from the kitchen and with wireless internet access provided by the campground, the task should have been easy enough.

Instead, my traitorous brain kept wandering back to the kid from the fast-food restaurant. Cody Frazier. His eyes taunted me every time I closed mine, unless my thoughts were occupied somewhere else.

But there was only so much of Brock Dominguez I could research. I already knew his social security number, his mother's maiden name, his credit score, where he was born…the list went on.

I clenched my jaw. No, Cody was off-limits. For once, I was going to obey my father's direction. I'd leave Cody alone, and I'd deal with Brock. Surely, killing Dominguez would satiate the pervasive urge.

Rolling my shoulders, I reached for a pad of paper and a pencil. I wasn't a remarkable artist, but I'd found that drawing was one reliable method to keep my mind under control.

All I had to do was hold out for a few more hours, and then I could let the urges take control for a time.

It would be enough.

It had to be enough.

12

Based on the rapid-fire pace of the Sammie Howard investigation so far, Zane had begun to wonder when he'd finally get a moment to bring his information about Joseph Larson to the Special Agent in Charge. As he stepped into the short hallway leading to SAC Jasmine Keaton's office, he tightened his grip on the manila folder in his left hand. Finally, almost a year after transferring to Chicago, Zane had discovered enough proof to rid the field office of one of its major sources of corruption.

Joseph Larson had tried to blackmail Amelia into sleeping with him, and though the attempted sexual assault was the reason for the anger that burned in Zane's heart whenever he thought of Larson, it wasn't why he was at SAC Keaton's office today.

Firing the sick bastard would be a start. Without his badge and gun, Larson lost much of his power. From there, it was only a matter of time.

A matter of time until what, exactly?

Zane gritted his teeth and pushed aside the doubts. One thing at a time.

As he approached SAC Keaton's office, he noted the door was open, allowing the warm glow of a lamp to spill out onto the carpeted hallway. Clearing his throat, he rapped his knuckles on the doorframe.

The SAC's dark eyes snapped away from her computer monitor and over to him. "Afternoon, er," she checked her smart watch, "good evening, I suppose. I seem to have lost track of time. Come on in, Agent Palmer. What can I do for you?"

Stepping over the threshold, Zane held up the manila folder for the SAC. "I've got information for you. Time-sensitive, which is the only reason I stepped away from the work Agent Storm and I are doing on the Howard case."

From hospitable and welcoming to focused, the SAC's expression shifted almost instantly. "All right. Close the door, have a seat."

For good measure, Zane flicked the lock on the door's lever handle. As he took his spot in one of the squat armchairs across from the SAC, he set the folder atop her desk. With any other authority figure in the Bureau, Zane might have had second thoughts about boldly proclaiming Joseph Larson was a rat. Brian Kolthoff's pockets were deep, and his influence was undoubtedly pervasive enough to extend to others in the FBI.

Fortunately, Jasmine Keaton wasn't just another authority figure. She was the person who'd recruited him for this job in the first place. Her integrity was second to none, but she wasn't omnipotent.

Which was where Zane's expertise came into play.

Scooting to the edge of the chair, Zane tapped the manila folder. "I know who's been leaking information out of this office and to the Leóne family, among others. Agent Larson has a long-standing connection to Brian Kolthoff, AKA The Shark. Based on what we learned during the Leila

Jackson case, we know Kolthoff is affiliated with the Leónes."

Her expression remained level. Even if the news shocked her, she gave no indication. "Agent Larson, huh? Do you know if he was affiliated with Glenn Kantowski, by any chance?"

"I've been searching for a link but haven't found one so far. That being said, I think it's certainly possible. Even if they weren't aware of it, they might have been working for the same people. But so far, I've found nothing to indicate they even knew one another outside of the FBI office."

The SAC gestured to Zane's folder. "All right. What's the information you've got on Joseph Larson, then? I'm assuming you have something solid, based on how you started this conversation."

Zane flipped open the folder, displaying the first glossy print of Brian Kolthoff and Joseph Larson in their Hawaiian shirts. He moved the image aside to display another photo of the two men on the deck of a different yacht, their attire now more befitting of a cocktail party than a spring break kegger.

"These two pictures were taken four years apart. The first, with the Hawaiian shirts, was taken off the coast of Florida on Kolthoff's yacht, the *Equilibrium*. The second was taken on Lake Michigan, five to six months ago, on another of Kolthoff's yachts, the *Server Not Found*."

As SAC Keaton studied the photos, her face changed little. The woman would make a fantastic poker player. "Where did *you* get them?"

"I didn't." Zane pushed the photos aside to display yet another picture of Kolthoff and Larson. In this image, which Zane had pulled from the CIA surveillance footage sent to him by Nate Tennick, the men were seated. "This is one of the photos I acquired. The first two were given to Agent Storm by a confidential informant. I had one of my contacts do a little digging to corroborate the photos and to get a little more information about each, such as when they were taken."

SAC Keaton nodded her understanding. "Then this means Agent Larson was affiliated with Brian Kolthoff well before the Leila Jackson case, which indicates a huge conflict of interest that he never felt the need to reveal to me or anyone else at the Bureau."

"Officially, yes, that's what these photos prove. But I think you and I both know what's *implied* by Larson's relationship with The Shark. That moniker was given to Brian Kolthoff *by* the Leóne family. Kolthoff is friendly with the Leónes, and Larson is friendly with Kolthoff. Then, we just so happened to be sandbagged by a rat during Leila Jackson's case? I don't think that's a coincidence."

"I agree." SAC Keaton held up her hands. "But officially, we don't have anything to prove that Larson was the rat. Based on that, I don't think this is enough to bring him up on criminal charges. Not anything that would stick, unfortunately."

Even though Zane had expected as much, disappointment still jabbed at his heart. "Criminal charges are a different story, I understand. But I think this is more than enough to call into question Joseph Larson's integrity as an agent, as well as the questionable legality of him working a case when he was friends with the prime suspect."

"Absolutely."

The single word brought on a wave of relief. His logical brain had known SAC Keaton would do the right thing, but barbs of anxiety had still grated on his nerves over the last couple days. "I also think it's worth noting that Glenn Kantowski never touched the Leila Jackson case. At the time, she was part of the Public Corruption Unit, and she was working an investigation regarding fraud in the Cook County Treasury."

"Well, that's another strike against Agent Larson. It's still not quite enough to prove he was the source of the leak at the time, but perhaps there's something out there that can. I'll look through personnel records to see if Kantowski and Larson ever worked together, or if there's anything in their work history that can connect them, or that can connect Larson and Officer McAdam."

FBI personnel records were one of the few places off-limits to Zane, though he figured Nate Tennick could access the information if he was motivated enough. Having SAC Keaton carry out that portion of the research was much easier. "That's a good place to start. I'll see if there's anything I can dig up on my end. I know I've mentioned it before, but the effort Agent Kantowski put into trying to frame Agent Storm for Ben Storey's murder screams there was more to the motive than just a bitter ex-lover."

"I won't argue that." SAC Keaton folded her hands on the desk. "Officially, the Ben Storey case is closed. Unofficially, keep doing what you're doing. In the meantime, I'll get Agent Larson in here as soon as I can. Sounds like he and I will be having a conversation about his future, or lack thereof, with the Bureau."

"He'll be fired, or at least forced to resign, correct?"

A sarcastic half-smile crept to SAC Keaton's face. "Correct. Of course, I have to corroborate this through confidential channels, but that's really just a formality. You were brought in to help find the rat, and I trust that you've done just that. Normally, I wouldn't share disciplinary action with anyone other than the person being disciplined, but I think this case warrants an exception. I doubt I have to tell you but don't mention this to anyone, all right? Not even Agent Storm. Not until I have a chance to talk to Larson."

"Understood." Zane pushed the folder closer to the SAC as he rose to his feet. "The dates and locations of all these images, as well as the names of the vessels are written down. Let me know if there's anything else you need from me."

SAC Keaton stood, extending her hand for a parting shake. "I appreciate everything you're doing for this office, Agent Palmer. I think you've got a very bright future with the FBI."

Even as the reality of Joseph Larson being forced out of the Bureau settled in, Zane noted the appearance of a new storm brewing on the horizon.

They'd take Larson's gun and badge, but the man would still be free.

Free and no longer bound to secrecy regarding his and Kolthoff's friendship.

Who would be first on Joseph's shit list? Amelia, or his recent ex-girlfriend, Assistant U.S. Attorney Cassandra Halcott?

Getting Joseph Larson out of the FBI was a good start, but it was merely a single battle in a much larger war.

13

Tapping a dry-erase marker against the heel of her hand, Amelia scanned the brand-new murder board. So far, the only victim on the whiteboard was Sammie Howard. As much as Amelia hoped there weren't other victims, she doubted the lunatic who'd cut Sammie's eyes out of her head was a first-time killer.

There were others. They just hadn't found them yet.

To Amelia's disappointment, Booker's effort to work with a sketch artist had been fruitless. Between his drunken state and the low light, Booker wasn't able to recall enough of the stranger's appearance to create even a rough approximation.

While Booker had been at the FBI office, he'd consented to a search of his apartment, which had turned up nothing. The lab had also collected his DNA, though they'd obtained no DNA evidence from Sammie's body.

At least we're being thorough.

Amelia groaned at the thought. They were straddling a line between "being thorough" and "wasting their time." For now, Booker was in the clear. Amelia and Zane had given him their business cards and had sternly advised him to remain in the city. Booker's response to the order had been a chortle and a reassurance he had no plans to leave Chicago.

Booker Gilbert was clearly going out of his way to prove he hadn't been involved in Sammie Howard's murder. While Amelia was inclined to believe he was innocent, there was an ever-present voice in the back of her head.

What if he's secretly a criminal mastermind? What if he has an IQ on the level of Ted Kaczynski, and this is him screwing with us? Are we going to find another body tomorrow with its eyes carved out like some kind of fucked up jack-o'-lantern?

Before Amelia's brain could spiral too far into the land of what-ifs, blinds clattered against glass as the door to the small room swung open to reveal Zane. He had excused himself not long ago, but he hadn't given any details of where he'd been going or what he'd been doing. Amelia wasn't the type to demand an explanation for each and every move he made, so she'd simply carried on with her work on the murder board.

With a grin, Zane held up his phone like it was a trophy. "Good news! I just heard back from the officers who responded to our request to canvass the neighborhood around the Fast Trip and Danny's Pub. They got some security camera footage from a thrift store across the street from the bar."

"That *is* good news. Have you watched it yet?"

He pulled out one of the office chairs and reached for his laptop. "Not yet. What time did Sammie's shift on Saturday end? Ten o'clock, right?"

"Right." Amelia's heart thrummed with anticipation as Zane powered on the laptop and opened his email.

As the video loaded, he glanced at her. "Did I miss anything while I was gone? Any epiphanies or breaking news from forensics?"

"Unfortunately not. Just me debating whether Booker's

an average guy who was at the wrong place at the wrong time, or if he's some secret Ted Kaczynski-esque mastermind with a collection of eyeballs hidden somewhere we'll never find."

"Well, we'll find out here in a second. Booker said he was sitting on the bench in front of this thrift store." He gestured to the still frame of the camera, which included a corner of Danny's Pub, as well as the alley beside the bar. In addition, the lens captured the sidewalk in front of the store, including the bench on which Booker claimed to have sat.

Amelia leaned in closer, her gaze fixed on the screen. She felt like a little kid about to unwrap her first present on Christmas morning. Would it be the drunk guy on the bench she'd been promised or a lump of coal?

Daylight gave way to darkness as Zane dragged the slider bar all the way to five minutes before ten.

"There he is." Amelia knew Zane saw the same image, but she pointed at the screen anyway. "That looks like Booker on the bench, doesn't it?"

"Sure does." Zane started to rewind the footage. "Let's see when he got there."

The timestamp in the lower righthand corner ticked backward. When the clock reached 9:45 p.m., Booker rose from his seat and ambled across the street where he disappeared in the direction of Danny's Pub.

Amelia glanced to Zane, noting her own curiosity mirrored in his face. "So, he got booted out of Danny's at quarter 'til ten, then went across the street and sat on the bench in front of the thrift store."

Zane pressed his lips together and hit play. The pace of the video was accelerated to two times normal, making Booker seem as if he was running across the street.

Once they were back at 9:55 p.m., Zane slowed the pace of the playback to its regular speed. Booker swayed slightly as he stared at his phone, glancing up every so often as if he was waiting for someone.

Eight minutes later, at only a few seconds past 10:03, Sammie entered into the frame from the left-hand side—the direction of the Fast Trip gas station. Her gaze was fixed straight ahead, both hands tucked in the pockets of the same faux Sherpa coat in which she'd been found.

Watching the dead come to life on a television or computer screen never ceased to raise goose bumps on the back of Amelia's neck. There was something surreal, even otherworldly, about witnessing a person's final moments.

Sammie was only a few feet away from the bench when Booker stood and waved a hand at her.

This is it. Time to find out if our witness is what he claims to be or if he's a closet psychopath.

As Sammie spoke, Amelia silently cursed the lack of audio. Booker held out his hands, and Sammie's expression—or what they could make of it in the darkness—grew contemplative.

Zane circled the cursor around the pair. "That must be his offer to pay her for buying him the booze. She's thinking about it."

Before Sammie could decide one way or the other, a young man hurried across the street, gesturing vehemently to Booker. Shoulders slumped, Booker made his way to the curb where he tripped, stumbled, and was caught just short of a fall by the mysterious stranger. Relief was written on Sammie Howard's face, along with a healthy dose of skepticism.

Amelia knew that look. "She doesn't know him. She's just as surprised by him showing up as Booker was."

The stranger and Sammie exchanged a few words before the young man reached out for a handshake. For the duration of the short conversation, he kept his head turned toward the street. Amelia clenched her jaw and willed him to turn around, to glance toward the thrift store, or even to move closer so they could get a better look at the side of his damn head.

Zane paused the video as Sammie and the stranger started down the street. "It's like he knows where the camera is."

"He might. It's not like a store is going to try to *hide* it, you know? A lot of the time, being able to see the security camera is what deters people from shoplifting. He could be a keen observer, or he might've just gotten lucky. We've got no way to tell without finding him and asking. Did the officers get us any other footage?"

Zane rubbed his chin, appearing contemplative. "No, actually. They said they spotted a couple other cameras, but they were either nonfunctional or deleted their footage on a rolling twenty-four-hour basis. Unfortunately, this is all we've got."

Slumping back in her chair, Amelia sighed. "Well, at least this confirms what Booker said about the strange guy who showed up. His description seems pretty accurate, at least as far as what we can see on the video, which isn't much."

"If it hadn't been so dark, we might've gotten a clearer picture of the side of his head, at least. But this isn't the highest quality camera in the world, and the guy stayed near the curb, so he didn't get close enough."

"Either way, we need to find this guy. We can print off some of the stills and see if anyone at Fast Trip recognizes him. They're low-quality, but we might get lucky. We've got the ouroboros tattoo on his wrist too. If we combine the tattoo with the print, that could help."

Zane perked up at the idea. "That's a good plan. Maybe we can send the images to the local officers, and they can ask around about him. Booker said he didn't see the guy in the bar, but maybe someone else did."

The renewed hope of finding a lead dispersed Amelia's momentary haze of disappointment. Before she or Zane could move to put their newest plan in motion, Zane's email pinged. Less than a second later, Amelia received a similar notification on her phone.

"It's forensics." Zane rolled his chair away from the table. "They've finished analyzing the trace evidence found on Sammie's clothes."

Amelia was on her feet before he finished the announcement. "Let's go see what they have for us."

The trip down to the lab took only a couple minutes, and they only passed two other agents. At six o'clock in the evening, the FBI office was notably less populous than it was during the day.

Tall, tinted windows—the only windows in the center of the FBI building's second floor—framed the glass and metal door leading to one of several different labs. Amelia hadn't been down to the lab since shortly after the new year, but aside from losing the Christmas decorations that had hung along the hallway, the place hadn't changed.

A vaguely familiar man with an impressive handlebar mustache and a black and gray ponytail approached the other side of the door. He offered a nod of greeting as he held the door open for the two of them. "Evening, Agents. Nice to see you down here so quickly. I'm Eduardo Arellano," he smiled and pointed to where his surname was embroidered onto his white lab coat, "I'm the lead forensic geologist on shift right now. You can call me Ed or Dr. Arellano. It's up to you."

Though the man appeared as if he was the president of a motorcycle club, his kind, relaxed tone and demeanor reminded Amelia of the humorous uncle on a sitcom. "Nice to meet you, Dr. Arellano. I'm Agent Amelia Storm, and this is my partner, Agent Zane Palmer."

Plucking a steaming mug from the edge of a long, rectangular table running along the wall next to the door, Dr. Arellano ushered them toward a computer on the other side of the room. Though drinks and food were prohibited in the section of the lab where expensive, top-of-the-line equipment was used to conduct analyses, rules for the room full of computers were more lax. The techs who worked in this windowless, cave-like environment needed a place to safely ingest their caffeine.

Dr. Arellano typed in his password and gestured to a pair of nearby office chairs. "Have a seat, Agents. We've wrapped up the analyses of the trace evidence on your vic's clothes, and the lab writeup is just about ready to send over. I wanted to make sure I gave you an overview before I sent it."

Amelia had been sitting for most of the afternoon, but she accepted the offered seat. As she rolled to sit on Dr. Arellano's right side, Zane took his spot on the geologist's left. "We appreciate it. What have you found so far?"

Sipping his coffee, Dr. Arellano maximized an image of particles taken from a microscope. "This is the first piece of trace we found. These are tiny metal fragments, many of which are so small they look like dust to the naked eye. Under a microscope, however, you can see they're many different shapes, but most are circular in appearance."

Amelia leaned closer, scrutinizing the image, though she wasn't entirely sure what she was looking at.

Dr. Arellano seemed to sense their curiosity. "What the shapes of these particles tell me right away is that they're from a location where metal was cut. As the metal particles, which are molten from the tool that's being used to cut the item, fly through the air, they cool very rapidly. The trajectory, along with the cooling, is what causes them to take on this circular shape."

Geology hadn't ever been Amelia's specialty, but she saw where Dr. Arellano's explanation was headed. "Okay, so the particles wound up on her clothes either when she was working with metal, or they were transferred from someone who works with metal."

Dr. Arellano lifted a finger. "Correct. You can see from looking at these particles that they're different colors and that the material itself varies quite a bit."

Zane spoke up before Amelia had the chance. "Which means that, wherever these particles originated, the location must've worked with multiple types of metal?"

"Exactly." Dr. Arellano clicked over to a second picture of more particles and then a third.

Though Amelia was hard-pressed to make out the difference between the metal shavings, she assumed such a visual comparison was second nature to an expert like Dr. Arellano. "We'd have to check to be sure, but I don't think there are any metal shavings like this at Sammie Howard's place of work. We can check with her mother to see if working with metal was a hobby of hers."

"It could very well be." Dr. Arellano shrugged. "One of my nephews makes sculptures of video game characters to sell online, and he uses metal in a lot of them."

Amelia typed a note in her phone, so she would remember to follow up on Sammie's hobbies. "This still seems like a significant find. We'd be able to compare these fragments to any we found on a suspect, or even another victim, right?"

"Absolutely. One of the most commonly used metals in construction and manufacturing is steel, and the composition of steel can vary quite a bit. Basic steel is composed of iron and carbon, but the percentage of carbon used is often different across manufacturers. There are also steel alloys, which add yet another element to the composition. It's not as unique as something like a fingerprint, but a comparison of metal fragments like these can tell us quite a lot."

The news was good, even great. They just had to find a suspect, provided the metal shavings weren't from Sammie. "Did you find anything else? Hairs, DNA, anything like that?"

Another click brought up a photo of what appeared to be a fiber or a hair. "Biological evidence isn't my strong suit, but I was briefed on everything by my colleagues. They're available if you'd like to speak to one of them, but unfortunately, they were unable to find anything usable."

Zane waved a hand at the monitor. "What about this? What're we looking at, Doctor?"

"This is a light gray polyester fiber, one of a few that was found in the victim's hair. Crime scene photos indicated the trunk where she was found was lined with black material, so we did a quick microscopic visual comparison." He brought up side-by-side images of the fibers in question.

Unlike the metal particles, these were easily distinguishable, even to a layperson.

The geologist turned to Amelia and Zane as if he were a parent trying to make sure his kids were paying attention. "Both are triangular in shape, which is consistent with the types of fibers used in cars. However, the color is quite clearly different. The fibers from her hair could have been transferred from a different source. Perhaps the upholstery of her own vehicle?"

"No, she didn't have a car." Amelia recalled Dr. Francis's summary of the rigor mortis that had seized Sammie's body in place. "These could be from the vehicle that was used to transport her body."

"It could." Dr. Arellano swirled his coffee. "We can certainly compare the fibers found on the victim to any that are found during your investigation. A positive match in this regard wouldn't be as valuable as an energy dispersive x-ray analysis of the metal fragments, but having both would be very significant."

We just have to find something to compare it to.

As she and Zane exchanged glances, Amelia knew where they'd start. Forensics wasn't finished combing through the dirt and debris around the site where Sammie's body was found, but Amelia didn't want to rely on evidence that may or may not be present. She and Zane would use what they currently had, and they'd squeeze every last drop of usefulness before letting it go.

She only hoped they wouldn't have to wait for another body before finding a case-breaking clue.

14

I paused just outside the door of the RV, patting the pocket of my jeans to ensure I'd remembered my keys. I doubted I had to worry about anyone breaking into the camper out here in the middle of nowhere, Wisconsin, but I knew I had the eyes of the family on me after the incident at the junkyard, so I couldn't be too careful. After double-checking the silenced nine-mil holstered at my back, I turned and started toward Brock Dominguez's luxurious RV. At only eight in the evening, I wasn't surprised by the light glowing through the windows.

Though I could have waited for the middle of the night, I figured I'd have an easier time getting into the RV if Brock was conscious. Sure, I could've picked the lock, but he might have rigged up an alarm system. I'd much rather deal with *him* than a screaming siren announcing my presence.

Over the past few hours, as I'd waited for the sun to sink behind the horizon, I'd had plenty of time to come up with excuses to knock on his door. I'd entertained some wild stories, but the tall tales were primarily to keep my mind from wandering back to the kid at the fast-food restaurant.

Cody.

A combination of anger and unease crawled up my spine at the name, and I gritted my teeth.

I'm dealing with Dominguez. Killing him will take care of this...need I can't seem to shake.

Not only that, but I'd make a few bucks in the process, and I'd get my old man off my case. Hell, maybe he'd even be proud of his son for once in his life.

Working at the chop shop, I'd done plenty of useful work for the family. However, like my father was keen to remind me, our surname entitled us to far more than physical labor.

This was it. *Dominguez* was it—the start of a real future for me in this fucked up world of organized crime.

I straightened my spine as I started toward my target's RV, rolling my shoulders. Perhaps I should have been overcome with anxiety as I walked toward my first solo murder for hire, or maybe I should have been excited like the killers portrayed in popular media.

To my dismay, I felt neither excitement nor nervousness. If I was honest with myself, closing in on the location of a man I was slated to kill wasn't much different than another day of work at the chop shop.

I silenced the emotions and rapped my knuckles on the door of the RV. Shifting my weight from one foot to the other, I painted a look of trepidation on my face as I waited for Dominguez. The blinds in one window parted briefly as the man peeked at his visitor.

I knew what he'd see and how he'd view me. A young man, a wholesome bumpkin, some random idiot. I'd taken the extra care to change into clothes that screamed rural kid out camping. I had removed any hint of mafia from my appearance.

Dominguez muttered a few words I couldn't understand, and for a beat, I was convinced he planned to ignore my presence altogether. Of course, this was a scenario for which I had planned, and I wasn't especially worried.

For good measure, I knocked again. "Hey, sorry to bother you, sir. I'm just...I need a little help."

The door swung open, revealing the lanky Brock Dominguez and his burgundy robe. Apparently, he fancied himself some sort of wealthy playboy. With those squinty eyes and his receding hairline—the type that told the world he knew he was balding but refused to accept the reality—I doubted women were flocking to him. Prostitutes likely charged him extra for that ugly mug.

Swallowing the laughter at my joke, I allowed the smile to creep to my face when the Hugh Hefner wannabe didn't respond. "I was about to head into town to get some groceries, but my truck won't start. I was wondering if you could give me a jump?"

Dominguez's eyes narrowed, telling me his answer before he actually spoke. "No, I can't. I'm busy right now. Get lost, kid."

What a dick.

I debated trying to bribe Brock into helping me but decided against it. I'd rather deal with this asshole and get the job done.

As the man moved to shut the door in my face, I threw my weight into his smaller frame. He stumbled backward, cursing with each step. I yanked the door closed behind myself to block off sight to any curious campers who might be out and about at night during the middle of February. Unlikely, but I didn't want to take my chances.

In a fraction of a second, Dominguez's expression went from pissed to borderline terrified. He scrambled down a short hall toward the warm glow of a lamp in the living room.

I closed the distance in a few swift steps, retrieving my

nine-mil as I moved. I suspected Brock was hell-bent on getting to the living room so he could arm himself. By now, he had probably guessed who I represented and why I was here.

"Don't move." I trained the sight of the gun on the man's head. "Let me see those hands."

Dominguez froze in place like I was Medusa. He was only a couple feet from an end table, the drawer of which I assumed held a firearm. If Brock was smart, he'd have been armed when he answered the door. Because I was young, and because I came across as some dumbass from the country, he'd let down his guard.

Who was the real dumbass here?

Dominguez licked his lips, his chest rising and falling like an Olympic athlete as he slowly turned to face me. "Who... who are you? What do you want?"

"I'm an envoy for someone you screwed out of a hell of a lot of money."

"Who, though?"

The man was funny. Did he even think the question really mattered?

"Who? You've been borrowing money from that many people and failing to pay them back? Really?" I was aware he'd reneged on debts he owed to my family, but now I was curious. "Did you borrow from us to pay back someone else? That's not how loans work. You know that, right?"

"They came for me first, okay? I...I had to, or they'd kill me! Please, you have to believe me. I can fix this. I can make this right."

Under normal circumstances, the family might have elected to leave a debtor alive to try to recoup some of the lost funds. Dominguez, however, was an exception. Especially now that I'd learned he'd borrowed from us to pay someone else.

After letting the asshole sweat through an oppressive silence, I cocked my head. "I'm afraid we can't do that."

"Wait! But I can—"

I didn't let him finish the sentence. As I eased my finger back on the trigger, the weapon barely made a sound. Blood and brain matter spattered the wood-paneled wall at Brock's back, his body slumping gracelessly to the floor.

Whatever he'd been about to tell me was grade-A bullshit. The guy was a lifelong conman, and the world would be a better place without him.

For several long, drawn-out moments, I studied Brock's lifeless face. His flat brown eyes peered up at the ceiling, and his mouth gaped open in an expression of shock.

I watched and waited for the familiar sense of satisfaction to fill me. It never did.

Well? That was supposed to do the trick, wasn't it? Killing him was supposed to satisfy this urge, this monster in my head.

I imagined Dominguez on some schoolground play yard, pushing down the weaker kids and making fun of those who were different. He seemed the type to have bullied others in the past. He had the attitude that he'd sided with the bullies whenever it was convenient just so he could avoid becoming their next target. The onlookers were almost worse, in my experience.

Despite the picture of Dominguez I painted in my head, the imagery didn't bring me any semblance of relief. His eyes were different.

They weren't Cody's.

No, I could still picture Cody's mocking eyes, watching me, judging me. Just waiting for me to mess up so he could rub my face in it like an untrained dog.

Would Cody spit in my food? Would the hazel-eyed brat film himself hocking a wad of phlegm and spittle onto my burger, only for it to go viral on social media?

I already knew the answer.

He would. There was no doubt in my mind.

Glancing at Dominguez's lifeless form, I gritted my teeth.

I knew what I had to do.

15

Zane was still sipping his latte—studying the murder board as he willed the caffeine to clear the remaining cobwebs of sleep from his tired brain—when the door of the incident room flew open as if it had been propelled by the wind of a hurricane. His ass nearly left his chair as he jumped in surprise. If he wasn't fully awake before, he sure as hell was now.

Holding back a slew of four-letter words, he swiveled his chair around to face the door. Where he expected Amelia to be holding the photos she'd gone to print, he was greeted with Spencer Corsaw instead. Despite the circles beneath the Supervisory Special Agent's brown eyes, the man appeared far too awake and alert for such an early hour.

Spencer's gaze snapped to Zane. "Agent Palmer, where's Agent Storm? We've got news. Big news."

The surprise of the SSA's abrupt entry evaporated like fog on a sunny day. "She's printing a few pictures. Should be back any second."

On cue, Amelia strolled through the open doorway. Her green eyes shifted from Spencer to Zane and back, curiosity written on her face. "I'm right here. What's this big news? What happened?"

Spencer shoved the door closed. "Apparently, Forensics found a tooth under the car compressor at the junkyard yesterday."

"A tooth?" To Zane, the discovery had been both bizarre and unpromising.

"Yeah. It was sent for DNA analysis, but we don't have a lot riding on it. We know it isn't Sammie's because she still had all her teeth. But it could've come from anywhere."

Without any context, a tooth was just...a tooth. Strange? Yes. Groundbreaking? Not necessarily. Zane had put on hold any hopes for the strange piece of evidence until the lab had the opportunity to analyze the DNA.

Puzzle pieces snapped together in Zane's head before the SSA had a chance to speak. "Wait, did we get the DNA back for it? Was there a hit this soon?"

Spencer leveled an index finger with Zane like he was praising a student. "Bingo. There was a hit. Well, a partial hit. The mitochondrial DNA was a match to Gordon Mclaughlin. Gordon is doing a nickel for possession in Wisconsin, and since he'd been convicted of a felony, his DNA was added to the national database."

Amelia pressed her lips together, echoing Zane's mounting curiosity. "You said it was a partial match? The tooth didn't belong to Gordon?"

"It didn't." Spencer held up a hand. "However, Gordon's younger sister, Olivia, has been missing for almost two weeks. Olivia's last known address was here in Chicago, where she lived with her aunt. We're reaching out to see if she can provide us with a sample of Olivia's DNA for comparison. Forensics also located some dried blood in the seams of the metal at the bottom of the compressor. They were able to confirm it was human, but we'll have to see if it's viable for DNA analysis."

"Shit." Zane was glad for the new evidence, though he lamented the source was potentially a second victim. "Where are we on getting a warrant for the rest of the yard?"

Spencer glanced at his watch. "Judge should be signing it any minute now. We just had to wait for her to wake up. I'm about to head over to the site now, and I figured we could carpool. You know, help the environment and all that."

Amelia set her freshly printed photos on the table. "I do love the environment. Especially the air it gives me to breathe."

Spencer produced a set of keys from the pocket of his black slacks. "All right. Let's go."

Scooping up his phone and his latte, Zane followed Amelia and Spencer out to the parking garage. While Spencer drove, he went over his interview with the owner of the Nissan in which Sammie's body had been found.

Alice Crawford, a sixty-six-year-old retired nurse, had been visiting her daughter in Minnesota during Sammie's estimated time of death. Alice had the Nissan towed to the lot after the car had blown a head gasket. Rather than fork over the thousands of dollars such a repair required, Alice had sold the car to Paulie's Scrap and Salvage for a couple hundred bucks.

For three months, the Nissan had sat in the lot at Paulie's. Customers paid the junkyard to peruse the vehicles in the lot, searching for parts they might have had difficulty finding elsewhere. Once the yard was confident they'd sold all they could, they stripped the remaining valuable metal and crushed the vehicle.

Needless to say, Alice had been ruled out as a suspect. Paulie's was affiliated with the Leónes, but the junkyard also conducted legitimate business to maintain its front.

As they parked on the street across from Paulie's, Zane spotted a handful of K-9 squad cars. His stomach clenched as he considered what those dogs might find. Halfway across the street, a vaguely familiar FBI agent—Agent Stephanie Avila, a recent addition to the Organized Crime Division, if Zane remembered right—emerged from the driver's side of a black Town Car, the long rope of her black hair swaying from a low ponytail.

The woman held up a folded document, a victorious smirk on her face. "Good timing, SSA Corsaw. I just got back from having our warrant signed."

Spencer rubbed his hands together. "Perfect. It covers the entire yard, including the staff's offices, yeah?"

The agent nodded, her light brown eyes gleaming. "It does." She gestured to Amelia and Zane. "These must be Agents Palmer and Storm."

Zane extended a hand, followed by Amelia. "Nice to meet you, Agent Avila. Looks like the K-9 unit is here already. What's the game plan?"

Spencer pointed to the stacks of flattened cars near the compactor on the other side of the imposing fence. "The dogs will start there since those vehicles are nearest to the location where Sammie Howard's body was discovered. We'll have them go through the entire lot, just to be on the safe side. Agent Avila has been part of the team surveilling the junkyard looking for the Leóne chop shop, so she and her partner will help forensics look through VINs to find stolen vehicles."

The work was necessary, but Zane didn't envy Avila and her partner. "That leaves us with the offices?"

"It does." Spencer brushed a few strands of dark hair away from his forehead. Jet-black locks, dark brown eyes, and a lightly tanned complexion were all testament to Spencer's Italian heritage. "If this place has been used by the Leónes as a dumping ground for more than just scrapped stolen cars, and that's still a big *if*, then maybe there'll be some kind of paper trail."

Zane wasn't convinced but being thorough was one of the most important aspects of his job. So far, they'd been unable to find a link between Sammie Howard and the Leóne family. Although their current suspect—the man Booker had encountered the night Sammie disappeared—had an appearance consistent with an Italian lineage, it proved nothing. Italian immigrants had called Chicago home since before the twentieth century. Most Italian Chicagoans weren't affiliated with any mob of any kind.

He mulled over the possibilities as the four of them made their way to a pair of uniformed officers standing beside Russel Armstrong. Beneath several days' worth of scruff, Armstrong's cheeks were tinged a dark pink, his jaw clenched so tightly Zane wondered if he'd break a tooth.

The man's facial expression was neutral, but his overall demeanor betrayed him. He was pissed, and he was nervous.

Nervous about the Bureau finding flattened cars with VINs that had been reported stolen, or about the cadaver dogs?

That's the million-dollar question. What are you guys hiding in here, Mr. Armstrong?

Zane kept a diligent eye on Russel Armstrong as Agent Avila served him the freshly signed warrant. He half-expected Armstrong to bolt, but the man remained in place as a trio of officers and their canine companions marched through the gate.

A pang of sadness stabbed Zane's heart as he recalled the last search and rescue dog with whom they'd worked. Sir Sniffs, with help from his handler, Deputy McCannon, had led them to the discovery of a serial killer's dumping ground.

In the end, the Deputy had been killed by an explosion from a trap set at the killer's lair.

Shaking off the memory, Zane jammed his hands in his pockets and turned his attention to the officers. Spencer stood in front of the two men and one woman, waving his arms like the world's weirdest music conductor. He directed each officer to a different section of the junkyard. The woman was given the flattened cars around the compressor, and the two men were directed toward the rest of the lot.

As Zane stood beside Amelia and Spencer, watching the officer and her German Shepherd trot toward the flattened vehicles on a flatbed trailer, his blood pressure ratcheted up with each passing second. "Those cars were scheduled to be shipped out on Monday morning, weren't they?"

Spencer crossed his arms. "They were. Armstrong was bitching about how we were holding up their business by not letting them haul that trailer through our crime scene so they could ship it out to Korea or wherever it's going."

Amelia pointed to the shelved vehicles beside the compactor. The Nissan had been towed by forensics, but the other two derelict cars remained. "Those were supposed to be on the shipment too. They were running behind because they were short-staffed."

If the kid who'd made the 911 call on Tuesday night hadn't broken in looking for items to steal, there was a distinct possibility the FBI never would have found Sammie Howard let alone started looking for her murderer.

How many other shipments have gone out with a body flattened in the trunk? Was Sammie the first, or has this been ongoing?

Phantom spider legs skittered down his back, telling him the answer. Sammie wasn't the first or probably even the hundredth. They were in the midst of a real-life haunted house attraction. In February.

Before Zane could make a comment to continue the

conversation about the junkyard's shipping schedule, a single bark jerked his focus to the officer and the flattened cars. The German Shepherd gave the stack another sniff, glanced to the officer, and plopped down on the concrete.

Spencer swore, and Zane couldn't blame him.

Zane had seen this particular cadaver dog at work before and was well aware that the canine knew the difference between human remains and animal. Still staring intently at the car, the dog appeared confident in the discovery, and that was all the proof Zane needed.

Damn.

A body. Less than five minutes of searching, and the dog had found a damn body.

16

A s Amelia stepped out of her car, the mid-afternoon
sun beat down on her through the bare tree branches.
The faint scent of dried leaves swirled past her, and she
tugged up the collar of her coat. Though the forecast
promised snow for the weekend, Amelia wouldn't have
guessed based on today's sunny sky.

She hated to pull herself away from the Sammie Howard
investigation—and now the Olivia Mclaughlin missing
persons case—but she needed to meet with Alex Passarelli to
update him on what she'd learned from Josh. Alex claimed he
was busy with work, and if they didn't set aside the time to
talk today, then he wasn't sure when his next opening would
be. Amelia didn't know what "busy with work" entailed for a
mob boss, but she'd decided to avoid conflict and adhere to
Alex's schedule.

Inhaling the fresh air of Adams Park, located forty-five
minutes north of Chicago, Amelia stuffed her hands into her
pockets and glanced around the parking lot. Other than
Alex's Audi parked three stalls down from hers, the space
was empty.

Five months ago, Amelia had met Alex here for the first time. In the midst of an investigation into a corrupt Chicago police detective and fresh off a huge takedown of a Leóne forced labor trafficking ring, they'd deemed it too risky for Amelia to simply meet Alex at his condo. She hadn't been happy about the extended drive to Adams Park, but it was better than being spotted with a D'Amato capo—for both of them.

The park was centered around a lake at the bottom of the hill, but in the middle of February, the place was vacant. Rather than be annoyed at the distance she'd had to travel to get here, she took in another lungful of fresh, albeit frigid, air.

After soaking in the environment, Amelia turned to the gazebo. From her vantage point, all that was visible of Alex was his neatly styled hair. As she made her way along the sidewalk, the rest of his face came into view, and she lifted a hand.

His gaze snapped up from where he'd been focused on his phone. He lifted a hand and offered a weak wave in response. Based on the dark circles beneath his eyes, he had indeed been busy. Then again, Amelia doubted she looked much better.

Alex tucked his phone into a pocket of his black peacoat. "Nice to see you, finally. You called this meeting, and then you keep me waiting."

Amelia rolled her eyes. "You're not the only one in the middle of something at work, all right? But this news is important, and I wanted to get it to you as soon as possible."

Readjusting his scarf, he sighed. "We're both busy. What did you want to tell me?"

At his impatient tone, Amelia fought back the urge to offer up a sarcastic comment in response. If she hadn't also been in a hurry, she would have taken the opportunity to remind Alex that *she* had been the one to ensure his lieutenant didn't serve a life sentence for a crime he hadn't committed. As it currently stood, Alex owed *Amelia* a favor, not the other way around.

She cleared her throat instead, standing at the entrance to the gazebo, but making no move to sit. "Yeah, sure. I'll keep it short and get out of your hair. As you may or may not recall, I've been doing some digging into my brother's murder."

Alex opened his mouth to speak, but Amelia silenced him with an upraised hand.

"I don't want to hear it, okay? Yeah, it's dangerous. Yeah, it can get me killed. I'm a big girl, okay? I've got a gun, I've got a badge, and I know how to use them both. As you neglected to tell me until it suited you, my brother was investigating your little sister's disappearance when he was killed."

"I didn't tell you about it because I didn't know the significance at the time, and I didn't want to give you misleading information." An unmistakable defensiveness had edged its way into Alex's normally calm tone.

Rather than spit out another dry response, Amelia merely crossed her arms. "In any case, I've got it on good authority that Trevor was, in fact, killed because of his involvement in Gianna's case. I've also got it on good authority that your mother knows more about what happened to her daughter than she's let on so far."

For a split second, Alex's eyebrows shot up, but he quickly tempered the look of surprise. "My *mother*? What the hell does she have to do with anything?"

Amelia ignored the question. "Who were your suspects in Gianna's abduction? I know you had to have had some ideas."

Alex narrowed his eyes. "The Shark, Brian Kolthoff, was one. But there was so little evidence to implicate him that it seemed like a far-fetched theory. You don't start a war with someone like Kolthoff based on a far-fetched theory. There was Emilio Leóne, too, along with a couple of his guys. But other than just trying to piss us off, he didn't have any real motive. I don't think the Leónes would be stupid enough to go around kidnapping teenage girls from our family, anyway. Now, do you mind telling me what you think my *mother* has to do with this?"

Amelia couldn't find a reason to sugarcoat the information she'd received from Josh Young. "Back before your mother married Luca Passarelli, she had a fling or whatever you want to call it."

Alex blinked repeatedly, as if he had a hair in his eyes. "An fling? With *whom*, exactly?"

"With Stan Young."

In a blur, Alex was on his feet, his intense stare boring into Amelia. "Stan Young? The senator? *That* Stan Young?"

Amelia was sure plenty of mafiosos had withered under that glare, but she wasn't a D'Amato foot soldier. She wasn't a D'Amato *anything*. "Yes, with *that* Stan Young."

The muscles in Alex's jaw twitched. "Why? How?" He held his arms out to his sides and let them fall. "Who in the hell told you this, and where did they get *their* information from?"

Amelia suspected the abrupt rush of irritability wasn't due to the inaccuracy of her claims. Quite the opposite, in fact. Alex was pissed because he thought she was right. "I'm not going to tell you that. You already know I'm telling the truth. This isn't some grand attempt to slander Sofia Passarelli, trust me. It's all connected. To Gianna, to Trevor. All of it. Whatever fling Sofia and Stan had, it's what started all this shit."

Heaving a bedraggled sigh, Alex raked a hand through his hair. "If their fling is what started all this shit, then what? Is this some soap opera BS, and Stan is secretly Gianna's father? Did he kidnap her because she's actually his, or did he assassinate her as part of a plot to steal the Constitution?" He rubbed his temple, sarcasm dripping from his words. "Or did Stan have some of his goons kill my sister out of revenge for something that happened more than a decade earlier?"

Based on his dramatic tone, Amelia figured he'd meant for the synopsis to sound ridiculous and over-the-top. However, he was far closer to Amelia and Josh's theory than he realized.

"That's exactly what I think happened. Why? Do you picture Stan Young as the type of guy to live and let live? To let past transgressions slide without some form of retaliation? Plenty of men get overly aggressive when they're rejected by a woman. Hell, that's the first place we look when we find a female homicide victim."

Alex tilted back his head and covered his eyes. For several tense moments, the faint whisper of the afternoon's chilly breeze was the only sound.

Amelia's muscles tensed, her mouth suddenly dry. She'd assumed Alex would listen to reason, and she realized with a start that she hadn't prepared for him to *refuse* to accept her newest piece of information. Alex Passarelli had always been a reasonable person, practical and level-headed. He wasn't the type to let emotions lead him to poor judgment—to deny a valid theory about his sister's kidnapping out of some misguided sense of family pride.

Or so she'd thought.

But as the seconds dragged on and Alex didn't speak, Amelia wondered if she'd misjudged him. Had she put too much trust in his good sense? Would he leave here and go straight to Sofia to tell her there was someone out there spreading rumors about her having screwed Stan Young?

Amelia studied the man before her. If lethal could be called a character trait, then Alex Passarelli was the very definition of it. She had always known of Alex's ties to the mafia but had considered him to be a man of integrity…as much as the word could be used in connection with the mob.

Had she been wrong? Had she underestimated Alex's ability to kill and destroy? From the expression on his face right now, she feared she had.

"Okay." Alex's voice was calmer when he finally broke the silence and returned his gaze to Amelia. "I'm sorry, I didn't mean to react like that. I'm not trying to be defensive about my mom's honor or something stupidly similar. I know she's no saint. I just…liked to think I'd covered every possibility when I was trying to find answers about who'd kidnapped Gianna. I looked to all my *father's* enemies but never considered that the entire thing might actually be about my mother."

Amelia couldn't say she was surprised. Misogyny ran deep in the Italian mob, and the sexist mindset was bound to rub off on Alex. "Well, now you know. How do you plan to get answers from Sofia about her and Stan's, um, relationship?"

Alex snorted. "I don't know yet. I'll figure it out." His clipped tone told her this wasn't the time to press for more details.

Their goodbyes were short, bordering on curt, but Amelia didn't mind. The faster they said their parting words, the faster she could get back in her car to return to the FBI office. To her case. To the real world. Away from this reminder of her past and the person she no longer was.

When her phone buzzed against the cupholder, she was relieved to note the caller was SSA Spencer Corsaw. She pressed a button on the steering wheel to engage the hands-free system. "This is Agent Storm."

"Storm, you sound like you're in a tin can."

Maybe I am.

She bit off the sarcastic comment, grinning to herself at

the stupid joke and the imagery it inspired. "I'm using the hands-free in my car. What's going on? Something new in the case?"

"Yes, we do have something new. Something pretty big. The team conducting the investigation into the chop shop has found what they believe to be the warehouse used for the operation. We've secured a warrant, and Tactical is about to head out to the location."

Anticipation surged through Amelia's system, and her grip on the steering wheel tightened. Discovering the chop shop might not necessarily be correlated with the Sammie Howard case, but it was an exciting development no matter what.

While the possibilities whipped through Amelia's head, Spencer continued. "Once Tactical has the area secure, we'll be able to question whoever's there. You and Agent Palmer might be able to dig up a lead."

Amelia had hoped to accompany the tactical team, but she was a big kid. Tactical had their role, and she had hers. "We might, yeah."

As Spencer rattled off the address of the warehouse, Amelia pressed her foot down on the accelerator.

She still wasn't sure if Sammie Howard's murder was related to the Leónes, but any blow she could deal to that family was a welcome development.

❄

THE STENCH of burnt oil still lingered in the air as Amelia followed Zane down a short hallway leading to the warehouse's production floor. Well, once upon a time, it had been a production floor—a space where employees of some now-defunct company had packed items into boxes stuffed with Styrofoam peanuts. All that remained now were four long rows of workstations and a wide-open space full of...nothing.

Whoever had been here before the Tactical team arrived had done a damn fine job of clearing the place out.

A handful of crime scene techs milled around the area, as well as Agent Avila and her partner. With as much anticipation as Amelia had experienced after learning of the discovery, she had to admit she was underwhelmed.

It looks like a whole lot of nothing to us, but maybe the crime scene techs will find something useful. I can still smell *the oil, for god's sake. They couldn't have cleared out everything.*

"How long do you think they've been gone?" Zane's question pulled Amelia out of her contemplation.

She swept her gaze over the empty, concrete floor, then back over the workstations. "Not long." Amelia pointed to the nearest stainless-steel table. "There's no dust on these tables. No debris or anything that I can see, nothing to indicate that a family of raccoons or opossums have broken in to make themselves at home."

Spencer turned around from where he'd been studying the next row of workstations. "Which is something I assume would happen pretty quickly this time of year. I'm guessing the place would be full of cats or other opportunistic animals if it had been vacant for longer than a week or two. Plus, power and utilities are still servicing the address."

One of Zane's eyebrows quirked up. "Under whose name?"

"Under a business's name, actually." Spencer shrugged noncommittally. "We'll look into it, but my money's on a shell corporation. Something they use specifically for this purpose. It's not hard to fake business incorporation documents to send to the electric company. Their primary concern is whether or not the bills are getting paid. That's not a dig at them, either. It's not their job to track down the mob."

Zane tilted his chin toward the open area. "It looks like there might be some oil stains on the ground over there. They must've cleaned the floor, though, because they're pretty faint."

Spencer sighed. "They cleaned everything. They probably started clearing the place out when we found Sammie Howard's body at the junkyard on Tuesday morning. They had plenty of time to relocate."

As disappointment began to squash Amelia's rush of hopefulness, she gestured to a hallway across the room. "I'm assuming that's where the offices are?"

Spencer followed her gaze. "And a breakroom. The CSU is starting out here to look for anything stolen vehicle related, but we might have better luck if we go through the offices." Without elaborating, the SSA turned to make his way to the hall.

Mentally, Amelia put a hold on her disappointment. She and Zane exchanged glances and started after Spencer, their pace brisk. There was no other part of the Sammie Howard investigation that required their immediate attention, so they might as well rifle around for clues before they called it a day.

She, Zane, and Spencer all snapped on vinyl gloves and took different rooms. As Amelia stepped into a break area, she finally let go of the sigh she'd been holding since they'd walked through the doors.

Like the rest of the warehouse, the break area was unadorned. Aside from a calendar that sported pictures of motorcycles, the walls were bare. A laminate counter sported a double sink and a microwave. To Amelia's surprise, a dishwasher was built into the cabinet beside the sink.

Turning away from the kitchenette, she shifted her focus

to a metal filing cabinet beside a wooden desk. She assumed either a computer or television had been removed from the desk, leaving behind only a single, damaged HDMI cable.

As she opened the top drawer of the desk, pens and pencils rolled along the red cover of a notebook. A renewed sense of curiosity flickered to life. Moving aside the writing utensils, she pulled out the notebook and flipped it open to the first page.

She'd hoped to find some sort of ledger the Leónes had left behind, but she was greeted with a realistic drawing of a tree instead. Not just any tree, but a tree that sported eyeballs where there should have been leaves.

"What the hell?" She hadn't expected to find this type of surrealist art in a chop shop. The next drawing was a bit more normal, though the giant eye on a tower in the background reminded her of *Lord of the Rings*. Two more relatively normal pictures followed, but a pervasive sense of curiosity kept her searching.

Flipping carefully to the next page, anticipation flared in her chest.

Like the first picture, the medium for the drawing was a ballpoint pen. The image depicted a snake curled in a circle, its tail in its mouth.

The ouroboros. The same tattoo Booker had spotted on the wrist of the man who'd crawled out of the woodwork when he'd been asking Sammie Howard to buy him a six-pack.

There was no way this was a coincidence. What were the odds their potential suspect had the ouroboros tattooed on his wrist, his presumed victim is discovered at a junkyard, and then they find a sketch of the same symbol at the chop shop that had been using the junkyard to dispose of stolen vehicles?

And the eyes?

If this truly was a coincidence, Amelia needed to go buy a lottery ticket.

Staring down at the detailed sketch, she slowly began to realize she had no way to back up her instinctual knowledge. Though the ouroboros wasn't an everyday symbol in Western society, it was more common in other cultures.

What other cultures would possibly be at a Leóne chop shop? The Leónes are Italian, through and through. They've been in this city since the days of Al Capone.

She clenched her jaw and began to rein in her expectations. This was a lead, sure, but she would keep a level head as it was evaluated.

There's a saying about counting your chickens before they're hatched. Or, in this case, about assigning meaning to your evidence before you've had a chance to vet all the possibilities.

Amelia wasn't ignoring her gut. She was balancing it with reality.

The sketches in this notebook were significant. She just had to figure out how.

17

A s Cody Frazier strode away from the train stop, he pulled up the hood of his parka to keep his ears from freezing off his head. He silently cursed his decision to attend college in Chicago and not somewhere with a more agreeable climate, like California or Florida.

I bet it isn't ten degrees in Los Angeles right now.

He huffed to himself at the thought. UCLA hadn't offered him a scholarship, and neither had Florida State. The University of Illinois at Chicago, on the other hand, had. Not just a couple thousand dollars, either, but a full-ride scholarship that included housing. As a native of the great state of Illinois, Cody had been relieved he didn't have to uproot and move across the country.

However, transplanting himself from a town near the Illinois-Missouri border to a city the size of Chicago had been a challenge. Where Cody came from, everyone knew everyone else, and people left their doors unlocked at night.

The first time Cody had forgotten to lock the door of his old dorm, his roommate had lectured him for a full fifteen minutes. That particular roommate had since transferred to a different school, leaving Cody the entire room to himself. Well, until the university filled the spot, anyway.

Despite the roommate's absence, he'd not forgotten to lock the door again.

Tucking both hands in his pockets, Cody looked down to avoid the brunt of another gust of wind. He hurried his pace, eager to get back on campus, into the warmth of his room, and then into a scalding hot shower. He didn't have to touch his face to know his skin was coated in a thin layer of grease. Even the air of the restaurant where he worked was comprised partially of grease, he was sure.

He hated his job. Hated that he had to navigate the L to avoid the brutal cold. But more than anything, he couldn't stand the entitled customers. Just because he worked in a fast-food joint, so many people viewed him as a sub-human servant. If there was one slice of onion too many on their burger, they granted themselves permission to act like petulant toddlers.

Who in the hell had raised these people? Cody had never worked in a customer-facing job before, so he couldn't say for sure if his experience was universal.

Every day, he left with a new, outlandish story to tell his friends. He'd even brought up some of the interactions in his classes—particularly his introduction to psychology course.

Tonight was no exception. A large, belligerent man had quite literally thrown his half-eaten order across the counter because he'd asked for no tomatoes. Problem was, Cody had remembered taking his order, and he hadn't made the request.

The man had demanded not only a new burger but a refund. Cody had been on break at the time, and the large man had made the cashier cry. The poor girl was only sixteen, and she'd been working at the restaurant for all of two weeks.

He blew out a long sigh, the wind whipping away the vapor of his breath. Two more years, and he'd have a bachelor's degree. Then he could…what? Most of the jobs in that field involved actually working with other human beings, and the human species was quickly becoming his least favorite mammal. Maybe he should switch to chemistry or botany. Plants didn't make teenage cashiers cry because they were entitled jerks.

Science had never been Cody's strong suit, but maybe if he just applied himself more…

Cody's musing was cut short by the figure of a man darting out from a shadowy parking lot a block ahead. The man threw his arms up in the air, waving to get Cody's attention as he jogged closer.

"Sir, hello, sir!" The stranger was only half a block away as he shouted the greeting in what could only be called an urgent tone.

Cody's knee-jerk response was to glance over his shoulder, searching for a second person. He'd returned too many waves only to be met with confused frowns because the true target of the greeting was standing behind him.

To his dismay, no one was there. Only the pale white glow of streetlamps and the faint lights of the train stop several blocks behind him. The stranger *was* talking to Cody.

Cody whipped his head around, nearly leaping out of his skin when he noticed how close the man had gotten. "Um… I'm sorry, can I help you?"

At the closer distance, Cody noted the stranger wasn't much older than him. He was dressed normally enough— worn jeans, work boots, and a bomber jacket.

That was where the normalcy ended.

The stranger's dark eyes were wide, fright written plainly on his sweat-beaded face. "Sorry. I'm so sorry. I…I need help. You were the first person I saw, and I just need your help, please. My phone, it's dead, and, and..." He gulped in a panicked breath, pointing toward the parking lot. "My baby, she, she..."

Renewed energy surged through Cody's tired muscles. The stranger's sense of panic was so intense, Cody could feel it permeating his own thoughts. "Your baby? What happened?"

"I don't know. I don't know! She just...I thought she was sleeping, but she's not, she's not breathing! Please, can you help me? Do you know CPR?"

The rapid-fire questions shattered any semblance of confidence Cody might have otherwise had. Back in Cody's hometown, one of his good friends had been a lifeguard at the local pool. Cody had helped him study for his certification, and he could still remember most of a standard CPR procedure. But aside from practicing on a dummy a couple times in high school, he'd never actually put the knowledge to use.

He swallowed in a vain attempt to displace the tightness in his throat. "I do...kind of, yeah." He'd rather call 911, but it was possible the man's child didn't have time to wait for the EMTs.

"Oh my god, thank you. Thank you. I pulled over in the parking lot here." The man turned, jabbing his finger in the direction he'd just run from as he took off.

Without a word or even a second thought, Cody followed, even as uncertainty weighed on his shoulders like a barbell at the gym he never attended. He was so nervous about having to perform CPR on a little kid that his wits had taken off like a frightened bird.

How could he turn away from a desperate father? If his rudimentary CPR knowledge could help keep the man's daughter alive until EMTs arrived, if Cody could save the little girl's life, how could he do nothing in good conscience?

Cody would have passed by the parking lot on his route back to campus anyway, so he didn't see what difference it would make if he followed the stranger. It's not like he was getting into a van with a creepy old guy offering him candy.

If this guy's driving a white panel van, I'll hightail it out of here.

The mental joke loosened the death grip of anxiety around his throat.

As he trotted past the building—a closed Indian restaurant—his gaze shot straight to the only vehicle in the adjacent parking lot. The sleek black Outback was nothing like the stereotypical panel van.

Cody's relief at spotting a normal vehicle was short-lived. How long ago had the little girl stopped breathing? Had the man even noticed in time? Was Cody about to try to perform CPR he barely knew on a tiny human corpse? Or was she still alive, and was he truly the difference between her living and dying?

His stomach lurched, bile crawling up the back of his throat. For a beat, he was certain he was about to throw up.

Sucking in a deep breath of the cold night air, Cody reached into his coat pocket and pulled out his phone. His hands shook so badly that he was surprised he could maintain his grip on the device. With the seemingly endless bleak possibilities swirling around in his head, Cody took the last few steps to where the grief-stricken father stood beside the Subaru.

Sniffling, the man swiped the back of one hand beneath his nose and reached for the door handle. "I can call 911 if you…if you can try CPR."

Cody barely saw his phone as he typed in the passcode. Performing CPR on a child was slightly different from adult resuscitation. Children's bones weren't as large or strong as adults', so chest compressions were done using only the index and middle fingers.

Or was that wrong? What if the child wasn't a baby but a toddler? Was that different?

Racking his brain, Cody passed his cell to the father. Through the tinted window of the SUV's rear passenger side, Cody could scarcely make out the shape of a car seat and its tiny passenger.

She's a baby. Index fingers, then. To the beat of "Staying Alive."

The father raised Cody's phone to his ear and pulled open the door. With a deep breath, Cody hunched down to bring himself eye-level with the car seat, sending out a quick prayer that the little girl was still alive.

As he turned his gaze toward the child, a combination of shock and confusion surged through his veins.

The little girl wasn't alive. She'd never *been* alive.

She was a doll.

Cody's stomach dropped all the way to the cold asphalt, but he didn't have long to consider the implications of his discovery.

In the same instant the truth washed over Cody, an arm wrapped around his neck like a python that had been lying in wait. The inside of the stranger's elbow closed in around Cody's airway as the larger, stronger man used his body weight to tackle him into the back seat. As Cody's cheek met the rubber floor mat, the stranger's body pinned him in place.

Cody desperately tried to drag in even a slight breath, but all he managed was a pitiable choking sound.

Fight back! Do something, dammit!

He was in such a state of shock that his brain hadn't fully caught up to the situation. By the time it did, darkness was already chewing at the edges of his vision.

With one hand, Cody clawed at the stranger's arm. As his nails dug into the man's leather jacket, the world around him dimmed.

He threw a mental lasso to bring back his departing consciousness, to regain control over his body. To *fight*.

It was a valiant effort, but the rope fell short.

Darkness overtook him.

18

Joseph Larson set down his steaming mug of coffee, draped his coat over the back of the chair, and lowered himself to sit. The past two days away from the FBI Field Office had been refreshing, but he couldn't play hooky forever. He was between cases, though he'd caught wind of an investigation unfolding that involved a junkyard affiliated with the Leóne family.

He swallowed a sigh. The Leónes were always throwing themselves into the limelight these days. Once upon a time, the family had been discrete and organized. Joseph wasn't sure when the transformation had occurred, but somewhere along the line, they'd grown overconfident. So much so that one agent at the FBI couldn't keep this much heat off those idiots.

If it were up to Joseph—which it wasn't, to his chagrin—he'd have Stan and Brian propose an alliance with the D'Amatos. High profit and low risk was the name of the game for the smarter of the two crime families. Where the Leónes dealt in drugs, human trafficking, and all manner of high-risk industries, the D'Amatos had migrated over to far more lucrative industries.

Counterfeit handbags and virtual theft weren't as glorious as an old-school contract killer or a drug kingpin, but the former practices came with little to no risk of hard time. More importantly, the profit margin was almost too good to believe.

Maybe if Stan hadn't lost his shit, kidnapped Gianna Passarelli, and then knocked her up, we'd have the option to befriend the D'Amatos.

Why the corrupt senator had decided to *keep* Gianna's child was beyond Joseph's comprehension. Maybe Stan planned to groom her so he could have his fun with her when she grew a bit older.

Disgusting.

He was no saint, but incest was a line even he wasn't willing to cross.

As Joseph powered on his computer, he tried to push away the thoughts of Gianna Passarelli and the Leóne family. Brian, ever the venture capitalist, had been building bridges with the Russians over the past few years, and Joseph hoped those seeds would come to fruition sooner rather than later.

Before Joseph could type in his password, his phone buzzed once in the pocket of his tailored slacks. As he went through a mental inventory of who would text him at eight in the morning, he retrieved the device and unlocked the screen.

A shot of unease rippled through his veins as he spotted the messenger's name—SAC Keaton herself.

Good morning, Agent Larson. I need to see you in my office as soon as possible.

He grated his teeth to keep his expression neutral. There weren't many others around the cluster of desks belonging to Organized Crime, but he didn't want to risk any other agent witnessing him lose his cool, even for a second.

The Special Agent in Charge wanted him to meet with her as soon as possible. She hadn't included case details or even a *reason* for the meeting.

Was she going to reprimand him for his poor attendance over the last couple months? He could deal with that. It wouldn't take much brain power for him to whip up a story about his and Cassandra's breakup and how he'd been devastated by the loss. Such a story might make him sound like a wimp, but if it meant keeping his job at the FBI, he'd make do.

Plus, if he played the part of the bereaved ex-boyfriend, perhaps he could usher SAC Keaton over to his corner. The setup could play out well in the future.

Like a pre-programmed android, he rose to his feet. Gulping down a drink of the bitter black brew, he typed a quick message to let the SAC know he was on his way. Dodging the text and pretending he hadn't received it would accomplish nothing. Whatever SAC Keaton planned for their meeting, he'd be better served by arriving in a timely manner.

Maybe she's decided on the next Supervisory Special Agent for Organized Crime. Maybe Spencer Corsaw is actually going to step down like he told us two-and-a-half months ago.

Excitement thrummed along Joseph's nerves. An SSA position would be a huge step in the right direction for him, Brian, and Stan. Especially if Brian's work with the Russians was leading them to a brand-new alliance. Having access to a man at that level in the FBI would be a huge selling point.

Joseph squared his shoulders and kicked aside the thought, enticing though it was. He needed his wits about him, and he couldn't stay sharp if his head was in the clouds as he daydreamed about a promotion.

By the time he arrived at the SAC's open door, he'd shaken off the moment of optimism. Clearing his throat, he knocked on the doorframe.

SAC Keaton's dark eyes flicked up from the document she'd just finished signing. Try as Joseph might to get a read on her, the woman's expression was a blank slate. "Good morning, Agent Larson. Come in, have a seat. Close the door behind you."

The hairs on the back of Joseph's neck rose to attention, his instincts screaming something was wrong. Wordlessly, he heeded the SAC's request, wading through the awkward silence to sit in front of the polished wooden desk.

Before he could even lean back, SAC Keaton pinned him with a scrutinizing stare, the likes of which few could imitate.

Was he meeting with his boss, or was he on the receiving end of an interrogation? During most of his time in the Chicago office, Joseph had operated outside the usual chain of command. Realistically, the only people to whom he answered were Stan Young and Brian Kolthoff.

Or so he'd thought.

The seconds of uneasy silence seemed to morph into minutes, or maybe even hours. Joseph couldn't tell. Every beat of his heart took an eternity as he forced himself to sit still, keep his expression neutral, and keep his mouth closed.

Let *her* reveal the reason for the meeting. If he tried to guess, he'd only land himself in deeper and deeper shit.

After what might have been an eternity or only a few moments, the SAC pushed aside the paper she'd been writing on when Joseph had arrived. Beneath the form, which he couldn't quite read from his place across from her, was an unlabeled manila folder.

SAC Keaton folded her hands atop the folder. "I'll cut

straight to the point, Agent Larson. I've called you in here today to ask for your resignation."

As if the SAC's words had thrown him into a deep freeze, Joseph's blood turned to ice, his mouth suddenly as dry as an ancient Egyptian tomb. "I'm sorry." He leaned forward in his seat, meeting the SAC's stare head-on. "Did I hear you right? You're seriously asking for my resignation?"

If the simmering vitriol in his voice had affected her, SAC Keaton gave no indication. Her face was as expressive as a brick. "You heard me right. You can either resign, or I'll be forced to fire you. By turning in your resignation, you ought to be able to keep media scrutiny off your back, as well as the scrutiny of your peers. Your *former* peers."

What reason could this woman have for firing someone like *him*? Had Amelia Storm made a report about his supposedly inappropriate advances? Had Cassandra crafted some lie to get him in trouble, or had Michelle's disappearance been linked to him?

No. He wasn't in handcuffs. The SAC was asking for his resignation, not pressing criminal charges.

This couldn't be real. Surely, Joseph had slept through his alarm, and this was all a dream.

He bit down on the inside of his cheek until he tasted iron.

No, this wasn't a dream. This was reality.

How did he play this? Did he act offended and reiterate all he'd done for this office, or did he stay calm and demand an explanation?

He didn't have time to weigh his options. The longer he sat in front of the SAC without speaking, the more control he gained over the conversation.

Silence was king.

Which was something the SAC was very aware of too. In fact, she appeared ready to wait all day for him to speak first.

Dammit.

After several minutes had passed, Joseph cleared his throat and straightened his back. "If I'm being fired, then I'd like to know the reason. I realize my attendance lately hasn't been the best, but I can assure you, there's a reason for it."

"No, Mr. Larson. Your attendance isn't the reason I'm asking for your resignation."

Joseph mentally cringed as she referred to him as *Mister* Larson. Not Agent. His gut told him there was no swaying the SAC's decision, but he wasn't about to give up without a last stand. "Then what *is* the reason?"

"What's your relationship with Brian Kolthoff?"

The question hit him like a Mack truck. For a beat, he came within a millimeter of losing his composure. Only years of practiced indifference kept him from spitting out a string of four-letter words. "My *relationship* with Brian Kolthoff? What does that have to do with anything?"

SAC Keaton's stare turned flat. "A lot. Now, if you'll answer the question."

Shit.

Joseph knew the SAC wouldn't have asked him about Brian if she didn't already have information of her own. There was no sense in denying he knew the damn Shark. He wouldn't let the SAC catch him in a lie.

Feigning a resigned sigh, Joseph slumped back in his chair. "We've been friends for a few months. He invited me to a fundraiser for victims of sex trafficking. Look, I know what he was accused of, but he told me his side of the story. It's not what any of us thought it was at first. He's just as much a victim of the Leónes and their sick business as anyone."

A muscle in SAC Keaton's jaw twitched, the first sign of emotion since he'd arrived. "I doubt that very much, Mr. Larson."

Still Mister? Shit.

Thinking quickly, Joseph held up his hands in a gesture of surrender. "You're right. I'm sorry. I didn't mean it like that. I don't mean to discredit what real victims of trafficking have gone through, but the point is that Kolthoff wasn't a part of any of that. He'd hired an...an escort to attend a cocktail party with him. Unbeknownst to him, the escort service was operated by the Leóne family. Instead of finding a *grown woman* to accompany him to the event, the Leónes pulled one of the underaged girls from their prostitution ring. I don't know why they did it. You'd have to ask Emilio Leóne. He's the prick behind all this."

SAC Keaton offered him a half-smile, but the look was far from friendly. "I won't argue that Emilio Leóne is a prick. I reckon his lawyers weren't quite as good as Mr. Kolthoff's. If they had been, he'd be free today too."

Joseph could tell he was up shit creek without a paddle. He was playing a chess match, and he was quickly running out of moves. "With all due respect, SAC Keaton, Brian Kolthoff is an innocent man in the eyes of the law. And in *my* eyes, too, because I sat down and listened to his side of the story. I don't see how a professional friendship with Kolthoff is grounds for action as drastic as termination."

"You're entitled to your opinion." She paused to flip open the folder, turning the top photo around for Joseph to view.

A lead weight plummeted his stomach down to the floor.

He could hardly believe what he was witnessing. The image—a four-year-old photo of Joseph and Brian on the deck of the *Equilibrium* off the coast of Florida—was one he knew, but he didn't have the first clue how SAC Keaton had acquired it.

She doesn't know when it was taken. She has no way to identify the date, does she?

As the excuse began to form in his head, she tapped the

lower righthand corner of the image. "There's the time stamp. This photo was taken four years and six months ago. You *knew* Brian Kolthoff well before the Leila Jackson case. And don't try to tell me this was a one-off, either. It's not the only photo I have."

How? How in the absolute hell had she gotten her hands on such an obscure piece of evidence?

Cassandra. Amelia. They had something to do with this. They had *to have.*

Joseph swallowed, but the effort did little to quell the desert in his mouth. "Where did you get these from?"

The malicious smile was back on the SAC's lips. "Surveillance footage from newly declassified operations conducted by the United States government in their efforts to combat terrorist threats. Since your friend Brian Kolthoff was added to the no-fly list for a few weeks over the summer, he caught the attention of our very own intelligence analysts."

Was her explanation true?

No. There's no way. The timing is too convenient. This isn't a coincidence. One of those bitches had something to do with this.

Teeth clenched, Joseph racked his brain for a new excuse. The quality of the image left no doubt as to either his or Brian's identity, so he couldn't claim they'd found his doppelganger. Photo tampering? No. A quick trip downstairs would rule that out.

Shit. Shit. Shit.

He ran through the Leila Jackson case, recalling how the majority of their efforts had focused on the Leóne family. The Shark had only come up in the last fourth of the investigation.

Joseph held up a hand and shook his head. "Okay. I'll admit I've known Kolthoff for several years. Trust me, I was as surprised as anyone when we found out that *he* was The

Shark. I'm sorry. I shouldn't have kept that to myself. I should've said something as soon as we learned who The Shark was."

In silence, the SAC studied Joseph, though he couldn't make heads or tails of what was going through her head. If he had to hazard a guess, he suspected he'd gotten through to her.

Sensing his opportunity, Joseph went on. "Look, I don't know who gave Kolthoff that moniker, but chances are it's the result of some rumor spread by the Leónes. Something they intended to use to discredit him when he wouldn't work with them or give them money. I had *no idea* that Kolthoff was The Shark. You've got to believe me. I'd have said something if I'd known."

Another spell of quiet followed, and Joseph fought the urge to turn away from the SAC's scrutinizing stare.

"Here's the deal, Joseph." SAC Keaton threaded her fingers together. "Maybe you're telling the truth. Maybe you genuinely didn't know the Leónes liked to refer to Kolthoff as The Shark. Personally, I think you're feeding me a line."

He opened his mouth to deny the accusation, but she cut him off before he could speak.

"What I think doesn't matter. What matters is this." She pointed to the photo. "Brian Kolthoff came within an inch of buying a sixteen-year-old sex slave who'd been kidnapped from her family at age twelve and forced into an underaged brothel. I know what his lawyers said, but after all your time in the Bureau, you ought to know there's always more to the story than what the lawyers say."

How was this happening? He'd made a damn good counterpoint, and he knew it. "Legally, you know everything I've said would hold up in court."

A malicious half-smile crept to the SAC's face. "Maybe. But

here's the thing, Joseph. We aren't in a courtroom. I can fire you for whatever reason I see fit, and I'm fairly sure I've found a damn good one. Your long-time friendship with the man who nearly purchased an underaged sex slave calls into question your integrity as an agent. Put simply, I can't trust you in this office anymore, and the Bureau can't trust you with a badge."

His stunned disbelief was abruptly burned away by the anger rising in his chest like a volcano. "I *will* seek legal action if you fire me, *Jasmine*."

Shit.

Using her first name was a mistake. He tightened one hand into a fist, forcing himself to focus on the pain as his nails dug into the sensitive skin of his palm.

She hardly seemed to notice his passive-aggressive insult. Maybe she hadn't. "This is what's going to happen, all right?" She pushed the form she'd signed across the desk. "You're going to sign this resignation form, and you're going to sign a nondisclosure agreement. You won't talk to the media about any of this, and you'll leave today without making a fuss. If you refuse, then I'll fire you, and I *will* have you charged with obstruction of justice. And, for good measure, I'll make sure every media outlet in this city knows about what Brian Kolthoff tried to do last June."

"You can't do that. That's illegal." Was it, though? Joseph didn't honestly know.

"No, Joseph. It's not. I'm in charge of this office, and I'm permitted to give information to the press as I see fit. If you want to test me, if you want to call my bluff, go ahead and try. See if Capitol Hill lets your lobbyist friend through the doors again when I'm through with him."

Joseph had come to the end of the line. He could tell by the SAC's calm, confident tone that she would undoubtedly carry through with her threat. Though Brian had his own means of retaliation, they all knew the SAC's record was squeaky clean.

There was no sense in furthering the vitriol in the room. If he was going to be forced out of the FBI, then he'd rather go quietly and not draw attention to himself.

Sliding forward in his seat, he reached for a pen.

This wasn't over.

Those two bitches, Cassandra and Amelia, would pay dearly for taking this from him. He didn't give a shit what Brian or Stan had to say.

They would live to regret this.

19

Though Amelia had gotten a late start to the day—the product of several nights' worth of sleep debt had resulted in her and Zane waking up closer to eight than their usual six—she was energized and motivated as she and Zane returned to the incident room. She'd almost forgotten what a difference a full night of sleep made.

Turning over a dry-erase marker in one hand, Amelia studied the murder board. Olivia Mclaughlin, whose tooth had been found near the car compactor at the junkyard, had been added beside Sammie Howard. Though Olivia's body hadn't been found, Amelia doubted they'd ever find more than the tooth.

The body found in the stack of crushed cars was a different story. So far, all they knew from the preliminary DNA analysis was that he was male. Hopefully, over the next few days, the forensic anthropologist would be able to piece together more about his background.

For the time being, he was simply known as John Doe.

The clatter of blinds against glass turned Amelia's attention to the door as Zane stepped into the room, a handful of freshly printed papers in one hand. To her surprise, Spencer Corsaw was right behind him.

Amelia offered the two men a smile and a nod. "Morning, SSA Corsaw. I'm guessing you're here for a debrief on what we've found over the past day?"

Corsaw returned her pleasant expression as he closed the door. "That's part of it. I've also got news for the two of you. It's nothing we're making a big announcement about, but..." He lowered the volume of his voice to a conspiratorial murmur. "SAC Keaton asked for Joseph Larson's resignation a little while ago. I escorted him out of the building."

Blinking as if it would clear the sudden surprise from her brain, Amelia fought the urge to laugh inanely.

Screw you, Joseph. Enjoy life without your badge. See how useful you are to The Shark and the Leónes now.

She only wished she could have been a fly on the wall to witness the look on Larson's smarmy face when SAC Keaton —a *woman*—had sent him packing.

"I assume she had a good reason for it." Zane shrugged noncommittally. "Not that it's any of my business. Me and Larson never got along anyway."

Spencer snorted out a laugh. "I don't think anyone's going to be heartbroken that he's gone. Even for the people who got along with him, he had a way about him." The SSA made a face like he'd just bitten into a lemon. "Like he was always sizing you up, you know?"

Zane sipped his coffee and chuckled. "Oh, I know."

Amelia waved her marker and gestured back to the whiteboard. "Believe me, I could talk shit about Joseph Larson for days, but I think we can make better use of our time."

Clearing his throat, Spencer pulled out a chair at the oval table. "Right. That's the other reason I'm here. Agent Avila and her partner have traced the VINs of one of the crushed cars back to a vehicle reported stolen approximately two weeks ago. The only reason they even found the VIN was because some luxury car manufacturers take extra security precautions and print the VIN in hard-to-find places."

Zane lifted his thermos in a half-toast. "Innovation defeating the mob. That's what I like to see. Who was the owner of the car? Do we think they might be the body we found in the crushed cars?"

"No, it's not." Spencer's chair creaked as he leaned back. "Agent Avila was able to talk to the car's owner. She's alive and well, though a little irritated about having her stolen car destroyed."

"Understandable." Amelia had hoped for a connection between the corpse and the chop shop, something to make the motive behind the murders make sense. "Well, as you may already know, we've positively identified the tooth found beneath the car compressor. Olivia Mclaughlin's aunt provided us with her toothbrush, and the lab was able to match the DNA."

Spencer scooted forward, his dark eyes fixed on the whiteboard. "No body, though. Just the tooth?"

Disappointment weighed down Amelia's shoulders, though only for a moment. "No body. She's been missing for about two months, and her brother is doing a nickel in Wisconsin for drug possession. We've looked through his case and weren't able to find any connection to the Leónes. It seems unlikely Olivia was killed as a form of retribution against Gordon Mclaughlin."

Zane took a seat next to Spencer. "We're going through her last days, trying to find a possible link between her and Sammie. So far, it hasn't seemed likely, though. At nineteen, Olivia was a couple years younger than Sammie's twenty-one. Unlike Sammie, who'd lived in Chicago her entire life,

Olivia had moved to the city from Sheboygan, Wisconsin when she turned eighteen."

Amelia looked back and forth between Olivia and Sammie's information on the board. "Neither of them even had a car, so we can cross the potential for carjacking gone wrong off the list." Though Amelia hadn't given much consideration to the possibility to begin with, it wasn't likely that a carjacker would stick around to carve out the driver's eyes.

Spencer drummed his fingers against the table. "Not that there's any guarantee they were killed by the same person. Unfortunately, we don't have Olivia Mclaughlin's body to examine to see if the cause of death was the same. But if the bodies are being disposed of in a junkyard, there's still the possibility we're looking for more than one killer. Dumping a body in a car that's about to be crushed isn't exactly an original play."

He was right. Amelia had considered the possibility as well, but her instincts told her there was *some*thing connecting the two victims. They just had to figure out what in the hell that *thing* was.

A generic ringtone abruptly drew Amelia's attention to Spencer. The Supervisory Special Agent pulled out his cell and furrowed his eyebrows. Swiping the screen, he raised the phone to his ear. "SSA Corsaw."

As a tinny voice responded, Amelia shot Zane a curious glance. He lifted a shoulder and took a long swig of coffee.

"Really?" Spencer's tone contained a hint of surprise, further raising Amelia's interest. "Okay. Thanks for the call, Dr. Francis. I'll send my agents down there right away."

Excitement buzzed through Amelia as the SSA disconnected the call.

Spencer patted the table and stood. "That was the M.E.'s office. The CPD found another body this morning, pulled him out of Lake Michigan. The vic's name is Cody Frazier. He had a school ID in his pocket, but his wallet was gone. They didn't realize the case was connected until Dr. Francis had a look at his eyes. They were cut out, just like Sammie Howard's."

If Amelia had been sitting, she'd have jumped out of her seat. "All right. We'll head down there right away."

"If you don't mind," Spencer pocketed his phone and straightened his black suit jacket, "I think I'll go with you. I'm supervising this case but haven't had a chance to touch base with the M.E.'s office."

After donning their coats, the three of them set off for the parking garage. Amelia was glad to have another set of eyes on the case, and she hoped the victim's death wouldn't be in vain. For most of the trip, Amelia researched the newest victim as Zane informed Spencer what else they'd learned about Olivia Mclaughlin.

As they pulled into a parking spot in front of the concrete fortress that was the medical examiner's office, Amelia tucked the tablet back into its soft case and headed inside with Zane and Spencer.

Down in the lower level of the building, the strange, sterile scent of chemicals greeted them—a smell Amelia would forever associate with the morgue. Halfway down the hall, Dr. Adam Francis emerged from an exam room on the right.

"Good morning, Agents." The pathologist ushered them toward the open doorway. "I've finished the victim's postmortem, if you want to come in and have a look."

"Of course." Spencer followed Dr. Francis into the exam room. "I appreciate the call. From what I understand, the scene was processed by the Chicago PD, correct?"

Dr. Francis stepped aside to make room for Amelia and Zane to enter, closing the door once they were all inside.

"Correct. I noticed at the scene that the victim's eyes were missing, but since his body had been pulled from Lake Michigan, it seemed possible the marine life was responsible. Eyes, tongues, lips, and other similar soft tissues are the first things scavengers will go for. And considering Lake Michigan's ecology, it isn't unusual to see those parts gone by the time a body gets to my table."

Amelia's gaze was drawn to the mostly covered body of a young man in the center of the room. "What made you realize this case was different?" If they truly were dealing with the same killer, she suspected she already knew the answer.

The pathologist grabbed a pair of gloves from a box on the counter beside a stainless-steel sink. "Like Sammie Howard, this young man's optic nerve was cleanly severed, as well as the surrounding muscle. Only a sharp blade or scalpel could have made these incisions, not marine scavengers."

Just like Sammie Howard.

While Amelia didn't have concrete evidence to back up her hunch that Olivia Mclaughlin was killed by the same person who'd murdered Sammie, she could say with some confidence that Cody Frazier and Sammie's murderer was the same. She could triple check ViCAP—a national database containing details of homicides across the country—but she already knew she'd come away empty-handed.

She filed away the contemplation for later. "What's his official cause of death?"

The pathologist pulled down the sheet, revealing a garish wound on the young man's chest. "A single stab to the heart. I compared the measurements of the injury with those from Sammie Howard's autopsy, and it appears the wounds are nearly identical. Very likely made with the same blade or at least the same type of blade. Serrated on one side, smooth on the other. And the angle of penetration and damage to the underlying tissue indicate the killer was left-handed."

Zane crossed his arms, his gaze fixed on Cody's body. "It's got to be the same killer, then. We kept the part about the eyes being removed away from the media, so it's not a copy-cat. Did he sustain any other injuries? Any defensive wounds?"

Dr. Francis pulled up the sheet and pointed to a darkening mark around the young man's neck. "No defensive wounds. He might've been taken by surprise. There are contusions around his neck, though."

Spencer lifted an eyebrow. "Just like Sammie Howard?"

"Almost identical." The pathologist held his forearm against the victim's throat, comparing the width of it to the mark on his neck. "The pattern of these bruises leads me to believe the killer used his arm to put the victim into a choke-hold, perhaps to knock him unconscious. I measured the abrasions and compared them to Sammie's, and they are very nearly the same."

Amelia peered down at the young victim. Cody Frazier had only been twenty years old, and he'd been a straight-A student at the University of Illinois at Chicago. From what Amelia had glimpsed of his social media accounts, he was a kind, geeky kid from a small town in the southern part of the state. On occasion, he complained about entitled customers at his job, but Amelia doubted anyone could blame him. Well, aside from those same customers, at least.

How was he tied to the Leónes? *Was* he tied to the Leónes, or had a serial killer simply picked a mob junkyard to dispose of his victims?

Spencer walked around the table. "Do we have an approximate time of death?"

"Yes, quite recent, actually." Dr. Francis pulled the sheet over Cody's face and snapped off his gloves. "Decomposition was slowed by the cold temperature of Lake Michigan, but even taking that into consideration, I've put his TOD at last night between eight p.m. and one a.m."

Amelia almost asked how his body had been found so quickly, but she kept the thought to herself. She doubted anyone in the room could answer that question. None of them were experts on the currents of Lake Michigan.

However, they'd be able to consult with scientists who *were* experts. Using the location where Cody's body had been pulled from the water, along with the strength and direction of currents around the area, they could get an approximation of where he'd been dumped.

Dr. Francis ran through the rest of his report, including his doubt that forensics would be able to pull any trace evidence from Cody's clothes. The young man's wrists sported markings similar to Sammie Howard's, as well as traces of an adhesive. Samples had been sent to the lab to determine if the two were similar.

In addition to the adhesive, one of Cody's ankles had been rubbed raw by another type of bind. According to Dr. Francis's experience with bodies pulled from Lake Michigan, he assumed the mark was due to a weight that had been tied to Cody to keep him underwater.

As Amelia, Spencer, and Zane left the M.E.'s office, Amelia took her spot in the back seat of the Town Car. Finding a body in a mob-affiliated junkyard had begged the question of whether the Leónes had used Paulie's Scrap and Salvage as a clever method to dispose of the corpses of their enemies.

However, the more Amelia dug into the backgrounds of the victims, and now that they'd found a victim who'd been dumped outside the junkyard, the more she became convinced the murders had nothing to do with the business operations of the prolific crime family.

A coincidence? Perhaps. Or perhaps a clever serial killer had recognized the junkyard as a mob hotspot and had chosen the location to dispose of his victims to throw suspicion onto the Leónes. The police presence at the junkyard could have forced the Leónes to dump bodies elsewhere, but it also could have forced an unrelated killer to dump *his* victims at a new location.

There were many questions unanswered, but one aspect of the case was certain upon the discovery of Cody Frazier's body.

If they were dealing with a serial killer, then he was escalating.

And he was escalating quickly.

20

Leaning back in the office chair to stretch his legs, Zane was glad he'd chosen to remain at the FBI office to conduct the not-so-glorious research on Cody Frazier. Though he usually preferred to be in the field, the howling wind and sub-zero temperature made him grateful that the powers that be had recently replaced the field office's HVAC system with one that didn't set him ablaze in the winter. He sure as hell didn't envy the forensic techs who were still hard at work at Paulie's Scrap and Salvage.

Just thinking of spending most of the day outside made Zane shiver. He'd spent much of his younger years in the frigid tundra of Russia, but the older he got, the less he enjoyed freezing his ass off. He still liked the cold, but he liked it even better when he was inside.

Maybe I'm just turning into an old softy.

He chuckled quietly to himself. Thirty-four, almost thirty-five, was far from old.

Well, it's the oldest I've ever been.

Zane rubbed his eyes and reached for his coffee. Having mental conversations with himself was a sure sign he was tired. To his dismay, he didn't have time to be tired. Amelia and Spencer were on their way back to the field office from where they'd been conducting interviews with Cody Frazier's friends, coworkers, and classmates.

While Amelia and Spencer had been out, Zane had coordinated with the local police to obtain security camera footage from Cody's usual route home. Unlike Sammie Howard, Cody *had* boarded the L on the night he was killed, leading Zane to believe he'd been abducted somewhere between the train stop and his college dorm.

As Zane absentmindedly spun the paper sleeve around his coffee cup, the door at his back brushed open. Spinning his chair around, he flashed a pleasant smile to Amelia and Spencer as they entered the incident room. "Afternoon, or, well," he glanced to his watch, "almost evening. How'd the interviews go?"

Amelia shrugged out of her coat, and the faint scent of greasy food wafted over to Zane. "They were fine."

Spencer raised an arm to sniff the fabric of his own coat, frowning as he started unfastening buttons. "I'm going to smell like a cheap burger for the rest of my career."

"You and me both." Amelia dropped down to sit across the table from Zane. "I knew we should have just done those interviews outside and made everyone freeze their asses off."

Zane had interrogated suspects in far less enviable conditions. "It's a valid tactic. Make the subject uncomfortable while you pepper them with questions. They're more likely to slip up."

"I know." Spencer waved a dismissive hand and took his own seat. "But the problem with that is then *I'd* have to freeze my ass off too. Besides, none of Frazier's coworkers or friends were suspects to begin with. No need to go full-on interrogator when we're talking to innocent witnesses, you know?"

"True." Zane shook the wireless mouse to bring his laptop's screen to life. "Speaking of, what did you guys find?"

Amelia glanced at Spencer and shook her head. "Nothing groundbreaking. We were able to talk to Cody's manager from last night, plus the other employees who were on shift at the time. None of them noticed anything out of the ordinary in Cody's demeanor, nor did they see any suspicious looking individuals lurking around the restaurant."

The SSA's chair squeaked as he leaned back and stretched both arms above his head. "We asked if there were any particularly disgruntled customers that night, but one of the cooks who'd been working said no one had gotten mad at Cody. One customer yelled at a cashier and made her cry, but Cody and the manager diffused the situation before the guy could get any more belligerent."

"Otherwise." Amelia rested the backs of her hands on the table, palms up, and shrugged. "We didn't learn anything useful, honestly. Cody was a good student, didn't have any enemies, and hadn't reported anyone following or stalking him. His most recent relationship ended six months ago, and she's living in Cody's hometown on the Illinois-Missouri border."

Another nice kid, killed for absolutely no reason. Zane gestured to the whiteboard. He'd scrawled out Cody's information, though his handwriting was nowhere near as legible as Amelia's. To the side of Cody and Sammie's details was a taped photo of Olivia Mclaughlin with a large question mark next to her headshot.

They had no proof that the young woman was dead, but no one had questioned her picture being added to the board.

"One common thread, the *only* common thread between the three victims we've identified, aside from their ages, is their jobs. All three of them worked in customer-facing positions. Cody at a fast-food joint, Sammie at a gas station, and then Olivia was a server at a chain restaurant." Zane powered on the projector and lowered the lights. He wasn't sure how promising his discoveries would be, but they were better than nothing.

Amelia stood and walked closer to each picture, studying them closely. "Their eyes are all hazel." She shook her head. "Surely eye color wouldn't make them a target," she turned to face the other agents, "would it?"

Zane blew out a breath, fluttering his lips. "I've seen crazier things."

Amelia studied the photos again. "Very true."

She scooted to the side so she could view the projection. "If we're dealing with a serial killer, then he could just be picking victims he runs into around town."

Spencer scratched his cheek. "Most serial killers hunt for their victims in an area they know relatively well."

"Right." Zane pulled up a map of the city with three red dots indicating the workplaces of their victims. "Sammie and Cody worked on the same side of town, but Olivia is a bit farther away." He pressed another button, displaying a trio of blue markers. "These are their addresses. None of them had cars, so they worked pretty close to where they lived. And now, here's Paulie's Scrap and Salvage."

Amelia pressed her lips together, glancing to Zane and then back to the map. "It's not close to any of the victims. The killer would've had to go out of his way to dispose of the bodies there."

"Right. I thought that was worth noting." Zane's area of expertise trended in the direction of organized crime, not necessarily serial killers. However, he'd picked up a few bits of knowledge from the cases he and Amelia had worked with their colleagues in the Violent Crimes Division. "If we're considering the serial killer angle more seriously, it might be a good idea to get the BAU's take on this pattern. Although the crimes are bizarre to me, someone like Agent Redker might be able to make sense of it."

Spencer nodded and tapped out a message on his phone. "I'll get ahold of the BAU and see when we can get someone to take a look at what we've got so far." The SSA's dark eyes flicked up to study them both. "I *was* in VC before I came over to Organized Crime, for what it's worth. Speaking generally, serial killers are going to be familiar with some part of their hunting and dumping ground. Now, I think Agent Storm made a good point earlier. This killer could have chosen Paulie's junkyard to dump his victims because he knew it was affiliated with the mob. He'd realize what a huge red herring this would be for us."

Amelia gestured to the map. "And the only reason he'd have changed that dumping ground for Cody is because we're still at the junkyard. But I'll bet he doesn't go back to Paulie's even after we finish up out there."

"Probably not." Zane couldn't help but feel like they were on the cusp of a breakthrough, that a missing puzzle piece was just out of reach. "What about the ouroboros drawing we found at the chop shop? Any thoughts on how that fits into this?"

Pressing his lips together, Spencer exchanged a quick look with Amelia before shaking his head. "Not really. We asked Cody's coworkers and friends if the symbol had any significance to Cody, but they didn't think it did. We're still waiting to see if forensics can pull any prints from that notebook, not that we can necessarily connect it with our killer. Not right now, anyway."

"All right." Zane minimized the map and opened the video he'd been reviewing not long before Amelia and Spencer's return. "Well, this is the most promising lead I've found today. I got the CPD to send me surveillance footage from Cody's route to his dorm. I found him on the L and watched him get off the train at his stop. I followed the path, and this is where it led me."

As the image of a closed Indian restaurant came into view, Amelia and Spencer's attention was glued to the projection screen.

"This was taken from the camera of a mom-and-pop electronics store." He circled the cursor over the parking lot beside the Indian restaurant, much of which was obscured by the building. "Pay attention to this area on the right."

In silence, the three of them watched a red truck drive past the store front. A solid minute of nothingness followed before what appeared to be a Subaru pulled into the lot beside the Indian restaurant. The vehicle was obscured by the building, but it hadn't left.

Zane could sense the anticipation mounting in Amelia and Spencer's heads as a man moved from the parking lot to the sidewalk. Shortly afterward, Cody Frazier came into view on the left-hand side of the screen.

Without wasting a moment, the man from the parking lot sprinted over to Cody. The stranger's face was only visible for a split second, but that was all the time Zane needed. He paused the feed, took a screenshot, and zoomed in.

Amelia's eyes widened. "Leather bomber jacket, dark hair, jeans. That matches Booker Gilbert's description almost exactly. It also matches the guy we saw on camera with Sammie and Booker."

Zane swallowed a sigh as he moved the still to the middle of the screen. "The camera doesn't have a good enough lens to get details, unfortunately. All we can make out are the basics." If there was one aspect of the CIA Zane missed, it was their unfettered access to top-of-the-line technology. "But that's not the end of their interaction."

Closing the screenshot, he resumed the playback of the surveillance footage. As the man approached Cody, the college student's body language stiffened. The stranger appeared to be imploring Cody for something, but Zane didn't have the first clue what.

After a moment of consideration, the man in the bomber jacket hurried away, Cody close on his heels. The pair vanished around the corner of the Indian restaurant.

And then...nothing.

Zane minimized the video. "Neither of them come back into view of that camera. I also checked a couple cameras farther down the block, but I didn't find Cody anywhere. This parking lot is where he disappeared." He paused to pull up the feed from a new camera. "But don't worry, all is not lost. The CPD found this security camera from a gas station on the other side of the street, behind and catty-corner to the Indian place. It shows the entrance to the alley that leads to that parking lot."

Neither Amelia nor Spencer commented, their attention rapt on the projection screen.

Adjusting to the same timestamp as the start of the first video, Zane pressed play and waited. Less than a minute in, the sedan slowly turned into the alley.

As he hit pause, Amelia and Spencer sat up a little straighter.

Spencer turned his curious stare to Zane. "That's the same car, yeah? Same make and model, same time stamp?"

"Yep." Zane took yet another screenshot, zooming into the Subaru until the car took up the entire frame. "The lights from the gas station are shining on the windshield this whole time, so I couldn't get a look at the driver, unfortunately. The good news is that the license plate is plain as day."

Amelia frowned. "All right. What's the catch?"

Zane couldn't help but let out a self-deprecating chuckle. Amelia could read him like a book, and for a reason he had yet to comprehend, he wasn't bothered by it. "The catch is that I ran the plate, and this is what it turned up."

A new image lit up the screen, and Spencer swore. "Of course. Those plates belong to a red Volkswagen, and the owner of said Volkswagen is dead."

Amelia pushed her hair back from her face. "Of course. Do we know what happened to the Volkswagen, though?"

"Sure do." Zane had a hard time keeping the disappointment out of his voice. "The owner's daughter sold it after he died, and the new owner totaled it within a month. It's been out of operation for the past six months."

One of Spencer's eyebrows quirked up. "Where was it towed after the driver totaled it?"

"I know what you're thinking. I had the same idea. But it wasn't towed to Paulie's Scrap and Salvage. By the time it was wrecked, the plates were long gone anyway. I tried to backtrack and figure out when the plates could've been stolen, but there's honestly no way to tell."

Amelia patted the table. "This is still a good development, though. License plates aside, we can still safely link Sammie Howard and Cody Frazier's murders together. Both vics were killed in the same way, both had their eyes cleanly cut out of their head, and both were dumped at a location different from where they were killed. We've got security camera footage from just before both victims disappeared, and the same guy appears on both recordings. If we find the perp for one murder, we find the perp for both."

Spencer set down his phone. "But then we've still got Olivia Mclaughlin and the John Doe we found in the stack of crushed cars. We have no idea if they're connected to Cody and Sammie, or if they're casualties of the Leóne family, or if they're none of the above."

"True." Amelia lifted a shoulder. "We'll focus on what we can solve for the time being, and we can keep digging into

Olivia's background to see if there's anything that links her to Sammie or Cody."

They were hunting for a serial killer. One smart enough to throw off the Bureau's suspicions by dumping his victims in a mob-affiliated junkyard.

Zane hoped no one else would have to die for the Bureau to get its next clue.

21

Slumping into the cushioned seat of a small booth in the corner of the coffee shop, I let out the sigh I'd been holding. Popping the lid off the largest cup they offered, I savored the scent of the fresh brew. It would cool faster if I kept the lid off, and right now, I desperately needed the caffeine.

Fortunately, my efforts over the past twenty-four hours hadn't been in vain. I'd purchased my Subaru Outback because of how easy the interior was to clean and had detailed every inch after transporting that kid the night before. I had another car, but everyone I knew was used to me in this one, especially in the winter, and I didn't want to call attention to myself by switching vehicles.

Right now, attention was the absolute last thing I wanted.

My father didn't know about Cody Frazier, and I'd hoped that's the way it would stay. I'd dumped Cody's body in Lake Michigan, weighing him down with a cinder block tied to his ankle. I doubted his corpse would *stay* at the bottom, but I'd hoped the makeshift anchor would buy me a little time.

No such luck for me.

To my chagrin, the subject of the afternoon news—and now the evening news, according to the television mounted near my booth—had been none other than Cody Frazier. The kid's body had been fished out of Lake Michigan that morning, and authorities were reporting that he'd been killed by a single stab wound to the heart.

Accurate, but there had been no mention of his damn eyes. Those mocking eyes, filled with a sense of entitlement and self-righteousness I'd never understand.

No matter. Like Sammie Howard, I knew I hadn't left behind any clues for the authorities. I was operating under the assumption that the Feds would have their nose buried into the new case. They were at the helm of the investigation into Paulie's Scrap and Salvage, as well as Sammie Howard's murder.

But would they link Cody to Sammie?

Of course they will. How many bodies do they find in this city with the eyes cut out? Single stab wound to the heart? They have to know Cody and Sammie were killed by the same person. I knew I should change the method used to kill them...but those haunting eyes wouldn't die if the heart kept beating.

I'd had to do it right. Didn't people understand that?

Frustrated to my core, I turned my stare down to the black coffee. Reaching for a sugar packet, I mentally ran through last night's events.

Cody hadn't scratched me, and when I cut those cursed eyes out, I'd worn gloves and a poncho—both of which I'd since burned—to keep the blood spatter off my clothes. I'd wrapped his body in a tarp before placing him in the trunk of my car, and I'd promptly driven out to one of the family's marinas north of the city. If there were any fibers, any hair, any *any*thing, it would have been washed away by the lake.

As far as the chop shop and the family went, no one knew I had anything to do with Cody Frazier's murder. Killing

Brock Dominguez had gotten my father off my back and had even earned me a few praises from the boss. According to him, I'd carried out the contract without a hitch.

We'd taken Brock's fancy RV to our relocated chop shop and had promptly stripped it down to nothing. The value of the parts we'd recovered paled in comparison to Brock's debt to the family but killing him had sent a powerful message to anyone who might think to screw with us in the future.

My father had been quite clear about how much risk I'd exposed the family to with the necessity to relocate the chop shop on such short notice. I'd brought unwanted attention into our own backyard. If the family learned I had killed Sammie and forced them into this predicament…

I shook off the rest of the thought. The Feds *wouldn't* find out who'd killed Sammie Howard. Our sources had already confirmed nothing of interest had been found in the raid of the chop shop.

Stirring the sugar into my coffee, my thoughts finally began to calm.

All I had to do now was lay low. I could do that. Maybe take a short vacation somewhere tropical and far away. With everything that had happened at the junkyard, the family would understand why I'd want to take a break from the city.

It's February in Chicago. What more do they really need to know?

I chuckled quietly to myself. A sunny beach would be a welcome reprieve from the gray skies and cold wind of Illinois.

A voice in the back of my head insisted being out of the country would come in handy if the Feds were to make any headway in Sammie Howard's case, but I ignored the thought.

They wouldn't make headway. There was nothing for them to find.

Shoving to my feet, I picked up the cup with one hand and the lid with the other. Last-minute plane tickets weren't cheap, but I'd made enough money off Brock to reward myself with a short vacation. To the family, that's exactly what it would look like—me rewarding myself for a job well done. With the chop shop's operations slowed at the moment, it was perfect timing.

As I went to replace the lid on the paper cup, something slammed into my shoulder. Coffee splashed down the front of my white button-down shirt, some of it sloshing onto the table. All I could do was be grateful the brew had cooled off in the last ten minutes or so. Staining my shirt was bad enough, but if I'd been burned by whatever klutz had run into me...

"Oh my gosh, I am *so* sorry!" A tremor of nervousness was unmistakable beneath the young woman's otherwise amiable tone. Clutching a small towel in both hands, she hurried around to the table. The burgundy polo and black slacks she wore were the same as the baristas behind the counter, but that's where my initial observation ended. I didn't want to go out into the frigid February day with a wet shirt. And if the stain sank in, I'd have to throw the costly garment away.

I bit off the slew of four-letter words that stabbed at the tip of my tongue and snatched a fist full of napkins. Annoying though the situation may be, I wasn't about to make a scene and draw attention to myself by cursing at some klutz of an employee. "It's all right."

"I'm so sorry, sir. It's my first day, and I didn't realize the tables were so close together. Here, let me clean this up, and I'll buy you a new coffee. Whatever you want from the menu, my treat." As she went to work cleaning the coffee off the table, her gaze flicked up to meet mine.

Terror and anger combined to freeze the blood in my

veins. Light brown eyes, ringed ever so slightly with olive green mocked me. Laughed at me. Tormented me.

She'd done this on purpose.

Backing up a step, I reached into my pocket before remembering how weaponless I was. That had been her plan, I could tell. Catch me off guard, embarrass me in front of others. The same others that forced me to control the growing forces churning inside me.

"Sir?"

The face staring at me looked worried, but the eyes...they taunted.

"Andre?"

It was only when her forehead knitted in confusion that I realized I'd spoken the name aloud and knew I needed to pull my shit together. Needed to get out of there right then.

More than anything, in that moment, I wished I could pull out a hunting knife and see those godawful eyes out of their sockets. If I made them mine, if I owned them, then I was the one in control.

Sure, I could deal with her, but how many millions of people in this country had eyes like hers? Eyes similar to Andre's, the ringleader of the older kids who'd tortured me when I was young. When I was small and weak, when my left eye turned in toward my nose because one of my optic muscles was too short.

I couldn't say how I knew, but I knew this barista was viewing me as that skinny little kid. Had she accidentally bumped into my shoulder, or had she done it on purpose? Did she *want* me to make a fool out of myself in front of the coffee shop's other patrons?

She did. I was certain she did.

I gave myself a mental shake. She was waiting for me to respond. My most current tormentor didn't even have to try to make me look like an idiot. Apparently, the skill set came naturally to me.

Rubbing my eyes, I shook my head. I'd play it off like I was tired. "No. You don't have to do that. I need to get some sleep anyway, and more coffee sure isn't going to help with that."

She smiled, and a sliver of the brown and green orbs disappeared. "I understand. Stop back in sometime tomorrow if you want, and I'll buy you a coffee then." She pointed to her name tag. "Just ask for Desiree."

Heartbeat pounding in my ears, my body so tense I likely could have been mistaken for a statue, I looked down and zipped up my coat. Anything to keep my eyes off hers. "All right. Thanks, Desiree."

I couldn't get out of this damn café fast enough.

How could my reaction to coming face-to-face with those eyes be so visceral already? I'd dumped Cody Frazier's body in Lake Michigan fewer than twelve hours ago. I *should* have been able to stand interacting with someone sporting Andre's eyes so soon after a kill.

As I shuffled out into the cold, I could feel the scrutinizing stares of the other customers glued to my back. What was she saying about me now? Was she and the other employees laughing at the jackass who'd gotten coffee spilled all over his nice shirt?

None of them had a single clue who I really was. They didn't know what I could do or what I had done.

Settling into the driver's seat, I stared at the warm glow of the coffee shop's windows without seeing them.

I'd have to abandon this place.

That means she won.

Over the past few weeks, it had become my favorite café. Close to home, close to the relocated chop shop, close to my dad's place…

It's hers now.

I gritted my teeth. I wouldn't let her win. I wouldn't let *Andre* win.

Then what are you going to do about it?

There was only one thing to do.

22

S liding behind the wheel of her trusty Toyota Camry, Desiree Bauer waved to her manager as Kimmy opened her own car door. Warm air rushed up to greet her, leaving her grateful for her mom's suggestion that she upgrade to remote start. The one-time installation fee was well worth the grief she'd saved by being able to start her car from as far as a block away.

Today had been the first day of Desiree's on-the-job training, and the day had gone...okay. The first half of her shift had been fine, though she'd messed up a couple orders and had to remake them. Fortunately, the customers were relaxed and understanding when she explained about being a total newbie.

The messed-up drinks weren't where her anxious brain was focused, however. She couldn't stop thinking about how she'd run into a customer, spilling coffee all over his shirt. Based on the rest of his wardrobe—the genuine leather bomber jacket, expensive watch, and his black, slicked-back hair—the shirt hadn't been cheap. She'd half-expected him to lose his shit and berate her for ruining a piece of clothing that cost more than her weekly wage, but instead, he'd been oddly silent.

No...not just silent. Strange.

Scary somehow. But at least he hadn't yelled or threatened her job. Besides, the poor guy had probably been embarrassed and had just wanted to get out of the café so he could go change.

Sinking down farther into her seat, Desiree sighed. She hoped he returned tomorrow so she could at least buy him a coffee to apologize.

Unfortunately, the awkward mishap hadn't been the end of the day's weirdness. For the last three hours of her shift, maybe even longer, she hadn't been able to shake the feeling someone was watching her.

She snorted. Of course someone had been watching her. Her manager and the other baristas to name a few.

They were making sure I didn't screw up any more lattes or bowl over any more customers.

She slumped a little more, cringing as the memory replayed itself for the eight-thousandth time. As much as she tried to tell herself the feeling of paranoia was just concern over her job performance on her first day, there was more to the creepy-crawly sensation on the back of her neck.

Straightening, Desiree fastened her seat belt and took in a deep breath. She tightened her grip on the steering wheel and glanced around the parking lot to reassure herself.

Kimmy had just pulled out onto the street, and the rest of the lot was empty. Partially melted snow was piled in the back corner, but Desiree doubted anyone would hide in such a spot.

She shook off the lingering unease and shifted the car into gear. A year ago, even three months ago, she wouldn't have thought much of the strange sensation that had followed her for the last few hours. Until she'd ended things with her now ex-boyfriend, Elias Rasmussen, she'd had no reason to look over her shoulder.

Come on, Desiree. Pull yourself together. You're being ridiculous. Eli's an asshole, but he's not a killer. He's not even violent unless he's been drinking, and even then, he takes out his rage on inanimate objects and drywall.

How long until the walls no longer satiated his bursts of rage, though? She hadn't received any of Eli's drunken voicemails or texts in almost two weeks, but she wasn't convinced he'd finally moved on.

She'd rather be safe than sorry. Every abuser and murderer started somewhere, and a bad breakup was often a precursor to much more sinister behavior. She'd witnessed firsthand how quickly her friend's ex had gone from "just annoying" to full-on lunatic.

"*He* cheated on *me!*" Desiree exclaimed to the metal angel hanging from her rearview mirror. "That dickhead's got no right to harass me after I broke up with him for screwing someone else."

Not that it mattered to Eli. Twice, three times per week, he'd get wasted and send her texts that started off sappy and sad, then got progressively meaner until he was simply berating her. When she was particularly unlucky, he'd call and leave a voicemail.

Desiree had changed her number, but one of their mutual friends—who was no longer a friend of Desiree's—must have given him the new contact information. The messages had gotten to her at first, but then they'd pissed her off. Now, almost three months after the breakup, they were just annoying.

Better safe than sorry.

Sighing, she pulled out onto the street and sped away

from the café. Elias was the reason she carried mace in her handbag, and he was why she'd installed a doorbell alarm and camera on the front porch of her duplex. For good measure, she'd even placed a motion-activated camera on the bookshelf in the living room.

Though she desperately wanted to get a pet now that she officially lived on her own, she was putting off the adoption until she was confident Elias was out of her life for good. The absolute last thing she wanted was to come home to find her psychopath ex-boyfriend had murdered her furry friend.

The mental imagery brought a red-hot rush of anger to her veins. If Elias *was* stalking her, she'd mace him until his eyes melted out of his damn head. Maybe then he'd finally get the picture.

With her attention split between the road and an NPR news recap, Desiree didn't notice the constant pair of headlights in her rearview mirror until she was less than five minutes from her home.

Blood pounded in her ears, rendering the radio host's voice tinny and distant as she turned left and waited for the car to turn left too.

How long had they been following her?

Were they even following her? Or had she officially become overly jumpy and paranoid for no reason?

Not no reason. Eli.

Elias doesn't have a car or a driver's license. It can't be him... unless he got a friend to drive him around.

She had difficulty picturing any of Eli's friends possessing enough patience to chauffeur him around to stalk his ex-girlfriend.

Maybe it's someone who lives in the same neighborhood as me. That's not unheard of, right?

Desiree didn't believe her own excuses.

As she pulled closer to the next intersection, she flicked

on her right blinker as if she planned to turn off the main street and into the residential neighborhood.

Sure enough, the car behind her slowed as if to turn.

At the last second, Desiree veered away from the inter-section to continue traveling straight ahead. She was no expert on losing a tail, but the move would ostensibly tell her whether or not the person was following her or simply driving to their own destination.

Her heart sank as the headlights remained in the rearview. The other car—the make of which she couldn't quite tell, though she'd discerned the color was dark—started to lag behind, causing Desiree to make note of her speed.

"Shit." She spat the word more than said it. In her haste to get away from the stalker, she'd sped up to more than fifteen miles-per-hour over the speed limit.

Being pulled over wouldn't be the worst thing in the world. Maybe she could ask the cop for help, and she could tell them...

What, exactly? That she thought her ex-boyfriend might have possibly convinced one of his friends to follow her around as she drove home from work? Or that there was a stranger in a car going the same direction as she?

It'd be better than nothing. Then at least if you turn up dead, the cops might have a lead about who did it.

Desiree shook off the ridiculous scenarios. One thing at a time. First, she'd ditch whoever in the hell was or wasn't following her, then she'd try to figure out if the driver was Eli or someone else. Eli shouldn't know where she lived. After their breakup, she'd secretly moved to her new home. If he couldn't find her home, would he really stoop to following her? Stalking her?

Adrenaline thrummed through her body as she neared an upcoming traffic light. The light had just switched from green to yellow, and while she'd normally start to slow in preparation to stop, Desiree dropped her foot down on the accelerator instead.

As the golden-yellow glow gave way to red, her little Toyota zipped through the intersection like she was fresh off a NASCAR race.

Only when she was a block past the light did she slow back down to ten over the speed limit. Glancing in the rearview mirror, she almost pumped a victorious fist into the air as she noted the car stuck back at the light. Now, she just had to take a few more erratic turns so the driver couldn't follow her.

By the time she finally pulled into the driveway of her duplex, her fingers had started to cramp from how tightly she'd been gripping the steering wheel. To her relief, she hadn't spotted another pair of headlights in the rearview mirror. Whoever had been following her out on the main street hadn't managed to track her home.

Now, she just had to get inside.

Turning the key back in the ignition, she shifted in her seat to scan the quiet neighborhood. If it wasn't for Desiree's mom being friends with the owner of the duplex, there was no way she could have afforded to live somewhere this nice. Not in Chicago, and not on a retail worker turned barista's salary. The residential area was home primarily to working-class families, and Desiree felt safe walking from her car to the front door at night.

Normally.

Her scan of the gloomy street revealed nothing out of the ordinary. No creepers hiding behind bushes, no idling white panel vans. No sign of the car that felt like it was following her. Only the occasional glow of a window to remind her she wasn't the only night owl in the neighborhood.

Desiree breathed deeply, reminding herself she was only ten or so feet from the front porch. Streetlamps dotted the area in regular intervals, their glow partially obscured by the leafless branches of tall, old trees. She had light, she had her mace, and she had her keys ready to go. She was a modern woman who was about to walk into her very own duplex in the middle of Chicago, not a camp counselor at Camp Crystal Lake circa the late seventies. There was no immortal psychopath with a hockey mask and a machete lying in wait.

"Come on, Desiree. Get it together. The car's gone. You lost them. Right? Just get inside, turn on every single light, triple check the locks, and then do a voice call with someone until you can walk around without jumping at your own shadow."

Her pep talk was half-assed, but it worked. Keys in one hand, mace in the other, she elbowed open the car door. She was so preoccupied with surveilling her immediate surroundings she barely noticed the cold. As she rushed to the porch, she permitted herself a moment of relief at the stillness around her.

See, no monsters lurking in the dark.

No Elias, either.

Thank god.

Desiree was grateful, but she didn't linger to test her fate. Sliding the key into the lock, she breathed a sigh of relief as she stepped over the threshold and into the gloom of the pint-sized foyer.

Her shoulders sagged with relief as she flicked the deadbolt into place. She'd made it. And she was also a silly woman with crazy notions and shouldn't be allowed to go out on her own.

The chuckle that escaped her vibrated with nerves. "I'm seriously going craz—"

A hand snapped out of the shadows and clamped over her mouth a second before an arm grabbed her around the waist.

The powerful grip pulled her out of the foyer, and she tried in vain to dig her heels into the carpet of the living room.

Desiree had no idea what was happening. All she knew was she had to fight.

Tightening her grip on the mace, she squirmed against the man's iron grasp, struggling to put herself at an angle that would allow her to spray him without hitting herself.

As if he'd read her mind, the assailant leaned back, lifting her feet from the floor. Before she could lash out with either foot, he slammed her onto the ground with the full weight of his body. Stars danced in front of her vision like in an old cartoon while pain seared through her head as the dull crunch of her nose breaking was audible in the otherwise silent room.

To Desiree, however, the worst sound of all was the quiet thud of both her mace and keys hitting the carpeted floor. Fallen like her chances of getting out of this with only a broken nose. Those items had been her last and only line of defense against whoever this madman was.

With the man on top of her and blood running into her mouth, Desiree struggled to take a full breath. Though time moved at the speed of cold molasses, adrenaline rushed through her veins with every beat of her heart. To her chagrin, adrenaline wasn't the miracle it was portrayed to be on television. Her muscles were taut, her senses acute, but she didn't possess the strength of a superhero.

Hopelessness swirled around her like a dark fog. One good breath, and maybe she could mount a fight.

You don't need to be able to beat him in the Octagon in an MMA match. You don't even need to be able to beat him in a fight. All you need to do is give yourself an opening so you can scramble away and make a break for it. Once to safety, she could call the cops and let them sort this out.

Desiree tried to jerk her body like a bucking bronco to

throw the man off her, or at least to allow her lungs some precious air. If she could knock him off balance, maybe that would give her the opening she needed to get back to the front door, her car, and safety.

Mustering as much strength as she could manage, she wildly jerked under her assailant's weight. If she'd caught him by surprise, it didn't last long.

Before she could crawl toward freedom, he grabbed her by the ankle, knocking her prone once again. With the speed of a coiled snake striking its prey, he rolled her onto her back and climbed on top of her, pinning her hands under his knees with superhuman force.

The sliver of hope from only seconds earlier vanished, gone like a tendril of smoke on the winter wind.

Her gaze settled on a face covered almost entirely by a ski mask and hood. She had no idea who this man was. His upper body was covered by a rain poncho, but she didn't have time to ponder the garment's significance.

Desiree opened her mouth to scream, but before a single decibel could leave her lips, a knife glinted in his hand. Serrated on one side, the blade took on an almost ethereal glow in the blue light of the digital clock on the bookshelf.

The shelf. The camera. It's still there. He didn't notice it.

Her assailant hadn't spotted the camera planted in an otherwise benign bookend, but how much good had it done her tonight?

"Look at me." The quiet command plowed through the haze that had begun to permeate Desiree's brain. "Look at me, Desiree."

She forced herself to comply with his demand, and as soon as she did, his hand slipped away from her mouth. This was her last chance.

The scream that escaped her lips didn't last long before

the breath was knocked from her lungs by something burning into her chest.

"You're evil," the man muttered a moment before pain became a living thing under her skin. Blade scraped bone, and she could almost hear the sound it made before a new explosion of agony ripped through her.

Then nothing.

23

A melia arrived at the FBI office bright and early—or, in this case, she and Zane got to the office *dark* and early. While Zane headed to the copy room to print more photos for the murder board, Amelia scanned the whiteboard, hoping a new clue would jump out at her, but knowing the prospect was unlikely. After all, she was still waking up, and they had a busy day ahead of them.

As much work as she and Zane had on their plates, the forensic team had even more on theirs. A snowstorm was predicted for mid-week, and the crime scene techs were scrambling to ensure they hadn't missed a crucial piece of evidence at Paulie's before the weather could ruin it.

The night before, right around the time Amelia and Zane were heading to bed, they'd received a call from the lab. They'd been busy trying to identify the corpse found by the K-9 unit in the stack of crushed cars, and they'd made a huge breakthrough. As luck would have it, one of the body's hands was relatively intact, and forensics had been able to lift a print.

Norris Lowery, age twenty and missing for two weeks,

had been fingerprinted for a theft he'd been involved in during high school. Though the charges were expunged from his criminal record, his prints had remained on file.

Rather than get to work at ten o'clock at night, Amelia and Zane had put in the requests for Norris's case files and set their alarms for the buttcrack of dawn. Special Agent Layton Redker of the Bureau's Behavioral Analysis Unit was scheduled to provide his expertise in less than an hour, and Amelia wanted to know more about Norris before he arrived.

By the time Zane returned with a freshly printed collection of photos, Amelia was almost finished reading through Norris's missing persons case. Not that Zane had taken long —the case file was just lacking.

Zane shot her a curious glance and made his way to the whiteboard. "Learn anything new about Norris Lowery while I was fighting with the printer?"

Sighing, Amelia leaned back in her chair. She wished she'd found anything, but rarely was their work that straightforward. "Not really. There's next to nothing in the case file from when he went missing. He was twenty, lived in an apartment by himself, and was attending a trade school to become an electrician. He worked part-time at a hardware store, and his parents helped him close the financial gap to pay rent."

"Who reported him missing?"

"The hardware store." Amelia scrolled back up to scan the parents' information. "His parents live in Chicago as well, but according to their statement, their son is very independent. They have a daughter who's a senior in high school and still lives at home. Between their busy schedules and Norris's trade school and work, they said it wasn't unusual for them not to hear from him for a few days at a time."

Taping the photo of a smiling young man with shoulder-length, chestnut brown hair to the whiteboard beside Olivia Mclaughlin's information, Zane shook his head. "This killer's motivation might have been decipherable when the vics were only women, but now we've got two males. All the vics are around the same age and work in customer-facing jobs."

Amelia glanced at the clock in the lower left of the laptop screen. "Layton will be here in a little bit. Hopefully, we gave him enough time to make heads or tails of what's going on here."

For the next forty-five minutes, Amelia and Zane dug through Norris Lowery's background, making notes of the friends and family members they'd be contacting later that day. Reviews of Norris's social media accounts revealed nothing new, and background checks of his family were clean. The theft case from Norris's sophomore year in high school was a dead end, not that Amelia had expected a six-year-old misdemeanor to lead anywhere.

When Agent Redker arrived, all they'd learned was that Norris's background was just as uneventful as Sammie Howard's, Cody Frazier's, and Olivia Mclaughlin's.

They gave Layton a rundown of the case, including its potential ties to the Leóne family. Fortunately, aside from Norris, Layton was well-versed in the victims' backgrounds.

Behind black-rimmed glasses, Layton's brown eyes flitted over the whiteboard as he stood beside the oval table. Flecks of silver were visible at the base of the behavior analyst's temples, but his toned-down faux hawk hairstyle lent him a youthful appearance. Otherwise, his tailored black suit and pastel purple tie were every bit as neatly pressed as Zane's attire.

"You were right." Layton offered Amelia and Zane an approving smile. "When you said you think this guy is escalating, I agree. Now, obviously, we don't have a list of *all* his victims, so it's difficult to discern whether this fits a previous pattern. So far, from the junkyard he used as a dumping ground, we've located the remains of two previous victims, correct?"

Zane nodded. "Olivia Mclaughlin and Norris Lowery. We only have Olivia's tooth, and Norris has been dead for a while, so the information from his postmortem is limited. However, it does appear he was killed with a single stab to the heart."

Layton held out his hands. "All right, I think that's enough to include him. He went missing two weeks ago, and then Sammie Howard was killed approximately a week later. Cody Frazier was killed only a few days later. Even with just these three, the interval between each kill is shortening. It's possible this is his pattern, but it's also possible his urges are becoming more difficult to control, which could explain why he's getting sloppier with each kill."

In the grand scheme of killers, Amelia wouldn't quite call their suspect sloppy, but Layton had a point. "We've reviewed the timeframe before Olivia Mclaughlin disappeared, and there was nothing. No security camera footage, just a coworker who saw her leave after she punched out for the night. But with Sammie, there was Booker…"

Zane finished the thought for her. "And with Cody, there was the security camera and the license plate. It sure does seem like he's getting sloppier, doesn't it?"

"It does." Layton flipped through a thick file. "It's interesting to me that there are male and female victims, but the age range is approximately the same. And him cutting out the victims' eyes is also telling. I don't think he's killing because he enjoys it. I think he's killing because he feels he has to. He's being compelled by something he believes he can't control."

That was a change of pace from Kenny MacMillan and James Amsdell. Both men were serial killers, but their crimes had been meticulously planned and executed almost to perfection. Though Kenny and James had vastly different motivations, each believed they were serving a higher purpose by killing their victims.

Layton pulled out a chair and sat. "To put it into perspective, serial killers typically fall into one of three categories. Organized, disorganized, and mixed. Organized serial killers are your Ted Bundys and Dan Giffords. They vary in how much they plan, but they're similar in that they do indeed plan. Disorganized serial killers, on the other hand, tend to obey an uncontrollable urge to kill. This means their kills aren't nearly as ritualistic as an organized killer's. They'll use whatever weapon is handy, and they'll work to cover up their tracks *afterward*."

Amelia had been introduced to the realm of serial killers for the first time when they'd tracked Dan Gifford, a man who'd abducted young men and women and then sold them to his list of sick clientele. "I'm familiar with organized and disorganized, and mixed seems self-explanatory."

Layton pulled out a familiar orange pack of his favorite candy. "It does, and I suppose it is. Mixed killers are a combination of organized and disorganized. They obey an urge to kill, but they're somewhat able to control it. Now, as their urges escalate in intensity, their crimes become less meticulously planned. They slip up, leave behind evidence, witnesses, damning camera footage, that sort of thing."

Zane took a seat across from the analyst. "It seems like that fits this killer to a tee."

As Amelia opened her mouth to add to the conversation, her phone began to dance across the table. "One second." She held up a hand and glanced at the screen. "Shit, it's Detective Hamilton. Hold on."

"No problem." Layton popped a Reese's Pieces into his mouth. "My schedule is clear. I'm here to help you guys."

Amelia offered him a grateful smile as she swiped her phone and raised the device to her ear. "This is Agent Storm."

"Good morning, Agent. I hope I didn't wake you. This is Detective Cordell Hamilton with the Chicago P.D. I'm at the scene of a homicide, and the M.O. is almost an exact match to the Sammie Howard junkyard case. The forensic pathologist just confirmed the cause of death is a match. Eyes cut out, single stab wound to the chest."

Amelia's heart fell. She'd desperately wanted to find this sick bastard before he claimed another life. "All right. Send me the address, and we'll be there as soon as we can."

"Will do. See you soon, Agent."

Before she ended the call, Zane and Layton's eyes were glued to her. "Well, Agent Redker." She pushed to her feet. "You're about to get a firsthand look at how this guy operates because the CPD just found another body with its eyes removed."

Zane muttered a few choice words as he rose to stand. None of them had wanted to find another body before they caught this psychopath, but Amelia would make sure the newest victim's death wasn't for naught. If Layton was right and the perp was getting sloppier, then perhaps he'd left behind something that would finally point them in his direction.

As usual, Amelia piled into the back seat of a sleek sedan, content to do research while Zane battled with Chicago's traffic. She'd have called the passenger seat, but Layton was a good six or seven inches taller than she, and she'd been raised with manners.

The trip wouldn't have been long at any other time of day, but thanks to the morning rush hour, they didn't pull up behind the CSU van for a good forty-five minutes. Rather than allow herself to be frustrated by what seemed like a needless wait, Amelia had used the time to brush up on the background of their victim.

Desiree Bauer was only twenty, but her lack of social media presence had surprised Amelia. It wasn't unheard of for the younger generation to shun online platforms, but Amelia never expected it. The last update made to Desiree's Facebook account was nearly three months old, and it had merely been a post she'd shared.

Oddly enough, Desiree's mother, Nellie Bauer, was more active online than her daughter. Cursory background checks of the Bauer family had come back clean. Desiree's younger brother was in his freshman year of college at Michigan State, and their father lived in Milwaukee with his second wife, to whom he'd been married for almost a decade.

As far as Amelia could tell, there was no bad blood between Nellie and her ex-husband. Nellie was an executive assistant, and she'd worked for the same company for more than twelve years. Desiree had just been hired by a coffee shop not far from her duplex, and before that, she'd worked in retail.

In other words, Desiree and Nellie Bauer were two normal women.

Stepping out of the back seat, Amelia lowered her head against a gust of cold wind. She hurried across the street, Layton and Zane on her heels. The three of them showed their badges to the pair of uniformed officers stationed at the sidewalk leading to a modest duplex. No sooner had they signed the logbook and ducked beneath the crime scene tape did Detective Hamilton emerge onto the front porch to greet them.

"Good morning, Agents. Hope the drive out here treated you well." Cordell Hamilton's tone was the sort Amelia expected from a coworker at a call center, not a detective at the scene of a brutal murder. Then again, how many years had Detective Hamilton been working homicides? For him, this *was* like any other morning.

"Good morning to you as well, Detective. This is Agent Redker of the BAU. He's consulting on the case." Her fellow agent nodded at the detective. Amelia gestured to the adjacent porch. "I don't see a car in the other driveway. Is the neighbor gone?"

Detective Hamilton shook his head. "Not gone. The unit is vacant right now, so there is no neighbor."

There went Amelia's hopes for a witness. As she scrutinized the unadorned porch, her gaze caught on a small electronic device mounted just beneath the porch light. Anticipation rushed through her veins, far more effective than any amount of caffeine.

She turned back to Detective Hamilton and pointed at the device. "Please tell me that's one of those little wireless cameras you can install in lieu of a home security system and it's not a dummy."

The detective's gaze followed hers. "It sure is. It appears to be functional too. It's all motion sensor, so if the perp used the door and not a window, it should have caught something. The company stores video footage for up to sixty days on all active accounts."

Hell, yeah.

Layton was right. The killer had screwed up and badly.

24

Amelia had a hard time pulling her stare away from the camera mounted to the porch light of Desiree Bauer's duplex. She could hardly believe their stroke of luck—the killer's first real screwup.

Had the camera caught their killer breaking into this poor woman's house?

Provided he didn't just avoid the camera like he had on every other damn security camera footage we've reviewed.

She pushed aside the pessimistic thought. "Do we have access to her account?"

"Legally, yes. The victim's mother pays for the service, so she's the administrator on the account. We've been granted permission to access anything we need."

Zane lifted an eyebrow. "But?"

Detective Cordell sighed. "But the mother had to be taken to the hospital for shock. She's the one who found her daughter's body. Poor woman went to surprise her daughter on her second day of work at her new job as a barista, but her daughter wasn't there. So, Mom came here to check on her, and that's when she found her. It was just a few minutes ago she was even able to give us permission to access the account, and now we're waiting on a password."

Amelia spotted a sliver of hope. "Maybe Desiree wrote the password down somewhere."

The detective appeared thoughtful as he turned back to the front door. "Maybe. My kids are always harping on me not to write mine down, but I'm sure plenty of people do."

Amelia clenched one hand in her pocket to keep her face neutral.

It's me. I'm people. I can't help that I need six-thousand pass-words, and I'm not allowed to make any of them identical.

If she knew Detective Hamilton better, she'd have thrown a friendly jab at him for the comment. Maybe after they'd collaborated on a few more cases.

She, Zane, and Layton all followed Detective Hamilton inside, slipping on booties over their shoes before proceeding across the threshold.

Layton snapped on a pair of blue vinyl gloves. "Desiree Bauer was a barista, wasn't she? You mentioned she'd just started working a new job. How could she afford a place like this?"

Detective Hamilton beckoned them toward the living room. "Her mom worked something out with the owner. We talked to the landlord briefly, and he's actually worked with the vic's mother for close to a decade. He said he gave Desiree a lower price on rent because he knew she was a good kid. He'd rather have a good tenant than a few more dollars. The extra cash wasn't worth the headache."

As she neared the end of the foyer, Amelia braced herself for the gruesome sight awaiting her. No matter how many years she worked on murder cases, she suspected she'd never become used to witnessing the corpse of a young, innocent person who'd been killed so brutally. She wasn't sure she *wanted* to get used to such a sight. There were some parts of her job that should never cease to cause an emotional impact.

She was almost embarrassed at the relief that washed over her when she spotted the dark stain on the carpet where the girl's body had been. Curtains had been drawn over a single picture window, blocking out much of the morning sun, as well as any looky-loos who might have thought to sneak a peek at a crime scene.

The furnishings were typical—a sofa and a loveseat with a small, round table between them, an ottoman, a television mounted to the wall, and a bookshelf.

At Amelia's side, Zane tossed Detective Hamilton a curious glance. "Was she taken already or is her body in a different room?"

"Taken just before you guys got here. We've got a massive amount of photos, plus the usual video walkthrough. Dr. Francis wanted to get her on the autopsy table ASAP, so we processed this part of the scene first. The CSU still has a little work to do, but we're cleared to take a look. It's not a very big room, as you can see, so the techs are taking a short break, so we don't all trip over one another."

Amelia couldn't argue with the detective's point. Even just the four of them standing in the small room was nearly enough to bring on hints of claustrophobia. "That's good. We appreciate all your hard work while we were…stuck in traffic."

The detective offered her a reassuring smile. "Being stuck in traffic in this city is a common affliction, Agent. We've all been there." With a gloved hand, he pointed to the bookshelf. "At any rate, we've got some good news in this room too. See that book end, the little house right after the Stephen King novel on the second highest shelf?"

Taking a step closer, Amelia studied the decorative house.

As she leaned in, light caught the lens of a camera tucked in behind the front window. Smart girl. "Another camera?"

Detective Hamilton gingerly lifted the house from its base to reveal a camera nearly identical to the one outside. "Sure is. Linked to the same account, we're hoping."

As grateful as Amelia was to have discovered the cameras, part of the situation didn't quite add up. "Her criminal background check was clean. She'd never been charged with anything, nor had she ever pressed charges against anyone. The exterior camera I understand but putting a camera in your own living room seems…excessive. Or is it just me?"

Layton circled around the dark stain on the carpet. "There might've been something in her background we have yet to see that made her paranoid. Maybe a friend of hers had a break-in, and that prompted her to install the cameras."

Amelia wished Nellie Bauer hadn't been taken to the hospital for shock, but she understood why. Besides, their prime suspect most likely wasn't anyone who'd known Desiree personally. They were searching for a serial killer.

Detective Hamilton went over the details they'd learned from the scene so far. There were no signs of forced entry, but the CSU had noted scratches on the front doorknob, which were consistent with a lockpicking tool. Since the back door was sealed shut, they were confident the perp had entered through the front door.

Which meant he'd been picked up by the doorbell camera. The light on the front porch didn't have a motion sensor, so there was the possibility the perp hadn't even noticed it.

Nothing jumped out at Amelia as they went through the dining room and kitchen, though she noted Desiree kept a fairly detailed wall calendar, along with a bulletin board full of colorful notes. Amelia made a mental note to circle back to the area when Detective Hamilton was finished with the tour.

Less than a minute after they'd entered Desiree's bedroom, Detective Hamilton's phone squawked. Literally. The man's text notification was a parrot.

Amelia suppressed her laugh. She could swear a hint of pink crawled to the man's cheeks as he fished the device from his pocket.

To Amelia's relief, and likely the relief of everyone in the room, the message was from Detective Hamilton's partner, who'd headed out to the hospital to meet with Desiree's mother. Nellie Bauer had come out of her shocked state enough to provide the password to her and Desiree's security account.

Before Detective Hamilton had even finished reading the text, Amelia produced the tablet she'd used to conduct research on the trip to the duplex. Her fingers flew across the touch screen as she entered the login details.

The website populated, and Amelia held up the tablet victoriously. "Here it is. Nellie has her own two cameras, one for each door of her house. Then there are Desiree's. I noticed on the calendar in the dining room that Desiree worked last night, from four to ten p.m. My guess is we're going to look for footage from sometime after ten o'clock."

Detective Hamilton nodded. "That should be pretty easy. They only activate when they sense motion, so we won't have to sift through a ton of footage."

Thank god.

Amelia and Zane, along with the officers who'd helped them obtain video surveillance for both Cody Frazier and Sammie Howard, had done their fair share of sifting.

The room grew silent, the only sound the creak of the front door as the crime scene techs returned. Amelia navigated to the camera labeled "Living Room." To her relief, the video was sorted by timestamps, so she was easily able to scroll down to a dark frame labeled 21:47.

Her relief was short-lived. They were about to watch a young woman being brutally murdered for no discernable reason.

Mouth dry, blood pounding in her ears, she held out the tablet for the others and pressed play.

A dark figure entered the frame from the left side, which Amelia quickly identified as the edge of the foyer. As the man stepped into the living room, he glanced from side to side, to the ceiling, the floor, and the window. When his gaze settled directly on the camera, Amelia paused the footage.

Zane crossed his arms, his attention still glued to the tablet. "He's wearing a fucking ski mask and a hoodie. Dammit."

Layton held up a finger. "He wasn't disguising his identity at any of the previous scenes. The entire ritual for this one deviates significantly from the Frazier or Howard murders. Rather than abduct the victim, he's breaking into her home. And rather than transport the body to dump it in Lake Michigan or at another junkyard, he left her here for us to find."

"Why, though?" Zane pressed his lips together. "Why the sudden change? Is this even the same guy?"

Amelia took a screenshot. "It *looks* like the same guy, but that's not saying much. We didn't have a lot to go on to begin with. Maybe we'll get something more from this."

Her suggestion was met with a couple nods, and she resumed the playback.

The man's dark eyes scanned the bookshelf, but he didn't notice the cleverly hidden camera. He disappeared from view as he headed in the direction of the dining room. Though the glimpse of his back was fleeting, Amelia noticed a design on his coat. She paused the video to take another screenshot. Booker had mentioned a design on the back of the bomber jacket he'd seen on the man who broke up his conversation with Sammie. This had to be the same guy.

After thirty seconds of no movement, the camera automatically turned itself off. The next video in line was labeled 22:14, a full seventeen minutes after the start of the first.

What the hell was he doing in here for almost twenty minutes?

More importantly, had his lengthy stay resulted in any trace evidence? Desiree's room was one of the tidiest bedrooms Amelia had ever been in, aside from her own. Hopefully, Desiree's cleanliness made the task of finding potential evidence easier for the CSU.

The man emerged from the right this time—the direction of the dining room and the hall leading to Desiree's bedroom. Part of his attire was different this time, and the design on the back of his coat was no longer visible.

"Is he..." Zane leaned in, squinting at the tablet, "... wearing a poncho? What the hell?"

What the hell indeed.

Amelia pressed pause, taking another screenshot. "He's a combination of organized and disorganized, remember. Bastard probably brought it with him to avoid blood splatter on his clothes."

Layton's mouth was a hard line. "This wasn't a break-in gone wrong. He came here prepared. He came here to kill her."

Not that Amelia had any doubts. The Bureau and the Chicago Police Department had kept the details of the cases close to the vest. Nothing in the news so far had mentioned the victims' missing eyes. The likelihood of a copycat killer was slim.

For the next seven minutes, the man stood in place, occasionally shifting his weight from foot to foot. The recording reminded Amelia of more than one horror movie. The guy wasn't a demon, but with what she knew he was about to do, he might as well have been.

Another six minutes passed, and the man paced back and forth until a pair of headlights pierced through the slight gap between the curtains. Amelia's chest grew tighter with each passing second.

She *knew* what was going to happen. She knew Desiree's eyes would be cut from their sockets, and she would be stabbed in the heart. But she couldn't help her efforts to will Desiree to turn around, to go to her mother's house, a hotel, anywhere but this damn living room.

As expected, all Amelia's mental energy was for naught. Her stomach dropped like a stone when the man lunged forward to grab Desiree. The girl made an effort to fight back, flailing against the man and trying to make a break for the door.

She wasn't successful.

"Wait a second." Layton's calm voice cut in through the din of Amelia's thoughts as they continued to watch the scene play out. "He just stabbed her and killed her. Weren't the previous victims killed *after* their eyes were cut out?"

Amelia was glad to pull her attention away from the video. "Yeah. That's what Dr. Francis's postmortems showed."

Layton pointed to the screen. "He's doing this differently. He knows he's not on his own turf, and he doesn't want to put himself at more risk than he already has. That tells me he's obeying an urge to kill, but he still has situational awareness. The unit next door is empty, but all the blinds are drawn, so he might not have known his level of isolation with his victim."

Turning her focus back to the blood-stained hunting knife—smooth on one side and serrated on the other, just like the wounds from the previous victims indicated—

Amelia noted Layton was correct. Desiree's body was limp and lifeless. And the man was left-handed.

Amelia pressed play, but less than thirty seconds in, the man pushed up the sleeves of his jacket. Though the angle was awkward and the lighting wasn't the best, she immediately spotted the shape of a tattoo on the inside of the man's wrist.

"Shit," Zane spat, "is that the ouroboros?"

"It might be." She took a screenshot. "It looks like a circle from here, but maybe once we zoom in on it, we can get some more detail."

"Right. Let's see if we get a better angle on it in the video."

Mentally, Amelia crossed her fingers. As the killer went to work removing Desiree's eyes, she focused primarily on the location of his tattoo. A couple screenshots later, and the man had finished his grotesque task.

His back blocked out most of the frame, but when he stood up empty-handed, she could only assume he'd transferred Desiree's eyes to a bag or a storage container.

Until now, she hadn't been certain what he'd done with them. Well, she *still* wasn't completely sure, but the eyes hadn't been found at the crime scene. He'd taken them as some sort of sick trophy.

Sheathing the bloodied knife, the man stripped the poncho over his head, providing an unobstructed view of the scorpion on the back of his coat. His gloves came off next, though he produced a new pair from his pocket after he'd bundled the bloody ones within the poncho.

Amelia's gut told her they'd never find the bloody garments. They'd either been buried in a hole, burned, or somehow discarded.

At the end of the video, she straightened and put away the tablet. The sense of routine—of going through the motions after finding so many victims within the span of a single week—was disheartening, but Amelia reminded herself it was necessary.

They had to cover all their bases in each new crime like it was the very first.

Only this time, they had the entire crime on video. They'd been waiting for the killer to make a mistake, and he'd finally slipped up.

Now, they had to find a way to capitalize on the error before another innocent person was killed.

25

S lumping down in the driver's seat of my Subaru, I let out a long, steady breath. I knew I shouldn't be here. Sure, this had become my preferred coffee joint over the last few months, but there was a multitude of locations for this coffee chain throughout this city. I could go to any one of them, and it wouldn't be the workplace of a person I'd just killed.

But did dropping off the face of the planet after I'd killed Desiree make me more or less suspicious? I wasn't exactly friends with any of the staff, but I was sure they recognized me. Would they notice if I up and disappeared? Would they tie the two events together?

None of that mattered, of course. I was here for only one reason...this was *my* coffee shop. Desiree had stolen it from me. I needed to stroll inside and cleanse my soul of her and her damned eyes. Once I'd done that, she...*they* would haunt me no more. Just like with the others, it had to be done.

Had. To. Be.

Especially now, since I'd killed Desiree's heart before

taking the eyes. I needed to make sure that little slipup wouldn't follow me forever.

I'd driven by Desiree's duplex and noticed the crime scene van out front. I wasn't sure who had found her, but it didn't make a difference. While my actions had been impulsive, all I could do was hope I'd covered all my bases at the crime scene.

Normally, I'd make sure Desiree's body was never found. Or, if it was found, any trace evidence would've been washed away by the churning tides of Lake Michigan.

Last night, the desire—no, the *need*—to silence those mocking eyes had grown too strong. After locating her address and driving to her neighborhood, I'd been compelled by a force I couldn't control. Like some kind of marionette.

I shuddered. I hated marionettes and what they represented. And I hated that I'd become one, even just for a night.

This was becoming a problem, but I didn't have the first clue what to do about it. Did I dare ask my father, the great Arturo Piliero, for help?

Yeah, right.

Artie had always been a man's man, a pillar of inscrutable masculinity in the Leóne family. Between his competency and the weight of our surname, he'd carved out a place for himself in the upper echelon of mafia hierarchy.

How would someone like my father understand what I'd dealt with as a kid? The boys who'd tormented me had been led by none other than Andre Leóne, the boss's grandson. Even at my young age, I'd known there was no recourse for me when I was being bullied by one of the heirs to the Leóne throne.

So, I'd kept my mouth shut and endured. I'd bottled up all my hatred, all my wishful vengeance, and I'd let it simmer. After the operation that made me "normal," Andre and his posse moved on.

But I didn't.

Maybe if I'd been the one to kill the smug, pig-nosed Andre, to watch the life drain from his eyes, I wouldn't have these urges. But the boss's grandson had overdosed on Vicodin at nineteen.

Yet part of Andre lived on. His eyes. Those hateful, mocking eyes.

I'd kill Andre over and over again until I finally purged the scars his godawful eyes left on my brain.

The beep of a car horn ripped me out of the recollection. For a split second, I thought the honk was directed at me, but I was still parked.

I gave myself a mental shake. I had no idea how long I'd been sitting behind the wheel. Had I fallen asleep? I glanced at the clock, but the time did little to resolve my quandary.

Well, I've been sitting in this parking lot like a fucking weirdo for god knows how long. If I just drive away now, how weird will that look? At least if I go in to get a cup, I can play it off like I was just sitting here because I'm tired.

This wasn't the scene of the crime. I wasn't one of *those* people—the ones who returned to the crime scene to observe the havoc they'd wreaked on the victim's family. I could admit part of me was curious to witness the aftermath of Desiree's death but not curious enough to do something as stupid as stand outside her duplex and gawk. Casually driving by had told me all I needed to know.

Showing up to the coffee shop, on the other hand, was perfectly normal. I'd regularly visited the place—my place—for months. Once I was inside, I'd feel free to enjoy my coffee without her eyes haunting me, taunting me. I would be liberated, perhaps even at peace, inside this sanctuary.

I pondered how her death might affect her coworkers.

She worked with them for a whole day. I doubt they gave a shit she was gone.

I chuckled.

They'd all pretend to care, no doubt. That's what people did when they thought others were watching—they pretended to be sympathetic, even empathetic. But deep down, they all had the same sick curiosity. They wanted to see the crime scene photos, to see how I'd driven the blade into Desiree's heart, how I'd watched the life drain from those horrendous eyes.

I'd play pretend right along with them.

Pulling up the collar of my jacket, I stepped out into the cold morning air. I pocketed my keys and looked down to my hands, half-expecting them to be covered in Desiree's blood.

Not a speck. My hands were spotless, and so was my coat. Cutting out a person's eyes while they were still alive usually resulted in a bloody mess, and despite the bizarre fugue that had overcome me last night, I'd at least kept that little tidbit in mind. Driving away from the girl's duplex with the blood-stained poncho and gloves beneath the lining of my trunk was bad enough. I hadn't wanted to deal with blood on my face as well.

The poncho and gloves were little more than ashes now. Reluctantly, I'd even thrown the knife into Lake Michigan after cleaning the blade with bleach. I'd used the same knife to kill Sammie Howard, Cody Frazier, and Desiree Bauer. Though it held some sentimental value, after my screwup of killing Desiree and leaving her body for the cops to find, I'd known the time had come to dispose of the blade.

It didn't matter. I had more hunting knives. I had more gloves. I had more ponchos. And I had plenty of room in my storage unit.

Jamming both hands into my pockets, I prepared to shoulder open the door but hesitated as I caught a glimpse of myself in the mirror. I looked...different. Strange. Older somehow.

I thought I understood why.

The urges were becoming more difficult to control. As much as I wanted to tell myself killing Desiree had helped, I knew it was bullshit.

This was becoming a problem, and I didn't have the first clue how to solve it.

Maybe I didn't *want* to solve it.

26

Amelia craned her neck to catch a glimpse inside the coffee shop as Zane pulled into a parking stall in the back corner of the lot. The morning rush hour—patrons swinging by the café or the drive-thru to get their pre-work, Monday morning caffeine fix—had begun to abate, to Amelia's relief. They were here to talk to the staff, and she always felt a little pang of guilt when such interviews left the rest of the workers shorthanded during a busy time of day. Having been employed at a movie theater during high school, Amelia could still relate to the woes of customer-facing jobs.

She turned her attention to the two men in the front of the car. Rather than leave someone behind at a crime scene that was already mostly processed, all three of them had decided to venture to Desiree's former place of work. The idea was they could get through interviews with the employees more quickly if there were three of them, provided the flow of business allowed them to take three people away from their work at the same time.

Once they were done here, they'd comb through Desiree's

background, brief Spencer Corsaw on the morning's events, and split up to interview Desiree's friends and family. Time was of the essence, and Amelia was committed to working as quickly as possible.

The killer would strike again, there was no doubt about that. They needed to chase down leads and find the bastard before he had a chance.

As Amelia exited the back seat of the Town Car, she spotted a few flurries on the wind. A snow shower was predicted to roll in before noon, though the total accumulation was supposed to be just a light dusting. For the sake of the crime scene techs still at Paulie's Scrap and Salvage, she hoped the meteorologists' optimistic predictions were accurate.

To Amelia's side, Zane rubbed his hands together. "It's not weird if we buy coffee while we're here, is it?"

Amelia chuckled, hoping the sound wasn't as strained as it felt. "I don't think so. Seems like it'd be more polite than anything."

Ever since viewing the video of Desiree Bauer being murdered and mutilated by a madman in a ski mask, Amelia's nerves had been as taut as a tightrope. The hyper-awareness was reminiscent of the sort that had kept her alive during deployments in her ten-year military career. Her stomach clenched every time she thought about what must have been going through the poor girl's head when she'd been thrown to the ground in her own living room.

With the sadness came a familiar fire of anger, and the two sentiments coalesced into the bizarre form of anxiety that had been so prevalent in the Middle East.

She clenched her hands in her pockets. Flakes of snow were in the air, not dust and sand. The temperature for the day was slated to reach a whopping twenty-one degrees. A far cry from the burning heat of an Afghani desert.

Judging from the lack of dialogue as she, Layton, and Zane walked toward the front door of the coffee shop, the two men were experiencing their own versions of disillusionment.

A middle-aged woman emerged from the double doors, a coffee in one hand and a small paper bag in the other. Stepping aside to let the woman by, Amelia's gaze caught on a black Subaru Outback Wilderness parked in a stall near the drive-thru.

Could it be? Probably not. But...

Amelia stopped short of the door, glancing at her two companions. Once she had their attention, she tilted her chin in the direction of the car. "Check that out. An Outback Wilderness, same color as the one we saw in the videos from the Frazier case."

Layton looked at the vehicle and gave a slight nod. "Worth noting since we're at the victim's workplace, but chances are good it could just be a coincidence. That's not an uncommon color for a car."

"And not an uncommon car in this city. Too bad the perp didn't drive a hot pink Nissan Cube." In spite of Zane's humorous comment, his voice held no mirth.

Amelia offered him a smile to let him know his dry humor hadn't gone unnoticed. Pulling open the door, she stepped aside and ushered him and Layton through.

"Chivalry isn't dead, is it, Agent Storm?" Layton's joke lifted some of the tension from Amelia's stance.

Zane beat her to the next set of doors. "She's a true gentleman, Layton."

As Layton chuckled, a grin crept to Amelia's face. Tipping an invisible hat to her partner, she stepped over the threshold and into the café.

The warm aroma of roasting coffee was another dose of calm. Making a note of the number of patrons seated throughout the lobby—which fortunately wasn't many, leaving them space to sit down to talk to the employees— Amelia turned to the front counter.

Her smile vanished, and the pleasant scent of coffee gave way to dust, sand, and blood. In her mind's eye, she watched a small, black scorpion crawl across a dusty rock, behind which was the headless corpse of an insurgent fighter she'd sniped from nearly a mile away.

She kept her distance from the scorpion. Contrary to common assumptions, smaller scorpions were the more lethal of the species. The little bastards would make themselves at home in clothing or shoes, places where a bigger scorpion would have been easily noticed. Not only could they hide better, but they were usually more venomous.

Like a space traveler through a wormhole, her brain shot back to the present. To the coffee shop and the man waiting for his drink at the far end of the counter.

Blinking away the unexpected flashback, Amelia returned her focus to the man who'd caught her attention in the first place. His back was turned to her, giving her a full view of the scorpion embroidered on the back of his leather bomber jacket.

The Subaru outside easily could have been a coincidence, but the Subaru *and* a man wearing a jacket with a scorpion on the back of it?

Taller than average. Caucasian, dark hair. Jeans and work boots.

This wasn't a coincidence. This couldn't be a coincidence.

Swallowing to return moisture to her mouth, Amelia turned and elbowed Zane in the arm. "Counter." She mouthed the word carefully, catching Layton's attention as she did.

Zane's jaw tightened. "Shit."

Coincidence or not, Amelia needed to know. If the man

wasn't who they were looking for, then she'd apologize for the mistake.

Easy peasy, lemon squeezy.

Unfortunately, Amelia with her knee-length trench, Zane and his stylish black frock, and Layton in his smart peacoat, they couldn't have looked any more like Feds if they'd tried. None of their weapons were visible, but with their attire and the way they held themselves, they couldn't pass for civilian businesspeople.

Civilian businesspeople don't wear this damn much black. We should add some color to our wardrobes, so we blend in a little better.

She kicked aside the inane thought. Not even a minute had passed since she'd spotted the man in the scorpion jacket, but to her, they'd been standing at the front door like a trio of idiots for a half-hour.

Sliding one hand within easy reach of where her service weapon was holstered beneath her left arm but maintaining as nonchalant a stance as possible, she took the first step toward the man at the counter. Amelia lamented that she, Layton, and Zane hadn't been able to come up with a plan in case the entire situation deteriorated.

If everything went to shit, they'd have to improvise.

As much as Amelia wanted the guy in the scorpion jacket to be the psychopath who'd murdered Desiree Bauer and the others, a small voice in the back of her head told her it wouldn't be so bad if he was a normal patron. At least then they wouldn't risk him retaliating when they hadn't even bothered to don bullet suppression vests. Sure, his crimes had all been carried out with a knife, but Amelia operated under the assumption all suspects carried firearms.

Midway through her third step toward the man, he must have caught the movement in his periphery. His head snapped to the side, and for a beat, his brown eyes met hers.

His expression was unreadable, but there was a keenness in those dark orbs. Alertness. Paranoia.

He didn't *look* like a lunatic who derived some sort of sick gratification from carving the eyes out of an innocent person's head.

But they never did.

Time slowed to a crawl, and she couldn't help but feel like a dream version of herself. Shoving her hand the rest of the way into her coat was agonizingly slow like she was underwater or weighted down with lead. In reality, she was moving with reflexes far quicker than the average person.

Unfortunately, the man in the scorpion jacket wasn't an average person.

Her fingers had only just closed around the textured grip of her service weapon when the young man spun and grabbed another patron, pulling the middle-aged woman in front of him as a human shield. As he raised his left arm, revealing a handgun, a shot rang out.

Amelia dove to the ground, and in one fluid motion, pulled her Glock from her coat. His panicked expression was somehow still calm and composed, and Amelia could tell this wasn't the first time he'd fired a gun at another person.

Who's this calm with an FBI agent pointing a gun at them?

A couple screams belted out by the baristas behind the counter cut through the air as they all dove for cover. Shouts of surprise from the customers seated in the café followed, including a handful of four-letter words. Chaos ensued as terrified customers didn't know where to find safety in the sparsely furnished café.

In the fraction of a second following the deafening blast, Amelia almost convinced herself she had died. That the only reason she was still viewing the coffee shop was because she was a ghost, and her specter was here to haunt the location where she'd lost her life.

An eternity seemed to pass, but only a second or two had gone by. Still, Amelia was stricken by no onslaught of pain. The muscles in her neck were so tense, they might have turned to stone when she wasn't paying attention. Her heart thundered against her ribs like a car with the bass turned up too loud.

She bit the inside of her cheek, nearly flinching at the sudden sting.

He didn't shoot me. But if he didn't shoot me, then who the hell did he shoot?

Amelia could have sworn he'd been aiming at her. She'd been standing in front of Layton and Zane. If the bullet hadn't hit her, then had he missed, or had he…

The thought shattered her lingering sense of dissociation.

Zane!

Maybe he hadn't missed. Maybe he hadn't been aiming for her at all. Snapping her head to the side, her focus shot to her partner. He had also dived to the ground and taken aim to return fire. Okay, nothing in his body language indicated he'd been shot.

Where was Layton?

The clatter of Layton's Glock falling to the floor jerked her gaze to Zane's side. The BAU agent grasped at the drywall in an effort to keep himself upright, one hand pressed tightly against his stomach. Crimson stained his hand from the feeble attempt to contain the bleeding.

"I said don't fucking move!" The gunman's shout was tinny and distant through the ringing in her ears, and his handgun was now level with his hostage's temple.

Amelia hadn't even registered the first demand. She wasn't sure if her selective hearing was the result of being rendered temporarily deaf by the gunshot or if too much of her mental bandwidth had been devoted to her dying colleague.

Fighting past the imagined scent of desert dirt and blood —yet another flashback nipping at the heels of her coherent thoughts—Amelia jerked her gaze back to the man with the gun.

"Drop your weapons, both of you! I know you're cops!" His jaw tightened, his eyes flicking back and forth between Amelia and Zane.

A hostage changed everything.

Amelia was a trained sniper and a damn good one. But sniping with a scoped rifle was a far cry from the accuracy of her unsighted Glock. The middle-aged woman's terrified face and whimpers underscored how quickly things had escalated.

"Weapons! Now!" The man jammed the barrel of his gun into the side of the woman's head. "Don't make me tell you again!"

As the heat from the recently fired gun touched the hostage's skin, she yelped and winced in pain.

There was no choice but to comply with his demand. Layton had taken a bullet to the gut, and now this lunatic was threatening to shoot a random customer. With at least ten other people huddled throughout the space, plus the workers behind the counter, and then the three of them, he had plenty of targets to choose from if he carried through with his threat to shoot the woman he'd decided to use as a human shield.

Exchanging an uncertain glance with Zane, Amelia slowly placed her Glock on the concrete floor. If she'd anticipated traveling to a hostile location, she'd have hidden a second handgun on her person, either near her ankle or behind her back.

We were just supposed to come here to talk to Desiree's cowork-ers, for god's sake. How were any of us supposed to know it'd devolve into a hostage situation as soon as we walked through the damn doors?

The simple answer: they weren't. None of them could have anticipated walking straight into the sights of Desiree's killer that morning.

But here they were. Layton had been shot in the gut, and if they didn't figure out a way to diffuse the situation, his chances for survival were slim to none. If the bullet hadn't damaged any vital organs, then he'd bleed to death. Without immediate medical attention, the survival rate of a gut shot was far lower than popular media liked to portray.

"Put them on the floor, nice and slow. Then kick them over here." The gunman flexed his fingers against the grip of his weapon as if to remind them how close his index finger was to the trigger.

Wordlessly, Amelia and Zane complied. They had no other option, and they knew it. After putting their weapons on the floor, both slowly rose.

This is way too similar to the incident with Kenny MacMillan in the basement of the safehouse. I'm really done with forfeiting my service revolver.

"You," the gunman pointed to Zane, "lock the door."

Zane's sour expression held more malice than Amelia had expected. "I don't have the fucking keys."

The gunman motioned to the young women cowering behind the counter, both of whom had their hands raised in surrender. "One of you toss him the keys. The rest of you," he bobbed his head toward the seating area, "get out from behind the counter and go take a seat with everyone else."

Seconds crawled by like molasses on a cold day. The shorter of the two baristas unclipped her carabiner with the shop's keys from the belt loop of her black slacks, sliding them along the counter to Zane. She then scurried to huddle with her coworker at a table in the corner. All the while,

Amelia's gaze shot from where Layton had slumped to the floor, to the gunman, and then back.

If she went for him, he'd kill an innocent woman. And with the ten or so feet between them, he'd likely have enough time to turn the gun on her after executing his hostage.

Caught between a rock and a hard place like this was Amelia Storm's nightmare.

Someone out in the parking lot might have noticed what was happening and called the cops, but the arrival of backup would make little difference in their current situation. Eventually, a sniper might get a clear shot to take out the gunman, but how long would that take?

With Layton's injury, time wasn't a luxury they had.

She needed a plan, and she needed it yesterday.

27

As soon as Zane returned from locking the front door of the coffee shop, Amelia focused the entirety of her attention back on the gunman.

Amelia licked her dry lips. Her only weapons now were her voice and her intellect. "All right. The door's locked. You can see no one in here is on their phone, but that's not going to stop someone outside from calling the cops. You know that, right? They *will* show up."

The gunman's jaw tightened. "Yeah, maybe. They won't get inside when they do, though. If they try anything, I'll kill her." He prodded the woman's temple, then waved the handgun at the customers. "I'll kill whoever I have to. I'll kill *you*. Both of you. I'll take out as many people as I can if they try to storm this place."

Amelia believed him. Based on the desperation lurking behind the blatant anger in his dark eyes, he was prepared to die here. He saw no other way out.

If he thinks this is the end, then you need to make him realize it's not. He's more dangerous if he thinks he's got no hope for the future.

She gritted her teeth. How in the hell did she get a serial killer who'd just shot a federal agent to hope for a better tomorrow?

Had the man not shot Layton, then Amelia's task would be slightly less impossible. But if Layton died, and if the gunman knew he'd killed a Fed, then he'd be even more volatile. Though Illinois didn't employ capital punishment, federal law superseded the State's. Killing an FBI agent would all but guarantee the death penalty.

"What do you want from us?" Despite Zane's vitriol from only moments ago, his tone was now calm and non-accusatory. Amelia was grateful for the sudden change. They were dealing with a volatile human being, and navigating this conversation was about as treacherous as walking through a minefield.

The gunman's stance tensed, and for a beat, he appeared contemplative.

Amelia didn't give him time to finish the thought. He was volatile, sure, but they had to at least try to gain control of the conversation.

"The man you shot is a federal agent." She pointed to where Layton was hunched over on the floor, blood coating both his hands as he essentially tried to hold his entrails in place. Amelia had witnessed similar wounds before. Layton needed a hospital and an operating room, but the absolute minimum, he needed someone to help keep him alive.

"Is that supposed to surprise me? I knew you were cops." The gunman spat the words, but Amelia didn't miss the shadow of anxiety that passed over his face.

She saw the opening, and she'd use that trepidation for all it was worth. "You need to let us help him, or he's going to die. Look, I don't know what's been driving you so far, but whatever it is, this is different. This man," she jabbed her finger in Layton's direction, "is a *federal agent*." Amelia hated the way her diatribe implied civilians were less-than, but she had to get through to this lunatic. Convincing him the scenario in which he'd put himself today was more dire than his previous crimes was paramount to their survival.

Hopefully.

To her relief, Zane nodded his agreement. He was already on the same page. "If you kill a federal agent, there's nothing we'll be able to do to help you out of this."

Amelia jumped back in before the gunman could reply. "We already know about Desiree Bauer. That's why you're here today, isn't it?"

From the back of the coffee shop, a couple of the baristas gasped.

As the gunman clenched his jaw again, Amelia hoped he'd break one of his damn teeth. "What about Desiree Bauer? I don't know what you're talking about."

Amelia bit off a petulant response. Layton was dying, and she'd swallow her pride to play nice with this prick if it meant giving Layton a shot at surviving. "My point is that you were here because of Desiree, not to kill a federal agent. If you want to talk about Desiree, we can do that, but not if you let this man die."

The statement took some of the bluster from the gunman's features. For the first time, he seemed to understand what he'd done by shooting Layton. "Fine. What do you want for him?"

"We need to slow the bleeding. We need towels or something like that. I don't know. A gutshot from a nine-mil is a little out of the realm of the first-aid they taught me in Boy Scouts." Zane's observation was a figure of speech, Amelia figured. The man had never been a scout, at least as far as she knew. With both hands in front of himself, Zane swept his gaze over the haunted faces of the café patrons. "Is anyone in here a doctor or a nurse?"

A woman on the other side of the dining area slowly raised a hand. Her dark curls were streaked with gray and based on the steadiness of her arm, she was someone who'd been through her share of dire situations. "I'm a pediatric oncologist."

Finally, a stroke of good luck. Amelia noted Layton's ghostly complexion, and her hopes immediately fell. In just a few minutes, he'd traveled at least halfway to death's door. Dark circles were visible beneath his eyes and sweat beaded on his forehead. A streak of crimson followed him to the floor, and more blood had seeped from between his hands to darken the black fabric of his slacks.

They needed more than a stroke of luck. They needed a fucking miracle.

The gunman gestured to the oncologist with his free hand, then to Layton. "Fine. Go help him, but don't you even think about trying anything."

As the woman hurried over to Layton and Zane, she tentatively asked if she could retrieve some towels or cloths from behind the counter. After he nodded his consent, she grabbed a stack of towels from the other side of the granite counter. Amelia wasn't sure how much time they'd bought Layton, but she hoped it was enough. Layton was a quick-draw, and while normally being able to produce a weapon fast was a good trait, today it had the potential to cost Layton his life.

The only reason he'd been here at all was because Amelia and Zane had asked for his expertise to get a better idea of the type of killer they were dealing with.

Maybe if he wasn't fighting for his life right now, Layton would have been able to help Amelia get through to the crazy asshole with the gun. But with Zane helping the oncologist, Amelia was on her own.

Talk him down. Talk some sense into him.

She cleared her throat. "What's your name?"

Midway through fidgeting, he froze, his dark eyes snapping to Amelia. For a moment, he seemed like he might ignore her question altogether or perhaps tell her to go screw herself.

"Gavin." His response was terse, but the fact he was willing to reply at all spoke volumes to Amelia. Maybe, just *maybe*, she'd be able to talk some sense into him.

"Gavin, I'm Amelia. Listen, I need you to tell me what the next move is here, okay? You seem pretty cognizant of everything that's happening right now, including the fact that, whether you like it or not, your life is tied to his." She gestured to Layton. "And it also seems to me you didn't really want to be in this situation in the first place, did you?"

He let out a derisive snort. "Who in the hell would *want* to be here?"

So, he wasn't delusional. He didn't have a grand plan. He'd simply made them for law enforcement, assumed they were here to arrest him, and reacted.

But why? If he was backed by the Leóne family—which Amelia strongly suspected he was—then why not allow for the arrest to happen and immediately call an expensive defense attorney?

Like a lightning strike, it hit her. The murders of Sammie Howard, Cody Frazier, and Desiree Bauer weren't sanctioned by the Leóne family. Maybe even Norris too. That was why.

For the duration of the investigation, Amelia and Zane had been trying to determine if the killer they sought was a member of the crime family or if he was a serial killer.

They'd never stopped to consider he might be both.

"Excuse me." The pediatric oncologist's voice drew both Amelia and Gavin's attention. "This is far beyond what I can deal with here. This man needs a fully equipped operating room, and he needs it as soon as possible. His breathing is shallow, and the bullet may have compromised his diaphragm. That's not including the sheer blood loss. Without a transfusion, he'll experience hypovolemic shock within the hour."

Amelia's heart plummeted to the cold floor, but she didn't let her expression belie the surge of hopelessness. Glancing to Zane, she spotted the same sentiment in his expression.

Gavin swiped a hand along his forehead. "Just...do what you can. Give me a second."

Swallowing her fear for Layton's well-being, Amelia mentally avowed to do no such thing.

She had to keep the pressure on him. Had to force him to slip up. "Gavin, I found some of your artwork when we went through your...*workplace*. That chop shop we raided. I know it was your artwork because I know you've got the ouroboros tattooed on your wrist. That's the drawing that caught my attention. How long have you been working for the Leónes?"

For a split second, his eyes widened. Amelia realized he hadn't expected her to make the connection. "I don't know what you're talking about."

"You drew those pictures, and we found them at the site of a Leóne chop shop when we raided it. Deny it all you want, but I know you're involved with the family. You probably have been for a while, haven't you?"

"I don't know what you're talking about." He spoke through clenched teeth, and to Amelia's surprise, let his hostage go as he flailed his arms around in agitation.

Amelia had hit a nerve. As if she was disarming a bomb, she had to hope she'd hit the right nerve—the one that would either cause Gavin to make a mistake or realize the folly of his current situation. Not the nerve that would tell him to go berserk and kill them all.

In the distance, sirens wailed. Gavin's posture abruptly stiffened, his paranoid gaze darting from one window to another. "Someone draw the blinds."

No. Amelia didn't want them to be blocked in here with this unpredictable lunatic. Her gut told her closing the blinds would be the end of their hope for Layton Redker.

Sealing the café off from the outside world would give Gavin the sense he had time to figure out how to get away from the situation. Without the pressure of the police drawing nearer, Layton would be locked into his fate.

There wasn't time for her to work on earning Gavin's trust. Noting how unnerved he became at the mention of the Leónes, Amelia had a new tactic.

"Why their eyes, Gavin?" She took a slight step forward as he swiveled back toward her.

"What?"

Another half-step. Catching the gaze of the woman by Gavin's side, Amelia ever so slightly used her eyes to communicate for her to slowly increase the distance between her and the gunman.

The sirens grew louder, but Amelia wanted Gavin's full focus on her. She wasn't through with him. "Was taking their eyes symbolic? Were they witnesses? Did the Leónes tell you to get rid of them before they could testify?" She knew her hypothetical was incorrect, but she wanted to observe how Gavin reacted. "What did they see, anyway?"

A vein in his forehead was suddenly more noticeable. "I don't know what you're talking about."

"So, these murders *weren't* ordered by the Leónes?" She pinned him with a scrutinizing stare, steeling herself for the moment he decided to point the gun at her. "If they weren't sanctioned by the Leóne family, then what were they? Just an extracurricular activity for you?"

He balled one hand into a fist but still didn't bring the

handgun to bear. "Lady, I already said I don't know what you're talking about, all right?"

In the corner of the café, the blinds of one tall window went down. Amelia could tell the young woman attending to the task was taking her sweet time, and she silently thanked the girl for her effort.

"Yeah, okay." Amelia made a show of weighing her hands, edging a bit closer to Gavin while his attention was fixed on her gesture. Meanwhile, the woman by his side increased her distance from Gavin another couple inches. "Then consider this a hypothetical, yeah? Let's say you make it out of here today. Maybe you sneak through a vent like James Bond, and you run off to a safe house across state lines. What then? Even if you make it out of here, you're the prime suspect in at least three recent premeditated homicides, probably more if we can officially link them to you." She flicked her gaze to Layton. "And a Fed."

He seemed as if he might reply, but Amelia didn't give him time to think of a rebuttal.

"The first thing the Bureau will do is hold a press conference to update the public. Your face will be everywhere, and you might even make it into *America's Most Wanted*. But that's not the important part." She made a slight dismissive gesture with one hand. "The important part is that the Leónes are going to know what you did. They're going to know that their chop shop got raided by the Bureau because *you* decided to dump a body at Paulie's Scrap and Salvage. Not just one body, but multiple. Our original three, then Olivia Mclaughlin, Norris Lowery, and how many others? I don't know. We're still looking, but I suspect we'll find more."

Though barely noticeable at first, a slight flush had begun to creep up to Gavin's cheeks. "I don't—"

Amelia plowed ahead, praying she was cutting the right wire. "I know the Leóne family, Gavin. And I know they aren't going to react kindly to you losing them money and casting all this federal scrutiny on them. So, say you make it out of here and avoid the FBI. How do you plan to avoid the Leónes?"

Gavin threw his arms up in the air, and Amelia almost flinched away from the gesture of exasperation. "I don't know, okay! I know you all think I'm some kind of brain-dead...*thing*, but believe it or not, I'm perfectly aware that I'm between a rock and a hard place here."

As he tilted his head back and rubbed his eyes, Amelia spotted her opening. It was possible she could talk him down, but she didn't have time to dive into the intricacies of his crimes and his motivation. The third set of blinds had just been closed, and Layton's life hung in the balance.

She had to take the chance. She had no other choice.

Adrenaline pushed aside any hint of trepidation.

Like a tiger attacking its prey, Amelia sprang forward to take hold of his gun-wielding hand, whipping it up and out so hard she heard his finger crack as the trigger guard twisted it brutally, even as she drove her elbow into his jaw. He howled, and she used her forward momentum to jerk the limb behind his back, not stopping until she felt the sickening crunch of cartilage.

A grunt of surprise escaped Gavin, but to his credit, he didn't cry out a second time as Amelia jammed his wrist all the way up to his shoulder blade. As the handgun fell to the floor, Amelia wasted no time kicking the weapon away from them.

His body tensed, and Amelia sensed the incoming blow as much as witnessed it. Attempting to angle his body away from hers, Gavin swung wildly. Amelia's grasp on his arm never lessened, and she drove his elbow up higher, slowing his efforts to get away.

Amelia had no plans to relinquish her grip on his arm.

Gavin appeared to only be in his early twenties, and he was in prime physical condition. Standing at least five inches taller than her five-eight, his solid muscle mass had to have made him a good sixty pounds heavier than Amelia.

The size of a man's biceps had never stopped her before, and she didn't intend for it to slow her down today.

"Don't move!" The command came from Zane, who clasped a weapon in his bloodstained hands. "Gavin, I don't know what your last name is, don't fucking move."

Relieved to her core, Amelia caught a pair of cuffs Zane tossed her. She half-expected a fight, but the kid was still disoriented from the blow he'd taken to his jaw. As Zane rattled off Gavin's Miranda rights, Amelia cinched the handcuffs around his wrists.

All she could do now for Agent Redker was hope she'd diffused the situation in time.

28

Z ane paused just outside the open doorway of the hospital room, rapping his knuckles against the frame to announce his and Amelia's presence. Though Colleen Gibson—the pediatric oncologist who'd helped Layton Redker at the café and who also happened to work at the same hospital where Layton had been taken—had given them a dire outlook for Layton's health the morning before, the doctor had actually been exaggerating. She'd quietly warned Layton and Zane of her plan while Gavin was preoccupied by his discussion with Amelia.

By convincing Gavin that Layton was on death's doorstep, they'd hoped to put pressure on him. Sure enough, the tactic had worked. Colleen's quick thinking and her fake, dire outlook for Layton had given Amelia the edge she'd needed in their dialogue.

In reality, Layton had been seriously injured, but the bullet had missed his lung, as well as any other vital organs. Ironically, if Colleen hadn't faked his impending doom, Layton would have faced the very real possibility of death. With a gutshot, rapid access to medical care was imperative.

He'd been rushed to the nearest hospital and fast-tracked to the operating room. After a four-hour surgery and a blood transfusion, the doctors had advised that Layton's prognosis was good. With plenty of rest, he'd make a full recovery.

Zane shook off the memories of the intense standoff.

All's well that ends well.

Sure enough, Gavin was in custody, and Layton was on the mend. Twenty-four hours after he'd come out of surgery, and he was ready for visitors.

Layton's tired gaze shifted to them, along with a second set of nearly identical brown eyes. The young woman on the other side of Layton sported a Chicago Cubs hoodie, and despite her neat makeup and fashionably messy bun, she appeared as if she hadn't slept in at least a day.

Holding out an arrangement of orange lilies and bright green leaves, Zane offered the pair a wide smile. "Hey. Sorry if we're interrupting. We can leave these and stop by later if that works better for you."

Layton waved a dismissive hand. "No, you're fine. Good timing, actually. Deanna was just about to head out."

Shouldering a backpack, Deanna rose to her feet. "Yep, I was. Need to go let Ernest outside, or he'll start using the cats' litter box." She turned back to Layton and squeezed his hand. "I'll call you later, okay?"

"Sounds good, sweetie. Drive safe."

With a slight wave to Zane and Amelia, Deanna made her way to the door and disappeared down the hall. As the young woman departed, Zane realized how little he knew about Layton's background. He'd helped Colleen Gibson press blood-soaked towels against Layton's stomach to keep him from bleeding to death, but Zane didn't know the first thing about the agent.

He jerked a thumb over his shoulder, gesturing to Deanna. Though he could tell the young woman was a blood relative of Layton's, he hadn't concluded *who* exactly she was. "Was that your…sister?"

Layton laughed but quickly winced and rested a hand on his stomach. "Deanna's my daughter. She's house-sitting for me while I'm in here."

"Oh." Zane felt like a deer standing in front of a pair of headlights. Layton looked good for his age, but the girl who'd just left was easily nineteen or twenty. Which made Layton… forty? Fifty? Jesus, Zane didn't even know how old the guy was.

Amelia returned from closing the door, raising an orange bag of candy and mercifully cutting Zane's mental math short. "I had to ask around a little bit, but Spencer and Zane helped me figure out that your favorite candy is Reese's Pieces. We figured you could use some junk food while you're stuck in here."

Layton rubbed his hands together. "I could always use some junk food. I was never much of a fan until I quit smoking seven years ago."

Now *that* was a sentiment to which Zane could relate. "Quitting actually alters your taste buds. I had no idea until I kicked the habit. Went to eat a Butterfinger a few weeks after I quit, and it was the best tasting thing I think I've ever eaten in my life. Never appreciated it while I was smoking."

With a grin, Layton accepted the Reese's Pieces from Amelia. "Glad I'm not the only one. How's the case? Any developments?"

Dropping to sit beside the nightstand, Zane held back a sigh. "Nothing yet. The kid hasn't even asked for a lawyer. He hasn't said a damn thing since we left the café yesterday. He went through arraignment this morning, and the judge remanded him to custody without bail, so that's a positive."

Amelia took the chair on the other side of the bed. "My guess is he isn't asking for a lawyer because he knows any lawyer he gets will be in the Leóne family's pocket. Gavin is a Piliero, which is one of the more influential families in the Leóne operation, but that's not going to shield him from their wrath. Cassandra made her case to put him in protective custody for the time being, but who knows how long that'll last."

Zane didn't feel a sense of pity for Gavin Piliero so much as he worried the families of his victims would never see justice. If the Leónes killed Gavin, they might never even identify all the people he'd butchered over the years.

Layton scratched the side of his nose, appearing thoughtful. "I heard about the storage unit. I can't say I've heard of a serial killer keeping their victims' eyes in jars of formalin before, though it's not the first time someone like that has kept body parts as a trophy. Usually, we're talking about an extremity like fingers, though. Removing a person's eyes is… pretty involved."

Thinking back to the search of Gavin's storage unit, Zane barely suppressed a shudder. The jars of preserved eyeballs sitting in neat rows along the shelves of a gun safe would likely never dissipate from his mind. "We found some firearms, fake IDs, and cash, too. But that's all pretty normal for a guy with strong ties to the mob. The eyes were the really weird part. Forensics will be scouring everything in that storage unit and will run all the tests they can on the eyes."

Amelia held out her hands and slumped back in her chair. "But unless they're already in the system somewhere, who knows how useful it'll actually be."

"Right." Layton lifted a shoulder, glancing back and forth between Zane and Amelia. "I doubt he labeled them, but maybe we can find newspaper clippings or some sort of memorabilia related to the missing persons cases that correlate with each victim."

Amelia nodded. "We were thinking that too. We executed the search warrant for Gavin's condo, but we didn't see any news articles or anything. It's possible he kept all that stuff digitally, so we'll have to wait for the lab to go through his PC."

Before Zane could add to the conversation, his phone buzzed inside his suit jacket. He'd have ignored the call if they weren't still neck-deep in the case.

As Zane pulled the device out to check the screen, he held up a finger. "Hold on. It's Spencer. I should take this. It might be about Gavin Piliero."

"Definitely. No worries." Layton's smile was genuine and understanding. "Let us know if he gives you an update."

"Will do." Swiping the screen, Zane let himself out into the hallway and headed toward the nearest window. Service was spotty enough inside the hospital, and he didn't want to play phone tag with the SSA. "Morning, Corsaw."

"Morning?" the SSA echoed. "It's almost one, Palmer."

Zane reflexively checked his watch. Sure enough, Spencer was right. "Correction acknowledged. Thanks for letting me know. I assume that's why you were calling?"

"Yes, that's exactly it. I called to see if you knew what time it was." The SSA's voice was flat, but Zane knew the tone was feigned.

"All right, well, good talk. See you back at the office in a little bit."

Spencer chortled, but the mirth died out quickly. "Thanks for a laugh, but are you ready to be serious for a minute?"

Actually, Zane wasn't, but he prepared himself to be anyway. "What's the real reason?"

"We've got an...unexpected visitor. Arturo Piliero, Gavin Piliero's father. He says he wants to speak to the attorney in charge of his son's case, as well as the two agents who were behind the raid of the trafficking ring in Kankakee County this past summer."

A list of possibilities ran through Zane's mind at this bit of news, none of them good. Zane settled on a question. "Did he ask for us by name?"

When Spencer spoke again, his voice was quieter. "Yeah, and before you ask, I don't know how the hell he knew your names. We kept both of you out of the media."

Ice water trickled into Zane's bloodstream. "He knew because of Larson. What the hell does he want from Storm and me?"

"He wants to make a deal. Not for himself, but for his son. He wouldn't go into any more detail than that. He's waiting in an interview room on the first floor. I'll send you the info, but I need you and Storm back here ASAP."

As Zane and Spencer said their goodbyes, Zane went through the motions like a robot.

A Piliero wanted to make a deal. Whatever Arturo Piliero had in mind for them, it sure as hell wouldn't come with a vacation.

Out of the frying pan and into the fire they went.

29

Amelia elbowed open the door of the incident room she and Zane had used during the start of the Sammie Howard case. The oval table was home to scattered papers, photos, and manila envelopes as Amelia, Zane, and Spencer, with help from Cassandra, sorted through Gavin Piliero's previously unknown victims.

Cassandra Halcott glanced up from her laptop, the white of the screen reflecting off the lenses of her glasses. Brushing a piece of bright auburn hair from her shoulder, the Assistant U.S. Attorney reached out to accept one of Amelia's two paper cups of coffee. Zane and Spencer had set off to Herman's Sandwich Shop to get lunch, but Amelia and Cassandra had opted to drink their midday meal.

With a deep drink from the latte, Cassandra nodded her approval. "Thank you so much. This should get me through the next few hours."

"Yeah, I figured we'd need a recharge before the end of the day. Whenever that is. Did you hear back from the agents in charge of Artie Piliero's security?"

Cassandra set down the coffee and turned back to the

laptop. "I did, just a few minutes ago. I got confirmation that relocating him to the safe house went smoothly. The U.S. Attorney approved the plea agreement for Gavin Piliero this morning, so he'll be relocated before the end of the week."

At least the heavy lifting was over. Gavin Piliero, at his father's behest and with the guarantee he wouldn't be charged with the death penalty, had provided them with the identities of all his previous victims. Amelia had sat in the interrogation room beside Cassandra as the twenty-two-year-old had walked them through each individual crime. When it was all said and done, the interview had taken nearly six hours.

Artie Piliero, on the other hand, was currently facing no criminal charges. In exchange for his son's protection, as well as witness protection for himself, Artie was prepared to give the FBI information pertinent to the inner workings of the Leóne family.

Amelia was still curious—even a bit suspicious—of Artie's motive, but the man's distress when talking about his son was undeniable. He'd stressed his desire for Gavin to receive extensive therapy in whichever prison he was sent to, and at one point, the man had even teared up.

As someone familiar with Italian mob culture, Amelia knew how significant such an emotional display was. Artie had failed to protect his son when he was younger, but he was pulling out all the stops now.

Two days after meeting Artie Piliero for the first time, and Amelia still couldn't quite wrap her head around his and Gavin's family dynamic.

Fortunately, or maybe, unfortunately, as far as her sanity was concerned, Artie Piliero wasn't going anywhere. The Leóne capo still had a great deal of information to provide the Bureau if he wanted to ensure his own criminal immunity.

The door swung open at Amelia's back, jerking her from the contemplation like she'd been smacked upside the head.

She expected to spot Zane, Spencer, and the smell of their meatball subs, but to her surprise, the SSA and the food were nowhere to be found.

Zane's gaze darted from Cassandra to Amelia, a mixture of anxiety and uncertainty written on his face.

Right away, Amelia knew something was wrong. "What? What is it?"

With a paranoid glance over his shoulder, he stepped inside and closed the door. "We've got a visitor."

"Who?" Amelia and Cassandra asked simultaneously.

"Michelle Timmer's best friend...or adopted sister...or *both* really. She's a VC agent in the Las Vegas field office, and she wants to know what happened to Michelle."

The End
To be continued...

Thank you for reading.
All of the Amelia Storm Series books can be found on Amazon.

ACKNOWLEDGMENTS

How does one properly thank everyone involved in taking a dream and making it a reality? Here goes.

In addition to our families, whose unending support provided the foundation for us to find the time and energy to put these thoughts on paper, we want to thank the editors who polished our words and made them shine.

Many thanks to our publisher for risking taking on two newbies and giving us the confidence to become bona fide authors.

More than anyone, we want to thank you, our readers, for clicking on a couple of nobodies and sharing your most important asset, your time, with this book. We hope with all our hearts we made it worthwhile.

Much love,
Mary & Amy

ABOUT THE AUTHOR

Mary Stone lives among the majestic Blue Ridge Mountains of East Tennessee with her two dogs, four cats, a couple of energetic boys, and a very patient husband.

As a young girl, she would go to bed every night, wondering what type of creature might be lurking underneath. It wasn't until she was older that she learned that the creatures she needed to most fear were human.

Today, she creates vivid stories with courageous, strong heroines and dastardly villains. She invites you to enter her world of serial killers, FBI agents but never damsels in distress. Her female characters can handle themselves, going toe-to-toe with any male character, protagonist or antagonist.

Discover more about Mary Stone on her website.
www.authormarystone.com

Amy Wilson

Having spent her adult life in the heart of Atlanta, her upbringing near the Great Lakes always seems to slip into her writing. After several years as a vet tech, she has dreams of going back to school to be a veterinarian but it seems another dream of hers has come true first. Writing a novel.

Animals and books have always been her favorite things, in addition to her husband, who wanted her to have it all. He's the reason she has time to write. Their two teenage boys fill the rest of her time and help her take care of the mini zoo that now fills their home with laughter...and yes, the occasional poop.

Connect with Mary Online

Made in United States
Orlando, FL
24 April 2023

32410544R00153